THE FOUR OF HEARTS

Mollie Lee
Pryor

Books by Ellery Queen

And on the Eighth Day
Calamity Town
Face to Face
The Four of Hearts
The King Is Dead
The Origin of Evil
Ten Days' Wonder
There Was an Old Woman

THE FOUR OF HEARTS

Ellery Queen

HarperPerennial
A Division of HarperCollins*Publishers*

Reprinted by arrangement with The Ellery Queen (Manfred B. Lee and Frederic Dannay) Trusts and Scott Meredith Agency, Inc.

HarperCollins books may be purchased for educational, business, or sales promotional use. For information, please write: Special Markets Department, HarperCollins Publishers, Inc., 10 East 53rd Street, New York, NY 10022.

First HarperPerennial edition published 1994.

Designed by Elan M. Cole

Library of Congress Cataloging -in-Publication Data
Queen, Ellery.
    The four of hearts / Ellery Queen. — 1st HarperPerennial ed.
        p. cm.
    ISBN 0-06-097604-7
    1. Motion picture industry—California—Los Angeles—Fiction. 2. Hollywood (Los Angeles, Calif.)—Fiction. I. Title. II. Title: 4 of hearts.
PS3533.U4F67 1994
813'.52—dc   93-27181

94 95 96 97 98 ❖/CW 10 9 8 7 6 5 4 3 2 1

THE FOUR OF HEARTS

PART ONE

1

GOD'S GIFT TO HOLLYWOOD

It is a well-known fact that any one exposed to Hollywood longer than six weeks goes suddenly and incurably mad.

Mr. Ellery Queen groped for the bottle of Scotch on the open trunk.

"To Hollywood, city of screwballs! Drink 'er down." He guzzled what was left of the Scotch and tossed the bottle aside, resuming his packing. "California, here I go—unwept, unhonored, and unsung. And do I care?"

Alan Clark smiled that Mona Lisa smile by which you may know any member of the fraternity of Hollywood agents, fat or thin, tall or short, dewy-eyed or soiled by life. It is the sage's, the saint's, the cynic's smile of pure wisdom.

"All you wacks act this way at first. Them that can take it snaps out of it. Them that can't—they turn yellow and go squawking back East."

"If you're trying to arouse my ire," growled Ellery, kicking his prostrate golf-bag, "desist, Alan. I cut my eyeteeth on the tactics of scheming agents."

"What the hell did you expect—a Class A assignment your first week on the lot and a testimonial dinner at the Cocoanut Grove?"

"Work," said Ellery unreasonably.

"Phooey," said his agent. "It isn't work here; it's art. Rembrandt didn't get his start knocking out the Sistine Chapel, did he? Give yourself a chance to learn the ropes."

"By burying myself in that mausoleum of an office they gave me and sucking my thumbs?"

"Sure, sure," said Clark soothingly. "Why not? It's Magna's dough, isn't it? If the studio's willing to invest six weeks' salary in you, don't you think they know what they're doing?"

"Are you asking me?" said Ellery, flinging things into the trunk. "Then I'm telling you. No!"

"You've got to get the feel of pictures, Queen, before you can wade into a script. You're not a day-laborer. You're a writer, an artist, a—a sensitive plant."

"Flapdoodle, with onions on the side."

Clark grinned and tipped his hat. "Pleased to meet you. . . . Just the same, what's the rush? You've got a future out here. You're an idea man, and that's what they pay off on in Hollywood. They need you."

"Magna gives me a six-week contract with an option for renewal, the six weeks expire today, they don't take up the option, and that means they need me. Typical Hollywood logic."

"They just didn't like the contract the New York office wrote. Happens out here all the time. So they let your contract lapse and now they'll offer you a new one. You'll see."

"I was brought out here to do the story and dialogue on a horse opera. Have I done a single thing in six weeks? Nobody's paid the slightest attention to me, I haven't been able to see or talk to Jacques Butcher even once. . . . Do you know how many times I've called Butcher, Alan?"

"You've got to have patience. Butch is the Boy Wonder of Hollywood. And you're just another lous—another writer."

"You can't prove it by anything I've written, because I haven't written anything. No, sir, I'm homeward bound."

"Sure, sure," said the agent. "Here, you left out this wine-colored polo shirt. I know how you feel. You hate our guts. You can't trust your best friend here; he'll use the back of your neck for a stepladder the minute you turn your head. I know. We're twerps—"

"Illogical!"

"No art—"

"Synthetic!"

"Throw our dough around—"

"Dog eat dog!"

"Just the same," grinned Clark, "you'll learn to love it. They all do. And you'll make a hell of a lot more money writing for pictures than you ever will figuring out who wrapped a meat-cleaver around Cadwallader St. Swithin's neck in Room 202. Take my advice, Queen, and stick around."

"The way I figure it," said Ellery, "the incubation period lasts six weeks. After that a man's hopelessly infected. I'm taking it on the lam while I still have my sanity."

"You've still got ten days to pick up your tickets to New York."

"Ten days!" Ellery shuddered delicately. "If it hadn't been for the Sperry murder I'd have been back East long ago."

Clark stared. "I *thought* there was something screwy in the way Glücke's been pinning medals on himself!"

"Ouch, I've let the cat out. Keep it under your hat, Alan. I promised Inspector Glücke—"

The agent pulled a gust of indignation up from his shoes. "Do you mean to stand there and tell me you cracked the Sperry case and didn't have the brains to get your pan smeared over the front page?"

"It doesn't mean anything to me. Where the devil can I put these spiked shoes?"

"Why, with that publicity you could have walked into any studio in Hollywood and written your own ticket!" Clark became quiet, and when Ellery looked up he saw the old Mona Lisa smile. "Look," said Clark. "I've got a sweet idea."

Ellery dropped the shoes. "Now wait a minute, Alan."

"Leave it to me. I absolutely guarantee—"

"I gave Glücke my word, I tell you!"

"The hell with that. Well, okay, okay. I found it out somewhere else. You'll still be the white-haired boy—"

"No!"

"I think," mused the agent, pulling his lip, "I'll try Metro first."

"Alan, absolutely no!"

"Maybe I can ring Paramount and Twentieth Century in on it, too. Play 'em off against each other. I'll have the Magna outfit eating out of my hand." He slapped Ellery's shoulder. "Why, man, I'll get you twenty-five hundred bucks a week!"

In this moral crisis the telephone rang. Ellery fled to it.

"Mr. Queen? Hold the line, please. Mr. Butcher calling."

Ellery said: "Mr. *who*?"

"Mr. Butcher."

"*Butcher*?"

"Butcher!" Clark yanked his hat over his ears. "See, what did I tell you? Butcho the Great! Where's your extension? Don't mention dough, now. Feel him out. Boy, oh, boy!" He dashed into the bedroom.

"Mr. Queen?" said a sharp, nervous, young man's voice in Ellery's ear. "Jacques Butcher speaking."

"Did you say Jacques Butcher?" mumbled Ellery.

"Tried to locate you in New York for four days. Finally got your address from your father at Police Headquarters. What are you doing in Hollywood? Drop in to see me today."

"What am I do—" Ellery paused. "I beg your pardon?"

"What? I say, how is it you're on the Coast? Vacation?"

"Excuse me," said Ellery. "Is this the Jacques Butcher who is executive vice-president in charge of production at the Magna Studios in Melrose, in Hollywood, California, United States of America?" He stopped. "The planet Earth?"

There was a silence. Then: "Beg pardon?"

"You're not the gag man?"

"What? Hello! Mr. Queen?" Another dead moment in Time, as if Mr. Butcher were fumbling with a memorandum. "Am I speaking to Ellery Queen, Queen the detective-story writer? Where the hell— Madge. Madge! Did you get me the wrong man, damn it?"

"Wait," said Ellery hollowly. "Madge got you the right man, all right, all right. But my brain isn't functioning at par these days, Mr. Butcher. I'm slicing 'em into the rough on every drive. Did I understand you to ask if I'm in Hollywood on a vacation?"

"I don't get this." The edge on the sharp voice was badly blunted. "We seem to have our wires crossed. Aren't you feeling well, Queen?"

"Well?" howled Ellery, growing red in the face. "I feel terrible! Why, you incomparable nitwit, I've been employed by your studio for six interminable weeks now—and you ask me if I'm here on a *vacation?*"

"What!" shouted the producer. "You've been on our lot for six weeks? *Madge!*"

"I've phoned your office twice a day, six days a week, fathead—that makes seventy-two times not counting Sundays that I've tried to talk to you, you misbegotten apology for an idiot's stand-in! And you wire New York for my address!"

"Why—doesn't—somebody *tell* me these things!"

"Here I've parked on my chassis," roared Ellery, "in that doge's palace your minions gave me to doze in—a month and a half, do you hear?—losing weight, fretting my fool head off, dying by inches not a hundred feet from your office—and *you* look for *me* in New York!" Ellery's voice grew terrible. "I'm going mad. I *am* mad. Do you know what, Mr. Butcher? Nuts to you. *Double* nuts to you!"

And he hurled the telephone majestically from him.

Clark came scurrying back, rubbing his hands. "Oh, wonderful, wonderful. We're set. We're in!"

"Go away," said Ellery. Then he screeched: "*What?*"

"Hasn't been done since Garbo gave her last interview to *Screen Squeejees*," said the agent gleefully. "Telling Butch where he gets off! Now we're getting somewhere."

"Now," said Ellery, feeling his forehead, "now—we're—getting somewhere?"

"Great guy, Butch. Biggest man in pictures. What a break! Get your lid."

"Please. *Please*. Where are we going?"

"To see the Boy Wonder, of course. Come on!"

And the agent bustled out, looking delighted with life, the world, and the whole confused, thunderous march of events.

For a moment Ellery sat still.

But when he found himself putting a match on his head, sticking his hatbrim into his mouth, and rubbing a cigaret on his shoe, he made a gibbering sound and followed his personal representative from the apartment with the fogged air of one who will never understand.

Each studio in Hollywood has its Boy Wonder. But Jacques Butcher, it was admitted by even the other Boy Wonders, was the Boy Wonder of them all.

This paragon occupied a four-room bungalow office in the heart of the quadrangle of executive buildings on the Magna lot. The bungalow, thought Ellery grimly, was some unknown architectural genius's conception of the kind of Spanish edifice a Spanish executive in charge of the production of Spanish motion pictures would erect in his native Spain amid blood, mayhem, and the belch of batteries. It was very yellow, stuccoed, Moorish, and archified; and it was tiled and roofed and patioed as no structure outside a cocaine-addicted hidalgo's nightmare had ever been. In a word, it was colossal.

The Second Secretary's office in the edifice, having been designed in the same faithful spirit to house females, resembled the interior of a Moorish prince's zenana.

Ellery, scrutinizing this plaster and silken gingerbread, nodded unpleasantly. The Sultan of Production was probably lolling on an amethyst-studded throne puffing on a golden hookah and dictating to two houris in g-strings. As for Mr. Alan Clark, his manner had grown less and less enthusiastic as Mr. Queen grew more and more steel-dignified.

"Mr. Butcher will see you in a moment, Mr. Queen," said the Second Secretary piteously. "Will you have a chair?"

"You," said Mr. Queen with a nasty inflection, "are Madge, I presume?"

"Yes, sir."

"Ha," said Mr. Queen. "I will be delighted to have a chair." And he had a chair. The Second Secretary bit her budding lip, looking as if she wanted chiefly to burst into tears.

"Maybe we'd better come back tomorrow," whispered the agent. "If you're going to have an antagonistic attitude—"

"Let me remind you, Alan," said Mr. Queen complacently, "that coming here was your idea. I'm really looking forward to this audience. I can see him now—burlap bags under his eyes, dressed like a Radio City typist's conception of Robert Taylor, with a manicurist on one hand and a eunuch on the other—"

"Some other time," said Clark, rising. "I think maybe tomorrow—"

"Sit down, friend," said Mr. Queen.

Clark sat down and began to snap at his own fingernails like a tortured turtle. A door opened; he jumped up again. But it was only a washed-out male, obviously the First Secretary.

"Mr. Butcher will see you now, Mr. Queen."

Mr. Queen smiled. The Second Secretary looked faint, the First Secretary paled, and Clark wiped his forehead.

"Nice of him," murmured Mr. Queen. He strolled into the First Secretary's domain. "Ah, quite like my preconception. In the worst of possible taste. *Le mauvais goût.*"

"Yes, Mr. Queen," said the First Secretary. "I mean—"

"By the way, what's the proper form? Does one genuflect and kiss the royal hand, or will a deep bow from the waist suffice?"

"A kick in the pants would be more like it," said a rueful voice. "*Kamerad!*"

Mr. Queen turned around. A young man was standing in the doorway holding his hands high. He wore a soiled pair of slacks, openwork sandals on bare feet, and a lumberman's plaid shirt open at the throat. More wonderful than that, he was smoking a chipped clay pipe which fumed foully; his fingers were stained with ink; and he had not shaved his heavy young beard, judging from its vigorous sprout, in at least three days.

"I thought—" began Mr. Queen.

"I certainly rate one," said the Boy Wonder. "Will you dish it out now, or can we talk things over first?"

Mr. Queen swallowed. "Are you Butcher?"

"Guilty. Say, that was the dumbest stunt I've ever seen pulled in this town, and we've pulled some beauties here." He shook Ellery's hand crisply. "Hello, Clark. You Queen's agent?"

"Yes, Mr. Butcher," said Clark. "Yes, sir."

"Come in, both of you," said the Boy Wonder, leading the way. "Don't mind the spurious magnificence of this dump, Queen. The damned thing was wished on me. It was built by old Sigmund in the free-lunch days, when he was tossing away the stockholders' dough like a hunyak on Saturday night. I've tried to make my own workroom livable, anyway. Come on in."

Ellery almost said: "Yes, sir." He came on in.

It wasn't fair! With his sharp green eyes and red hair and boy's smile and beautifully disreputable clothes, Butcher looked like a normal human being. And the holy of holies! From the exterior and anteroom decoration, one had a right to anticipate lushness along Latin-Oriental lines, with tapestries and tiles and inlaid woods of precious pastels. But no drapes smothered the sun; the walls had been repaneled in clean pine; an old missionwood desk bearing the scars of golf-shoes and cigaret burns stood higgledy-piggledy in the midst of a congress of deep, honest chairs; the desk was littered with clues to toil—yellow paper covered with ink-scrawls, a clay model of a ballroom set, an old typewriter with a battered face, photographs, mimeographed scripts, a can of film; books that looked as if they were being read bristled in the pine walls; and a small portable bar beside the desk stood open, crowded with bottles, and accessible to a nervous elbow, as a bar should.

"Ripped out all the junk," said the Boy Wonder cheerfully. "You should have seen it. Sit down, boys. Drink?"

"It isn't fair," moaned Mr. Queen, getting into a chair and cowering.

"What?"

"He says he needs some air," said Alan Clark hastily.

"Shouldn't wonder, after the raw deal he got," said the young man, throwing open all the windows. "Have a slug of Scotch, Queen. Do you good."

"Brandy," said Mr. Queen faintly.

"Brandy!" The Boy Wonder looked pleased. "Now there's a man with discriminating boozing habits. It gets your ticker after a while, but look at all the fun you have waiting for coronary thrombosis. Tell you what I'll do with you, Queen. I'll crack open a couple of bottles of 125-year-old Napoleon I've been saving for my wedding. Just between friends?"

Mr. Queen wavered between the demon of prejudice and the Boy Wonder's grin. While he wavered, the tempter tilted a sun-scorched bottle and poured golden liquid.

It was too, too much. The would-be avenger accepted the fat glass and buried his nose in the seductive vapors of the aged cognac.

"Here—here's to you," said Mr. Queen one bottle later.

"No, no, here's to *you*," said Mr. Butcher.

The friendly sun was beaming on the Magna lot outside, the friendly room was cloistered and cool, the friendly brandy was pure bliss, and they were old, old friends.

Mr. Queen said fervently: "*My* m'stake, Butchie-boy."

"No, no," said Butchie-boy, beating his breast. "My m'stake, El ole cock."

Clark had gone, dismissed by the Boy Wonder. He had departed with anxiety, for the magic of Butchie-boy's executive methods was legend in Hollywood and as a good and conscientious agent Clark had misgivings about leaving his client alone with the magician.

Not without cause. Already his client was prepared to do or die for dear old Magna. "Don't see how I could've mis-misjudged you, Butch," said Mr. Queen, half in tears. "Thought you were a complete an' absolute louse. You my word."

"I *yam* a louse," said Butch. "No won'er people get the wrong impression 'bout Hollywood. A yarn like that! I'll be a laughing—a laughing-stock."

Mr. Queen grasped his glass and glared. "Show me the firsht man who laughsh—laughs an' I'll kick his teeth in!"

"My pal."

"But nob'dy'll spread the story, Butch. It's jus' b'tween us an' Alan Clark." Mr. Queen snapped his fingers. "Curse it, *he'll* talk."

"Cer'nly he'll talk. Di'n't you know all agents are rats? Down with agents!"

"The dirty shkunk," said Mr. Queen ferociously, rising. "Id'll be all over *Variety* t'morrow morning."

Mr. Butcher leered. "Siddown, ole frien'. I fixed his wagon."

"No! How?"

"Gave the shtory to *Variety* m'self jus' before you came!"

Mr. Queen howled with admiration and pounded the Boy Wonder's back. The Boy Wonder pounded his back. They fell into each other's arms.

The First Secretary discovered them on the floor half a bottle later among sheets and sheets of yellow paper, planning with intense sobriety a mystery picture in which Ellery Van Christie, the world-famous detective, murders Jacques Bouchêrre, the world-famous movie producer, and pins the crime with fiendish ingenuity on one Alan Clarkwell, a scurvy fellow who skulked about making authors' lives miserable.

2

STORY CONFERENCE

The First Secretary conferred with the Second Secretary and while the Second Secretary ran for raw eggs, Worcestershire, and tomato juice the First Secretary hauled the debaters into old Sigmund's pre-Butcher lavatory, wheedled them into undressing, pushed them respectfully under the needle-shower, turned on the cold water, and retired under a barrage of yelps to telephone the trainer in the studio gymnasium.

They emerged from the lavatory an hour later full of tomato juice and the piety of newly converted teetotalers, looking like a pair of corpses washed up on shore. Ellery groped for the nearest chair and wound his arms about his head as if he were afraid it was going to fly away.

"What happened?" he moaned.

"I think the house fell in," said the producer. "Howard, locate Lew Bascom. You'll probably find him shooting craps with the grips on Stage 12." The First Secretary vanished. "Ow, my head."

"Alan Clark will massacre me," said Ellery nervously. "You fiend, did you make me sign anything?"

"How should I know?" growled the Boy Wonder. Then they looked at each other and grinned.

For a time there was the silence of common suffering. Then Butcher began to stride up and down. Ellery closed his eyes, pained at this superhuman vitality. He opened them at the crackle of Butcher's voice to find that remarkable gentleman studying him with a sharp green look. "Ellery, I want you back on the payroll."

"Go away," said Ellery.

"This time, I promise, you'll work like a horse."

"On a script?" Ellery made a face. "I don't know a lap dissolve from a fade-in. Look, Butch, you're a nice guy and all that, but this isn't my racket. Let me crawl back to New York."

The Boy Wonder grinned. "I could really care for a mugg like you; you're an honest man. Hell, I've got a dozen writers on this lot who've forgotten more about scripts than you'll know in a million years."

"Then what the devil do you want me for?"

"I've read your books and followed your investigations for a long time. You've got a remarkable gift. You combine death-on-rats analysis with a creative imagination. And you've got a freshness of viewpoint the old-timers here, saturated in the movie tradition and technique, lost years ago. In a word, it's my job to dig up talent, and I think you're a natural-born plot man. Shall I keep talking?"

"When you say such pretty things?" Ellery sighed. "More."

"Know Lew Bascom?"

"I've heard of him. A writer, isn't he?"

"He thinks he is. He's really an idea man. Picture ideas. Gets 'em in hot flushes. Got his greatest notion—Warner's bought it for twenty-five thousand and grossed two million on it—over a poker table when he was so plastered he couldn't tell an ace from a king. The magnificent slugnut sold the idea to another writer in the game in payment of a hundred-dollar debt. . . . Well, you're going to work with Lew. You'll do the treatment together."

"What treatment?" groaned Ellery.

"Of an original he's just sold me. It's the business. If I turned Lew loose on it solo, he'd come up with the most fantastic yarn you ever saw—if he came up with anything at all, which is doubtful. So I want you to work out the plot with him."

"Does he know you're wishing a collaborator on him?" asked Ellery dryly.

"He's probably heard it by this time; you can't keep anything secret in a studio. But don't worry about Lew; he's all right. Unstable, one of Nature's screwiest noblemen, brilliant picture mind, absolutely undependable, gambler, chippy-chaser, dipsomaniac—a swell guy."

"Hmm," said Ellery.

"Only don't let him throw you. You'll be looking for him to buckle down to work and he'll probably be over in Las Vegas playing craps with silver dollars. When he does show up he'll *be* boiled on both sides. Nobody in town remembers the last time Lew was even relatively sober. . . . Excuse me." Butcher snapped into his communicator: "Yes, Madge?"

The Second Secretary said wearily: "Mr. Bascom just whooshed through, Mr. Butcher, and on the way he grabbed my letter-knife again. I thought you'd like to know."

"Did she say knife?" asked Ellery, alarmed.

A chunky man whizzed in like a fat thunderbolt. He wore shapeless clothes, and he had blown cheeks, nose like a boiled onion, frizzled mustache, irritated hair, eyelids too tired to sit up straight, and a gaudy complexion not caused by exposure to the great outdoors.

This apparition skidded to a stop, danced an intricate measure symbolizing indignation, and brandished a long letter-knife. Then he hopped across the rug to the Boy Wonder's desk, behind which Mr. Queen sat paralyzed, and waggled the steel under the petrified Queen nose.

"See this?" he yelled.

Mr. Queen nodded. He wished he didn't.

"Know what it is?"

Mr. Queen gulped. "A knife."

"Know where I found it?"

Mr. Queen shook his head at this inexplicable catechism. The chunky man plunged the steel into Jacques Butcher's desk-top. It quivered there menacingly.

"In *my* back!" howled Mr. Bascom. "Know who put it there—rat?"

13

Mr. Queen pushed his chair back an inch.

"You did, you double-crossing New York story-stealer!" bellowed Mr. Bascom; and he seized a bottle of Scotch from the Boy Wonder's bar and wrapped his lips fiercely about its dark brown neck.

"This," said Mr. Queen, "is certainly the second feature of an especially bad dream."

"Just Lew," said Butcher absently. "Always the dramatist. This happens at the start of every production. Listen, Lew, you've got Queen wrong—Ellery Queen, Lew Bascom."

"How do you do," said Mr. Queen formally.

"Lousy," said Lew from behind the bottle.

"Queen's just going to help you with the treatment, Lew. It's still your job, and of course you get top billing."

"That's right," said Ellery, with an ingratiating smile. "Just your little helper, Lew, old man."

Mr. Bascom's wet lips widened in a grin of pure camaraderie. "That's different," he said handsomely. "Here, pal, have a shot. Have two shots. You, too, Butch. Le's all have two shots."

Gentle Alan Clark, the peace and sanity of New York's quiet streets, the milieu of normal people, seemed light-years away. Mr. Queen, hangover and all, wrested the Scotch from Mr. Bascom with the artificial courage of a desperate man.

There was a spare workroom off the Boy Wonder's office which smelled slightly of disinfectant and was furnished with all the luxury of a flagellant monk's cell.

"It's where I go when I want to think," explained Butcher. "You boys use it as your office while you're on this assignment; I want you near me."

Ellery, facing the prospect of being caged within the four nude walls with a gentleman whose whimsies seemed indistinguishable from homicidal mania, appealed to the Boy Wonder with mute, sad eyes. But Butcher grinned and shut the door in his face.

"All right, all right," said Mr. Bascom irritably. "Squat and listen.

You're bein' let in on the ground floor of next year's Academy prize-winner."

Eying the door which led to the patio and possible escape in an emergency, Ellery squatted. Lew lay down on the floor and spat accurately through an open window, arms behind his frowsy head.

"I can see it now," he began dreamily. "The crowds, the baby spots, the stinkin' speeches—"

"Spare the build-up," said Ellery. "Facts, please."

"What would you say," Lew went on in the same drifting way, "if M-G-M should all of a sudden make a picture out of Garbo's life? *Huh?*"

"I'd say you ought to sell the idea to M-G-M."

"Nah, nah, you don't get it. And they should *star Garbo* in it, huh? Her own life!" Lew paused, triumphantly. "Say, what's the matter with you, anyway? Don't you see it—her virgin girlhood in Sweden, the meeting with Stiller the genius, Stiller's contract in Hollywood—he takes the gawky kid along, Hollywood falls for her and gives Stiller the cold mitt, she becomes a sensation, Stiller kicks off, the Gilbert romance, the broken heart behind the dead pan—for gossakes!"

"But would Miss Garbo consent?" murmured Ellery.

"Or s'pose," continued Lew, ignoring him, "that Paramount took John and Lionel and Ethel and slung 'em together in a story of *their* lives?"

"You'd have something there," said Ellery.

Lew sprang to his feet. "See what I mean? Well, I've got a real-life yarn that's got those licked a mile! Y'know whose lives we're gonna make? The dizziest, grandest, greatest names in the American theatre! Those dynamos of the drama—the screwballs of the screen—the fightin', feudin', first families of Hollywood!"

"I suppose," frowned Ellery, "you mean the Royles and the Stuarts."

"For gossakes, who else?" groaned Lew. "Get it? Get the set-up? On one side Jack Royle and his cub Ty—on the other Blythe Stuart and her daughter Bonnie. The old generation an' the new. A reg'lar four-ring circus!"

And overwhelmed by his own enthusiasm, Lew staggered out, returning a moment later from Butcher's office with the unfinished bottle of Scotch.

Ellery sucked his lower lip. It was an idea, all right. There was enough dramatic material in the lives of the Royles and the Stuarts to make two motion pictures, with something left over for a first-class Broadway production.

Before the War, when John Royle and Blythe Stuart had dominated the New York stage, their stormy love-affair was the romantic gossip of Mayfair and Tanktown. It was like the courtship of two jungle cats. They mauled each other from Times Square to San Francisco and back again, leaving a trail of glittering performances and swollen box-offices. But no one doubted, despite their fighting, that in the end they would marry and settle down to the important business of raising a new royal family.

Astonishingly, after the furious passion of their romance, they did nothing of the kind. Something happened; gossip-writers from that day to this had skinned their noses trying to ferret out exactly what. Whatever the cause, it broke up their romance—to such an accompaniment of tears, bellows, recriminations, escapades out of pique, and bitter professions of undying enmity as to set the whole continent to buzzing.

Immediately after the *débâcle* each married some one else. Jack Royle took to his handsome bosom a brawny Oklahoma débutante who had come to New York to give the theatre a new Duse, presented Royle with a son instead, publicly horsewhipped her husband a month later for an unexplained but easily imagined reason, and died shortly after of a broken neck as the result of a fall from a horse.

Blythe Stuart eloped with her publicity man, who fathered her daughter Bonnie, stole and pawned the pearl necklace which had been presented to her by Jack during their engagement, fled to Europe as a war correspondent, and died in a Paris *bistro* of acute alcoholism.

When Hollywood beckoned, the Royle-Stuart feud was already in the flush of its development, its origin long forgotten in the sheer fury of the feudists' temperaments. It communicated itself to their progeny, so that the hostility of Bonnie Stuart, who already was an important screen ingénue, for Tyler Royle, who was Magna's leading juvenile, became scarcely less magnificent than that of their parents.

From Wilshire to Hollywood boulevards the feud raged. It was said that old Sigmund, to whom Jack and Blythe had been under contract, had died not of cerebral hemorrhage but of nervous indigestion as a result of trying to keep peace on the Magna lot; and a few prematurely gray hairs at the back of Jacques Butcher's head were ascribed to his similarly futile efforts in the case of their respective issue. One studio wit stated that the Boy Wonder had proposed marriage to Bonnie Stuart as a last desperate measure, on the theory that love sometimes works miracles.

"That's right," said Ellery aloud. "Butch and Bonnie are engaged, aren't they?"

"Is that all you got to say about my idea, for gossakes?" snarled Lew, brandishing the bottle.

Butcher stuck his head into the room. "Well, Ellery, what do you think?"

"My honest opinion?"

"Give me anything else and I'll fire you out on your ear."

"I think," said Ellery, "that it's an inspired notion that will never get beyond the planning stage."

"See?" cried Lew. "You hooked me to a Jonah!"

"What makes you say that?"

"How do you propose to get those four to work in the same picture? They're mortal enemies."

Lew glared at Ellery. "The romance of the century, the most publi-cized cat-fight of the last twen'y years, terrific box-office appeal in four big star names, a honey of a human-int'rest story—an' *he* throws cold water!"

"Turn it off, Lew," said the Boy Wonder. "That's the major problem, of course, El. Attempts have been made before to cast them in teams, but they've always failed. This time I have a hunch it will be different."

"Love will find a way," said Lew. "The future Mrs. Butcher wouldn't throw her tootsie, would she?"

"Shut up," said Butcher, reddening. "As far as that's concerned, Lew has an in, too. He's Blythe's second cousin; aside from her father and Lew, Blythe hasn't any relatives, and I think she likes this screwball enough to listen to him."

"If she don't," grinned Lew, "I'll break her damn' neck."

"The four of them are broke, too—they always are. I'm prepared to offer them whopping big contracts. They simply won't be able to afford to turn it down."

"Listen," said Lew. "When I show 'em how they're gonna play a picture biography of themselves to an audience of millions, they'll be so damn' tickled they'll fall all over themselves grabbin' for the contracts. It's in the bag."

"I'll tackle Bonnie and Ty," said the Boy Wonder crisply, "and Lew goes to work on Blythe and Jack. Sam Vix, our publicity head, will start the ball rolling in the mags and papers."

"And I?"

"Hang around Lew. Get acquainted with the Stuarts and the Royles. Gather as much material on their personal lives as you can. The biggest job will be weeding, of course. We'll meet again in a few days and compare notes."

"*Adios*," said Lew, and wandered out with Butcher's bottle under his arm.

A tall man with a windburned face and a black patch over one eye came strolling in. "You want me, Butch?"

"Meet Ellery Queen—he's going to work with Lew Bascom on the Royle-Stuart imbroglio. Queen, this is Sam Vix, head of our publicity department."

"Say, I heard about you," said Vix. "You're the guy worked here for six weeks and nobody knew it. Swell story."

"What's swell about it?" asked Ellery sourly.

Vix stared. "It's publicity, isn't it? By the way, what do you think of Lew's picture idea?"

"I think—"

"It's got everything. Know about Blythe's old man? There's a character for pictures! Tolland Stuart. I bet Blythe hasn't even seen the old fossil for two-three years."

"Excuse me," said the Boy Wonder, and he disappeared.

"Park the carcass," said the publicity man. "Might as well feed you dope if you're going to work on the fracas. Stuart's an eccentric millionaire—I mean he's nuts, if you ask me, but when you've got his dough you're just eccentric, see what I mean? Made it in oil. Well, he's got a million-dollar estate on top of a big butte in the Chocolate Mountains—that's below the San Bernardino range in Imperial County—forty rooms, regular palace, and not a soul on the place but himself and a doctor named Junius, who's the old man's pill-roller, nose-wiper, hash-slinger, and plug-ugly all rolled into one."

"Pardon me," said Ellery, "but I think I'd better see where Lew—"

"Forget Lew; he'll turn up by himself in a couple of days. Well, as I was saying, they spin some mighty tall yarns about old man Stuart. Hypochondriac to the gills, they say; and the wackiest personal habits. Sort of hermit, I guess you'd call him, mortifying the flesh. He's supposed to be as healthy as a horse."

"Listen, Mr. Vix—"

"Call me Sam. If there's a trail down his mountain, only a goat or an Indian could negotiate it. Doc Junius uses a plane for supplies—they've got a landing-field up there; I've seen it plenty of times from the air. I'm an aviator myself, you know—got this eye shot out in a dog-fight over Boileau. So naturally I'm interested in these two bugs up there flying around their eagle's nest like a couple of spicks out of the Arabian Nights—"

"Look, Sam," said Ellery. "I'd love to swap fairy tales with you, but right now what I want to know is—who in this town knows everything about everybody?"

"Paula Paris," said the publicity man promptly.

"Paris? Sounds familiar."

"Say, where do you come from? She's only syndicated in a hundred and eighty papers from coast to coast. Does the famous movie-gossip column called *Seeing Stars*. Familiar!"

"Then she should be an ideal reference-library on the Royles and the Stuarts."

"I'll arrange an appointment for you." Vix leered. "You're in for an experience, meeting Paula for the first time."

"Oh, these old female battle-axes don't faze me," said Ellery.

"This isn't a battle-axe, my friend; it's a delicate, singing blade."

"Oh! Pretty?"

"Different. You'll fall for her like all the rest, from wubble-you-murdering Russian counts to Western Union boys. Only, don't try to date her up."

"Ah, exclusive. To whom does she belong?"

"Nobody. She suffers from crowd phobia."

"From what?"

"Fear of crowds. She hasn't left her house since she came to the Coast in a guarded drawing-room six years ago."

"Nonsense."

"Fact. People give her the willies. Never allows more than one person to be in the room with her at the same time."

"But I can't see— How does she snoop around and get her news?"

"She's got a thousand eyes—in other people's heads." Vix rolled his one eye. "What she'd be worth to a studio! Well, I'll ring her for you."

"Do that," said Ellery, feeling his head.

Vix left, and Ellery sat still. There was an eldritch chiming in his ears and the most beautiful colored spots were bouncing before his eyes.

His telephone rang. "Mr. Queen?" said the Second Secretary. "Mr. Butcher has had to go to the projection room to catch the day's rushes, but he wants you to call your agent and have him phone Mr. Butcher back to talk salary and contract. Is that all right?"

"Is that all right?" said Ellery. "I mean—certainly."

Salary. Contract. Lew. Paula. The old man of the mountains. Napoleon brandy. Gatling-gun Butch. The wild Royles and Stuarts. Crowd phobia. Chocolate Mountains. High pressure. Super-spectacle. Rushes. . . . My God, thought Ellery, is it too late?

He closed his eyes. It was too late. *Whoops!*

3

MR. QUEEN SEES STARS

After two days of trying to pin somebody into a chair within four walls, Ellery felt like a man groping with his bare hands in a goldfish bowl.

The Boy Wonder was holding all-day conferences behind locked doors, making final preparations for his widely publicized production of *Growth of the Soil*. The earth, it seemed, had swallowed Lew Bascom. And every effort of Ellery's to meet the male Royles and the female Stuarts was foiled in the one case by a nasal British voice belonging to a major-domo named Louderback and in the other by an almost incomprehensible French accent on the lips of a lady named Clotilde, neither of whom seemed aware that time was marching on and on and on.

Once, it was close. Ellery was prowling the alleys of the Magna lot with Alan Clark, who was vainly trying to restore his equilibrium, when they turned the corner of "A" Street and 1st and spied a tall girl in black satin slacks and a disreputable man's slouch hat matching pennies at the bootblack stand near the main gate with Roderick, the colored man who polished the shoes of the Magna extras.

"There's Bonnie now," said the agent. "The blonde babe. Ain't she somepin'? Knock you down. Bonnie!" he shouted. "I want you to meet—"

The star hastily dropped a handful of pennies, rubbed Roderick's humped back for luck, and vaulted into a scarlet Cord roadster.

"Wait!" roared Ellery, beside himself. "Damn it all—"

But the last he saw of Bonnie Stuart that day was a blinding smile over one slim shoulder as she shot the Cord around the corner of 1st and "B" Streets on two wheels.

"That's the last straw," stormed Ellery, hurling his Panama to the pavement. "I'm through!"

"Ever try to catch a playful fly? That's Bonnie."

"But *why* wouldn't she—"

"Look. Go see Paula Paris," said the agent diplomatically. "Sam Vix says he made an appointment for you for today. She'll tell you more about those doodlebugs than they know themselves."

"Fifteen hundred a week," mumbled Ellery.

"It's as far as Butcher would go," apologized Clark. "I tried to get him to raise the ante—"

"I'm not complaining about the salary, you fool! Here I've accumulated since yesterday almost six hundred dollars on the Magna books, and I haven't accomplished a blasted thing!"

"See Paula," soothed Clark, patting Ellery's back. "She's always good for what ails you."

So, muttering, Ellery drove up into the Hollywood hills.

He found the house almost by intuition; something told him it would be a sane, homey sort of place, and it was—white frame in a placid Colonial style surrounded by a picket fence. It stood out among the pseudo-Spanish stucco atrocities like a wimpled nun among painted wenches.

A girl at the secretary in the parlor smiled: "Miss Paris is expecting you, Mr. Queen. Go right in." Ellery went, pursued by the stares of the crowded room. They were a motley cross-section of Hollywood's floating population—extras down on their luck, salesmen, domestics, professional observers of the *scène célèbre*. He felt impatient to meet the mysterious Miss Paris, who concocted such luscious news from this salmagundi.

But the next room was another parlor in which another young woman sat taking notes as a hungry-looking man in immaculate morning clothes whispered to her.

"The weeding-out process," he thought, fascinated. "She'd have to be careful about libel, at that."

And he entered the third room at a nod from the second young woman to find himself in a wall-papered chamber full of maple furniture and sunlight, with tall glass doors giving upon a flagged terrace beyond which he could see trees, flowerbeds, and a very high stone wall blanketed with poinsettias.

"How do you do, Mr. Queen," said a pure diapason. *I do NOT know what THIS word means! mP Dec. 4, 2011!*

Perhaps his sudden emergence into the light affected his vision, for Mr. Queen indubitably blinked. Also, his ear still rang with that organ sound. But then he realized that that harmonious concord of musical tones was a human female voice, and that its owner was seated cross-kneed in a Cape Cod rocker smoking a Russian cigaret and smiling up at him.

And Mr. Queen said to himself on the instant that Paula Paris was beyond reasonable doubt the most beautiful woman he had yet met in Hollywood. No, in the world, ever, anywhere.

Now, Mr. Queen had always considered himself immune to the grand passion; even the most attractive of her sex had never meant more to him than some one to open doors for or help in and out of taxis. But at this historic moment misogyny, that crusted armor, inexplicably cracked and fell away from him, leaving him defenseless to the delicate blade.

He tried confusedly to clothe himself again in the garments of observation and analysis. There was a nose—a nose, yes, and a mouth, a white skin . . . yes, yes, very white, and two eyes—what could one say about them?—an interesting straight line of gray in her black-lacquer hair . . . all to be sure, to be sure. He was conscious, too, of a garment—was it a Lanvin, or a Patou, or a Poirot?—no, that was the little Belgian detective—a design in the silk gown; yes, yes, a design, and a

Thank you, Ellery Queen, for referring to Agatha Christie. mP note #2 of Dec. 4, 2011

23

bodice, and a softly falling skirt that dropped from the knee in long, pure, Praxitelean lines, and an aroma, or rather an effluvium, emanating from her person that was like the ghost of last year's honeysuckle. . . . Mr. Queen uttered a hollow inward chuckle. Honeysuckle! Damn analysis. This was a woman. No—Woman, without the procrusteanizing article. Or . . . was . . . it . . . *the* Woman?

"Here, here," said Mr. Queen in a panic, and almost aloud. "Stop that, you damned fool."

"If you're through inspecting me," said Paula Paris with a smile, rising, "suppose you be seated, Mr. Queen. Will you have a highball? Cigarets at your elbow."

Mr. Queen sat down stiffly, feeling for the chair.

"To tell the truth," he mumbled, "I'm—I'm sort of speechless. Paula Paris. Paris. That's it. A remarkable name. Thank you, no highball. Beautiful! Cigaret?" He sat back, folding his arms. "Will you please say something?"

There was a dimple at the left side of her mouth when she pursed her lips—not a large, gross, ordinary dimple, but a shadow, a feather's touch. It was visible now. "You speak awfully well for a speechless man, Mr. Queen, although I'll admit it doesn't quite make sense. What are you—a linguistic disciple of Dali?"

"That's it. More please. Yahweh, thou hast given me the peace that passeth understanding."

Ah, the concern, the faint frown, the tensing of that cool still figure. Here, for heaven's sake! What's the matter with you?

"Are you ill?" she asked anxiously. "Or—"

"Or drunk. Drunk, you were going to say. Yes, I am drunk. No, delirious. I feel the way I felt when I stood on the north rim of the Grand Canyon looking into infinity. No, no, that's so unfair to you. Miss Paris, if you don't talk to me I shall go completely mad."

She seemed amused then, and yet he felt an infinitesimal withdrawing, like the stir of a small animal in the dark. "Talk to you? I thought you wanted to talk to me."

"No, no, that's all so trivial now. I must hear your voice. It bathes me. God knows I need something after what I've been through in this bubbling vat of a town. Has any one ever told you the organ took its tonal inspiration from your voice?"

Miss Paris averted her head suddenly, and after a moment she sat down. He saw a flush creeping down her throat. "*Et tu, Brute*," she laughed, and yet her eyes were strange. "Sometimes I think men say such kind things to me because—" She did not finish.

"On the contrary," said Ellery, out of control. "You're a gorgeous, gorgeous creature. Undoubtedly the trouble with you is an acute inferiority—"

"Mr. Queen."

He recognized it then, that eerie something in her eyes. It was fright. Before, it had seemed incredible that this poised, mature, patrician creature should be afraid of anything, let alone the mere grouping of human beings. "Crowd phobia," Sam Vix had called it, homophobia, a morbid fear of man. . . . Mr. Queen snapped out of it very quickly indeed. That one glimpse into terror had frightened him, too.

December 4 2011

"Sorry. Please forgive me. I did it on a—on a bet. Very stupid of me."

"I'm sure you did." She kept looking at her quiet hands.

"It's the detective in me, I suppose. I mean, this clumsy leap into analysis—"

"Tell me, Mr. Queen," she said abruptly, tamping out her cigaret. "How do you like the idea of putting the Royles and the Stuarts into a biographical film?"

Dangerous ground, then. Of course. He *was* an ass. "How did you know? Oh, I imagine Sam Vix told you."

"Not at all. I have deeper channels of information." She laughed then, and Ellery drank in the lovely sound. Superb, superb! "I know about you, you see," she was murmuring. "Your six weeks' horror at Magna, your futile scampering about the lot there, your orgy the other day with Jacques Butcher, who's a darling—"

"I'm beginning to think you'd make a pretty good detective yourself."

She shook her head ever so slowly and said: "Sam said you wanted information." Ellery recognized the barrier. "Exactly what?"

"The Royles and the Stuarts." He jumped up and began to walk around; it was not good to look at this woman too long. "What they're like. Their lives, thoughts, secrets—"

"Heavens, is that all? I'd have to take a month off, and I'm too busy for that."

"You do know all about them, though?"

"As much as any one. Do sit down again, Mr. Queen. Please."

Ellery looked at her then. He felt a little series of twitches in his spine. He grinned idiotically and sat down.

"The interesting question, of course," she went on in her gentle way, "is why Jack Royle and Blythe Stuart broke their engagement before the War. And nobody knows that."

"I understood you to know everything."

"Not quite everything, Mr. Queen. I don't agree, however, with those who think it was another woman, or another man, or anything as serious as that."

"Then you do have an opinion."

The dimple again. "Some ridiculous triviality. A lovers' spat of the most inconsequential sort."

"With such extraordinary consequences?" asked Ellery dryly.

"Apparently you don't know them. They're reckless, irresponsible, charming lunatics. They've earned top money for over twenty years, and yet both are stony. Jack was—and is—a philanderer, gambler, a swash-buckler who indulges in the most idiotic escapades; a great actor, of course. Blythe was—and is—a lovely, electric hoyden whom every one adores. It's simply that they're capable of anything, from breaking an engagement for no reason at all to keeping a vendetta for over twenty years."

"Or, I should imagine, piracy on the high seas."

She laughed. "Jack once signed a contract with old Sigmund calling for five thousand a week, to make a picture that was scheduled to take about ten weeks' shooting time. The afternoon of the day he signed the contract he dropped fifty thousand dollars at Tia Juana. So he worked the ten weeks for nothing, borrowing money from week to week for tips, and he gave the most brilliant performance of his career. That's Jack Royle."

"Keep talking."

"Blythe? She's never worn a girdle, drinks Martinis exclusively, sleeps raw, and three years ago gave half a year's salary to the Actors' Fund because Jack gave three months' income. And that's Blythe."

"I suppose the youngsters are worse than their parents. The second generation usually is."

"Oh, definitely. It's such a deep, sustained hatred that a psychologist, I suspect, would look for some frustration mechanism, like Love Crushed to Earth. . . ."

"But Bonnie's engaged to Jacques Butcher!"

"I know that," said Paula calmly. "Nevertheless—you mark my words—crushed to earth, it will rise again. Poor Butch is in for it. And I think he knows it, poor darling."

"This boy Tyler and the girl aren't on speaking terms?"

"Oh, but they are! Wait until you hear them. Of course, they both came up in pictures about the same time, and they're horribly jealous of each other. A couple of months ago Ty got a newspaper splash by wrestling with a trained grizzly at one of his father's famous parties. A few days later Bonnie adopted a panther cub as a pet and paraded it up and down the Magna lot until Ty came off a set with a gang of girls, and then somehow—quite innocently, of course—the cub came loose and began to chew at Ty's leg. The sight of Ty running away with the little animal scampering after him quite destroyed his reputation as a he-man."

"Playful, aren't they?"

"You'll love all four of them, as every one else does. In Blythe's and Bonnie's case, it's probably an inheritance from Blythe's father Tolland—that's Bonnie's grandfather."

"Vix mentioned him rather profusely."

"He's a local character—quite mad. I don't mean mentally. He was sane enough to amass a tremendous fortune in oil. Just gaga. He spent a million dollars on his estate on Chocolate Mountain, and he hasn't even a caretaker to hoe the weeds. It cost him forty thousand dollars to blast away the top of a neighboring mountain peak because he didn't like the view of it from his porch—he said it looked like the profile of a blankety-blank who had once beaten him in an oil deal."

"Charming," said Ellery, looking at her figure.

"He drinks cold water with a teaspoon and publishes pamphlets crammed with statistics crusading against stimulants, including tobacco and coffee and tea, and warning people that eating white bread brings you early to the grave."

She talked on and on, and Ellery sat back and listened, more entranced by the source than the information. It was by far the pleasantest afternoon he had spent in Hollywood.

He came to with a start. There was a shadow on Paula's face, and it was creeping higher every minute.

"Good Lord!" he said, springing up and looking at his watch. "Why didn't you kick me out, Miss Paris? All those people waiting out there—"

"My girls take care of most of them, and it's a relief to be listened to for a change. And you're such a splendid listener, Mr. Queen." She rose, too, and extended her hand. "I'm afraid I haven't been much help."

He took her hand, and after a moment she gently withdrew it.

"Help?" said Ellery. "Oh, yes. Yes, you've been of tremendous service. By the way, can you suggest the surest means of treeing those four?"

"Today's Friday. Of course. You go down to the Horseshoe Club on Wilshire Boulevard tomorrow night."

"Horseshoe Club," said Ellery dutifully, watching her mouth.

"Don't you know it? It's probably the most famous gambling place in Los Angeles. Run by Alessandro, a very clever gentleman with a very dark past. You'll find them there."

"Alessandro's," said Ellery. "Yes."

"Let's see." She turned her head a little, trying to avoid his questioning eyes. "There's no opening tomorrow night—yes, they'll be there, I'm sure."

"Will they let me in? I'm a stranger in town."

"Would you like me to arrange it?" she asked demurely. "I'll call Alessandro. He and I have an understanding."

"You're simply wonderful." Then he said hastily: "I mean, so—

Look, Miss Paris. Or why not Paula? Do you mind? Would you—I mean, could you bring yourself to accompany—"

"Goodbye, Mr. Queen," said Paula with a faint smile.

"But would you do me the honor—"

"It's been so nice talking to you. Drop in again."

That damned phobia!

"I warn you," he said grimly. "You may live to regret that invitation."

And, a little blindly, Mr. Queen made his way to the street.

What a lovely day! he thought, breathing deeply, drinking in the lovely sky, the lovely trees, even the lovely Spanish-style houses all about that supremely lovely white-frame cottage which housed surely the loveliest self-imprisoned Juliet in the history of romantic heroines.

And suddenly he remembered Vix's cynical remark two days before: "You'll fall for her like all the rest." The rest. . . . That implied a host of admirers. Well, why not? She was delectable and piquant to the jaded male palate, like a strange condiment. And what sort of figure did he cut in this land of brown, brawny, handsome men?

The loveliness went out of everything.

Crushed, Mr. Queen crept into his car and drove away.

Saturday night found him in a dinner jacket at the Horseshoe Club, cursing his wasted years of singleness and, his thoughts still hovering over a certain white-frame cottage in the Hollywood hills, not greatly caring if he cornered his quarry or not.

"Where can I find Alessandro?" he asked a bartender. "In his office." The man pointed, and Ellery skirted the horseshoe-shaped bar, threaded his way across the packed dance-floor past the orchestra stand where a swaying quadroon moaned a love-song, and entered a silk-hung passage at the terminus of which stood a chrome-steel door.

Ellery went up to it and knocked. It was opened at once by a hard-looking gentlemen in tails who appropriately gave him a hard look.

"Yeah?"

"Alessandro?"

"So who wants him?"

"Oh, go away," said Ellery, and he pushed the hard-looking gentleman aside. An apple-cheeked little man with China-blue eyes wearing a huge horseshoe-shaped diamond on his left hand smiled up at him from behind a horseshoe-shaped desk.

"My name is Queen. Paula Paris told me to look you up."

"Yes, she called me." Alessandro rose and offered his fat little hand. "Any friend of Paula's is welcome here."

"I hope," said Ellery not too hopefully, "she gave me a nice reference."

"Very nice. You want to play, Mr. Queen? We can give you anything at any stakes—roulette, faro, baccarat, dice, chuck-a-luck, poker—"

"I'm afraid my quarter-limit stud is too rich for your blood," grinned Ellery. "I'm really here to find the Royles and the Stuarts. Are they here?"

"They haven't turned up yet. But they will. They generally do on Saturday nights."

"May I wait inside?"

"This way, Mr. Queen." Alessandro pressed on a blank wall and the wall opened, revealing a crowded, smoky, quiet room.

"Quite a set-up," said Ellery, amused. "Is all this hocus-pocus necessary?"

The gambler smiled. "My clients expect it. You know—Hollywood? They want a kick for their dough."

"Weren't you located in New York a few years ago?" asked Ellery, studying his bland, innocent features.

The little man said: "Me?" and smiled again, nodded to another hard-looking man in the secret passageway, "All right, Joe, let the gentleman through."

"My mistake," murmured Ellery, and he entered the gaming room.

But he had not been mistaken. Alessandro's name was not Alessandro, and he did hail from New York, and in New York he had gathered to his rosy little self a certain fame. The gossip of Police Headquarters had ascribed his sudden disappearance from Broadway to an extraordinary run of luck, during the course of which he had badly dented four bookmakers, two dice rings, and a poker clique composed of Dopey

Siciliano, an assistant District Attorney, a Municipal Court Judge, a member of the Board of Estimate, and Solly the Slob.

And here he was, running a joint in Hollywood. Well, well, thought Ellery, it's a small world.

He wandered about the place. He saw at once that Mr. Alessandro had risen in the social scale. At one table in a booth two wooden-faced house men played seven-card stud, deuces wild, with the president of a large film company, one of Hollywood's most famous directors, and a fabulously-paid radio comedian. The dice tables were monopolized—it was a curious thing, thought Ellery with a grin—by writers and gag men. And along the roulette tables were gathered more stars than Tillie the Toiler had ever dreamed of, registering a variety of emotions that would have delighted the hearts of the directors present had they been in a condition to appreciate their realism.

Ellery spied the elusive Lew Bascom, in a disreputable tuxedo, in the crowd about one of the wheels. He was clutching a stack of chips with one hand and the neck of a queenly brunette with the other.

"So here you are," said Ellery. "Don't tell me you've been hiding out here for three days!"

"Go 'way, pal," said Lew, "this is my lucky night." There was a mountain of chips before the brunette.

"Yeah," said the brunette, glaring at Ellery.

Ellery seized Lew's arms. "I want to talk to you."

"Why can't I get any peace, for gossakes? Here, toots, hang on to papa's rent," and he dropped his handful of chips down the gaping front of the brunette's décolletage. "Well, well, what's on your mind?"

"You," said Ellery firmly, "are remaining with me until the Royles and the Stuarts arrive. Then you're going to introduce me. And after that you may vanish in a puff of smoke for all I care."

Lew scowled. "What day is it?"

"Saturday."

"What the hell happened to Friday? Say, here's Jack Royle. C'mon, that wheel ain't gonna wait all night."

He dragged Ellery over to a tall, handsome man with iron-gray hair who was laughing at something Alessandro was saying. It was John

Royle, all right, in the flesh, thought Ellery; the merest child knew that famous profile.

"Jack, here's a guy named Ellery Queen," grunted Lew. "Give him your autograph and lemme get back to the wheel."

"Mr. Queen," said the famous baritone voice, and the famous mustache-smile appeared. "Don't mind this lack-brain; he's probably drunk as usual. Rudeness runs in the Stuart line. Excuse me a moment." He said to Alessandro: "It's all right, Alec. I'm filthy with it tonight." The little fat man nodded curtly and walked away. "And now, Mr. Queen, how do you like working for Magna?"

"Then Butcher's told you. Do you know how hard I've tried to see you in the past three days, Mr. Royle?"

The famous smile was cordial, but the famous black eyes were roving. "Louderback did say something. . . . Three days! Three, did you say? Lord, Queen, that's a hunch! Pardon me while I break Alessandro's heart."

See page 48

And he hurried off to the cashier's cage to exchange a fistful of bills for a stack of blue chips. He dived into the crowd at the roulette table.

"Five hundred on number three," Ellery heard him chortle.

Fascinated by this scientific attack on the laws of chance, Ellery permitted Lew to wriggle away. Number 3 failed to come up. Royle smiled, glanced at the clock on the wall, noted that its hands stood at nine-five, and promptly placed stacks on numbers 9 and 5. The ball stopped on 7.

Blythe Stuart swept in, magnificent in a black evening gown, followed by a tall Hindu in tails and a turban, with a brown impassive face. Instantly she was surrounded.

"Blythe! Who's the new boyfriend?"

"I'll bet he's a prince, or a rajah, or something. Leave it to Blythe."

"Introduce me, darling!"

"Please," protested the actress, laughing. "This is Ramdu Singh, and he's a Swami from India or some place, and he has second sight or something, I'll swear, because he's told me the most amazing things about myself. The Swami is going to help me play."

"How thrilling!"

"Lew darling!" cried Blythe, spying him. "Get out of the way and let me show you how to lick that thing. Come along, Mr. Singh!"

Lew looked the Swami over blearily and shrugged. "It's your cashee, Blythe."

A Russian director gave the actress his chair and the Swami took his place behind it, ignoring the stares of the crowd. The croupier looked a little startled and glanced at Alessandro, who shrugged, smiled, and moved off.

"Place your bets," said the croupier.

At this moment, across the table, the eyes of John Royle and Blythe Stuart met. And without a flicker they passed on.

With an enigmatic expression Royle placed a bet. The Swami whispered in Blythe Stuart's ear and she made no move to play, as if he had advised lying low until his Psyche could smell out the probabilities. The wheel spun, the ball clacked to a stop on a number, the croupier began raking up the chips.

"I beg your pardon," said John Royle politely, and he took the outstretched rake from the croupier's hand and poked it across the table at the Swami's turban. The turban fell off the Swami's head. His skull gleamed in the strong light—hairless, polished, pinkish-white.

The "Hindu" dived frantically for the turban. Some one gasped. Blythe Stuart gaped at the naked pink scalp.

Royle handed the rake back to the croupier with a bow. "This," he said in an amiable tone, "is Arthur William Park, the actor. You remember his Polonius, Sergie, in the Menzies *Hamlet* in 1920? An excellent performance, then—as now."

Park straightened up, murder in his eyes.

"Sorry, old man," murmured Royle. "I know you're down on your luck, but I can't permit my . . . friends to be victimized."

"You're riding high, Royle," said Park thickly, his cheeks muddy under the make-up. "Wait till you're sixty-five, unable to get a decent part, sick as a dying dog, with a wife and crippled son to support. Wait."

Alessandro signalled to two of his men.

"Come on, fella," said one of them.

"Just a moment," said Blythe Stuart in a low voice. Her hazel eyes blazed like Indian topaz. "Alessandro, call a policeman."

"Now, take it easy, Miss Stuart," said Alessandro swiftly. "I don't want any trouble here—"

Park cried out and tried to run; the two men caught him by his skinny arms. "No! Please!"

Royle's smile faded. "Don't take it out on this poor fellow, just because you're angry with me. Let him go."

"I won't be publicly humiliated!"

"Mother! What's the matter?" Bonnie Blythe, dazzling in an ermine cape, her golden curls iridescent in the light, appeared on Jacques Butcher's arm. She shook it off and ran to Blythe.

"Oh, darling, this beast put this man up to pretending to be a Swami, and he brought me here and—and the beast unmasked the Swami as an actor or something," sobbed Blythe, melting into tears at the sight of a compassionate face, "and I've never been so humiliated in my life." Then she stamped her foot. "Alessandro, will you call a policeman or must I? I'll have them both arrested!"

"Darling. Don't," said Bonnie gently, her arm about her mother's shoulders. "The man looks pretty much down in the mouth to me. I don't think you'd enjoy seeing him in jail." She nodded to Alessandro over her mother's sleek coiffure, and the gambler sighed with relief and signalled to his men, who hurried the man out. "But as for Mr. John Royle," continued Bonnie, her glance hardening, "that's—different."

"Bonnie," said the Boy Wonder warningly.

"No, Butch. It's time he was told—"

"My dear Bonnie," said Royle with a queer smile, "I assure you I didn't put Park up to his masquerade. That was his own idea."

"Don't tell *me*," sobbed Blythe. "I know *you,* John Royle. Oh, I could kill you!"

And she gathered her sweeping skirts about her and ran out of the gaming room, crying bitterly. Bonnie ran after her, followed by the Boy Wonder, whose face was red with embarrassment.

Royle shrugged with a braggadocio that did not quite come off. He pressed some bills into Lew Bascom's hand, nodding toward the door. Lew waddled out with the money.

"Place your bets," said the croupier wearily.

Lew came back after a long absence. "What a night! It's a conspiracy, damn it, to keep me from cleanin' up the joint. Just when I was goin' good!"

"I trust," sighed Ellery, "all's well that ends well? Nobody's murdered anybody?"

"Damn near. Bumped into Ty Royle outside, just comin' in. Alec's gorillas told him what happened and he tried to make Park take some dough. That kid gives away more dough to broken-down actors than half the relief-agencies in Hollywood. The old guy took it, all right. They're all outside now, raisin' hell."

"Then it wasn't a put-up job?"

"Hell, no. Though I'll bet Jack's sorry he didn't think of it."

"I doubt that," said Ellery dryly, glancing at Royle. The actor was sitting at the bar before a row of six cocktail glasses filled with Sidecars, his broad back humped.

"Park's got cancer or somepin', hasn't had more'n extra-work for two-three years. What'd he want to come around here for?" Lew made a face. "Spoiled my whole evening. Stiff old devil! I took him around the corner and bought him a couple. He wouldn't take Jack's dough, though."

"Curious ethics. And I can't say Blythe Stuart's spent a very enjoyable evening, either."

"That wacky dame! Sucker for every phony in the fortune-telling racket. She won't even take a part till she's read the tea-leaves."

Bonnie came stalking back, her face stormy. The Boy Wonder clutched her arm, looking harassed. He was talking earnestly to her; but she paid no attention, tapping the rug with her toe, glancing about. She caught sight of Jack Royle sitting Buddha-like at the bar and took a step forward.

"Hold it, me proud beauty," drawled a voice, and she stopped as if she had stepped on an electric wire.

A tall young man in evening clothes, surrounded by four beautiful young women, loomed in Alessandro's doorway. Alessandro looked positively unhappy, Ellery thought.

"You again?" said Bonnie with such colossal contempt that, had Ellery been in the young man's shoes, he would have made for the nearest crack in the wall. "You can spare that alcoholic breath of yours. He's got it coming to him, and he's going to get it."

"If this is going to be a scrap," said Ty Royle in a cold voice, "how about mixing it with me? I'm closer to your age, and dad's getting on."

Bonnie looked him up and down. "At that," she said sweetly, "he's a better man than you are. At least he doesn't flaunt *his* harem in decent people's faces."

The four young ladies surrounding Ty gasped, and for a moment Ellery thought there would be a general engagement in which the destruction of expensive coiffures would be the least of the damage.

"Ty. Bonnie," said the Boy Wonder hurriedly, stepping between them. "Not here, for the love of Mike. Here—" he glanced about desperately. "Queen! What luck. Darling, this is Ellery Queen. Queen— will you?" and Butcher dragged Ty Royle aside.

"If Butch thinks I'm going to let that conceited housemaid's hero," said Bonnie, her magnificent eyes smoking, "talk me out of giving his father a piece of my mind—"

"But would it be wise?" said Ellery hastily. "I mean—"

"Poor mother's positively *ashamed!* Of course, it's her fault for listening to every charlatan in a Hindu make-up, but a decent person wouldn't expose her that way in front of all the people she knows. She's really the dearest, sweetest thing, Mr. Queen. Only she isn't very practical, and if I didn't watch her like a nursemaid she'd get into all sorts of trouble. Especially with those detestable Royles just *watching* for a chance to humiliate her!"

"Not Tyler Royle, surely? He seems like a nice boy."

"Nice! He's loathsome! Although I'll admit he doesn't pester mother—he goes after *my* hide, and I can handle *him*. But Jack Royle. . . . Oh, I'm sure mother will cry herself to sleep tonight. I'll probably be up until dawn putting vinegar compresses on her poor head."

"Then don't you think," said Ellery cunningly, "that perhaps you'd better go home now? I mean, after all—"

"Oh, no," said Bonnie fiercely, glaring about. "I've got some unfinished business, Mr. Queen."

Ellery thought with desperation of some diversion. "I'm afraid I rather feel like an innocent Christian martyr thrown to a particularly lovely young lioness."

"*What?*" said Bonnie, looking at Ellery really for the first time.

"I talk that way sometimes," said Ellery.

She stared at him, and then burst out laughing. "Where've you *been*, Mr. Queen? That's the nicest thing I've ever been told outside a set. You must be a writer."

"I am. Hasn't Butch mentioned my name?"

"Probably." Her mouth curved and she took his arm. Ellery blushed a little. Her body felt terribly soft where it touched him, and she smelled delicious. Not quite so delicious as Paula Paris, of course, but still delicious enough to make him wonder whether he wasn't turning into a positive lecher. "I like you. You may take me over to the roulette table."

"Delighted."

"Oh, I know! You're the man who was with Alan Clark yesterday."

"So you remember!"

"Indeed I do. I thought you were an insurance agent. Did any one ever tell you you look like an insurance agent?"

"To the wheel!" groaned Ellery, "before I remind you of something you saw in your last nightmare."

He found a chair for her at the table. Butcher hurried over, looking warm but successful, and dumped two handfuls of chips before Bonnie. He winked at Ellery, wiped his face, bent over Bonnie, and kissed the nape of her neck.

Ellery, thinking instantly of a lady named Paris, sighed. Damn it, she would have to be a female hermit!

He saw Tyler Royle go over to the bar, put his arm about his father's shoulders, and say something with a cheerful expression. Jack Royle turned his head a little, and Ellery saw him smile briefly. Ty pounded his father's back affectionately and came back to herd his adoring feminine entourage over to the roulette table, opposite Bonnie. He ignored her elaborately, saying something in an undertone to his companions, who giggled.

Bonnie pursed her lips; but then she laughed and looked up at Butcher, whispering something; and Butcher laughed, not too gaily, while she turned back to place a bet. Young Mr. Royle, gazing quizzically at the board, also placed a bet. Miss Stuart smiled. Mr. Royle frowned. Miss Stuart frowned. Mr. Royle smiled.

The croupier droned on. The wheel spun. Chips made hollow, clicking sounds. Jack Royle sat imbibing Sidecars at the bar, gazing in silence at his handsome reflection in the mirror. Bonnie seemed absorbed in the play. Ty Royle placed bets carelessly.

Ellery was just beginning to feel relieved when a bray offended his left ear, and he turned to find Lew Bascom, grinning like a potbellied Pan, beside him.

"'Stoo peaceful," murmured Lew. "Watch this."

Ellery felt a premonition. The glint in Lew's bleared eye promised no advancement of the cause of peace.

The players were distributing their bets. Bonnie had pushed a stack of blue chips onto number 19 and, scarcely paying attention, Ty shoved a similar stack on the same number. At this moment Alessandro ushered into the room a very famous lady of the screen who had just married Prince Youssov, whose royal line was reputed to stand close to the Heavenly Throne; the Prince was with her, in full panoply; and everyone turned his attention from the table, including the croupier, to admire the gorgeous pair.

Lew calmly picked up Bonnie's stack and moved it from number 19 to number 9.

"My God," groaned Mr. Queen to himself. "If 19 should win. . . !"

"Nineteen," announced the croupier, and the hands of Bonnie and Ty stretched from opposite sides of the table to meet on the pile of chips shoved forward by the croupier. Bonnie did not remove her hand.

"Will somebody," she said in an ice-in-glass voice, "inform the gentleman that this is my stack?"

Ty kept his hand on hers. "Far be it from me to argue with a lady, but will somebody wise her up that it's mine?"

"The gentleman is trying to be cute. It's mine."

"The lady couldn't be if she tried. It's mine."

"Butch! You saw me cover nineteen, didn't you?"

"I wasn't watching. Look, dear—"

"Croupier!" said Ty Royle. "Didn't you see me cover number nineteen?"

The croupier looked baffled. "I'm afraid I didn't see—"

"It's Ty's!" said one of his companions.

"No, it vuss Bonnie's. I see her put it there," said the Russian director.

"But I tell you I saw Ty—"

"Bonnie—"

The table was in an uproar. Ty and Bonnie glared nakedly at each other. The Boy Wonder looked angry. Alessandro ran up.

"Ladies, gentlemen. Please! You're disturbing the other players. What's the trouble?"

Ty and Bonnie both tried to explain.

"That's not true," stormed Bonnie. "You let my hand go!"

"I'm sorry," barked Ty, "but I don't see why I should. If it were anybody else I might accept her word—"

"How dare you!"

"Oh, stop mugging. You're not doing the big scene now. It's a cheap stunt."

"Mugging, am I?" cried Bonnie. "You—*comedian!*"

Ty applauded. "Keep it up, sister; you're going great."

"Pretty boy!"

That stung him. "I ought to slap your face—"

"You took the words right out of my mouth!" And Bonnie whacked his cheek resoundingly.

Ty went pale. Bonnie's bosom heaved. The Boy Wonder whispered sharply in her ear. Alessandro said something to Ty in a curt undertone.

"I don't give a damn. If she thinks she can maul me and get away with it—" said Ty, his nostrils quivering.

"Insulting pup!" raged Bonnie. "Accuse *me* of cheating—"

"I'll pay you back for that smack if it's the last thing I do!" shouted Ty across Alessandro's fat shoulders.

"There's more where that came from, Ty Royle!"

"Please!" thundered Alessandro. "I'll credit each of your accounts with the winnings on that bet. Now I'll have to ask you, Miss Stuart and Mr. Royle, either to quiet down or leave."

"Leave?" shrieked Bonnie. "I can't get away from the contaminated air surrounding that fake old lady's delight soon enough!"

And she wrenched herself from the Boy Wonder's grasp and flew to the door. Ty shook Alessandro off and ran after her. The Boy Wonder dived after both.

They all disappeared to the accompaniment of screams and bellows.

"That," said Ellery to Lew Bascom, "was one damfool trick, my playful friend."

"Ain't it the truth?" sighed Lew. "C'mon, toots, let's watch the wind-up of this bout." And he dragged his brunette companion away from the wheel and hurried her after the vanished trio.

Something made Ellery turn and look at Jack Royle. The actor still sat at the bar, motionless, as if he had not heard a word of the quarrel behind him.

But in the mirror Ellery caught a glimpse of his lips. They were twisted into a bitter smile.

4

BATTLE ROYLE

The seven days following that quiet evening at Alessandro's whistled by Mr. Ellery Queen's ears with the terrifying intimacy of bullets; it was like being caught out in No Man's Land between two blasting armies. By the end of the week he had not only collected a smoking mass of notes but several lesions of the nervous system as well.

He was entangled in a mass of old Royle-Stuart clippings in the studio library, trying to unsnarl his notes, when he was summoned by page to Jacques Butcher's office.

The Boy Wonder looked gaunt, but triumphant. "*Mirabile dictu.* We're sitting on top of the world."

"Peace, it's wonderful," grinned Lew. "It sure is."

"They've agreed?" asked Ellery incredulously.

"Absolutely."

"I refuse to believe it. What did you use—hypnosis?"

"Appeal to their vanity. I knew they'd fall."

"Blythe put up a battle," said Lew, "but when I told her Jack didn't want her but was holding out for Cornell, she got tongue-tied trying to say yes."

"How about Jaunty Jack?"

"A pushover." Lew frowned. "It was hooey about Cornell, of course. Looked to me almost as if he *wanted* to play opposite Blythe."

"He has looked peaked this week," said Ellery thoughtfully.

"Hell, he ain't had a drink in five days. That would poop up any guy. I tell you something's happened to Jack!"

"Let's not pry too deeply into the ways of Providence," said the Boy Wonder piously. "The point is—they're in."

"I shouldn't imagine, Butch, you had quite so smooth a time winning the youngsters over."

The producer shuddered. "Please. . . . Ty finally gave in because I convinced him his public was demanding a real-life rôle from him—biography's the vogue, following the Muni hits—and what could Ty Royle's public like better than Ty Royle's own life on the screen? Know what he said? 'I'll show 'em real life,' he said, 'when I get my hands around your fiancée's lily-white throat!'"

"Sounds bad," said Ellery.

"Doesn't sound good," chortled Lew.

"Bonnie," said the Boy Wonder sadly, "Bonnie was even worse. The only condition on which she'd give in was that the script must include at least one scene in which she had to slap, scratch, and punch Ty into insensibility."

"Who's directing?" asked Lew.

"Probably Corsi. Swell Broadway background. And you know what he did last year with the human-interest situations in *Glory Road*. Why?"

"I was thinking," said Lew dreamily; "it's going to be a lot of fun. Corsi's the most finicky retake artist in pictures. After two-three days of slapping Ty around to Corsi's satisfaction for that one scene Bonnie'll have had Ty's pound of flesh—under her fingernails."

The historic ceremony of the Great Signing took place on the 11th, which was the following Monday. From the preparations he heard and witnessed in the office adjoining his, Ellery thought whimsically of a landing-field, with a crippled plane circling above, and fire-apparatus and ambulances scurrying about below in readiness for the inevitable crack-up.

But, all things considered, the contracts were signed without the blazing wreckage the Boy Wonder apparently anticipated. Peace was achieved by a simple expedient: the signatories did not open their mouths. Jack Royle, dressed even more carefully than usual, stared out of Butcher's windows until his turn came to sign; then he signed, smiled for the photographers, and quietly walked out. Blythe, eye-filling in a silver fox-trimmed suit, preserved a queenly silence. Bonnie, it was true, stared steadily at Ty's throat throughout the ceremony, as if contemplating assault. But Ty, to whose better nature Butch had appealed beforehand, ignored the challenge in her eyes.

The trade-paper reporters and photographers were plainly disappointed.

"For gossakes," said Lew disgustedly, when they had all left, "that's a hell of a way to build up the conflict angle. Look at the chance we muffed, Butch!"

"Until they signed," said the producer calmly, "I couldn't risk one of them blowing up the whole business by backing out. You don't fumble when you're playing catch with dynamite, Lew."

"Then it's okay to shoot the works now, Butch?" asked Sam Vix.

"We're rolling, Sam."

Vix proceeded to roll. Exactly how it occurred Ellery did not discover—he suspected a conspiracy between the publicity man and Lew Bascom—but on Monday night Bonnie and Ty collided at the bar of the Clover Club. Lew, conveniently present, tried with suspicious gravity to effect a reconciliation "for dear old Magna." Bonnie, who was escorted by a wealthy Argentine gentleman, flared up; Ty flared back; the Argentine gentleman resented Ty's tone; Ty resented the Argentine gentleman's tone; the Argentine gentleman pulled Ty's nose vigorously; and Ty threw the Argentine gentleman over the bartender's head into the bar mirror, which did not stand up under the strain. Whereupon Bonnie had Ty arrested for assault. Bailed out in the early hours of Tuesday morning by his father, Ty swore vengeance in the presence of half the newspapermen in Hollywood.

The Tuesday papers made Sam Vix look content. "Even Goldwyn," he told Ellery modestly, "would be satisfied with that one."

But Mr. Vix did not look so content on Friday. The very patch over his eye was quivering when he burst into the Boy Wonder's office, where Lew and Ellery were shouting at each other in a "story conference," while Butcher listened in silence.

"We're sunk," panted Vix. "Never trust an actor. They've done it. Paula Paris just tipped me off!"

"Who done what?" asked Butch sharply.

"The one thing that blows the Royle-Stuart picture higher than the Rockies. Jack and Blythe have made up!"

He sank into a chair. Lew Bascom, Ellery, goggled at him. Butcher swiveled and stared out his window.

"Go on," said Lew in a sick voice. "That's like saying Trotsky and Stalin were caught playing pinochle with J. P. Morgan."

"It's even worse than that," groaned Vix. "*They're going to be married.*"

"For gossakes!" yelled Lew, jumping up. "That screws everything!"

The Boy Wonder spun around and said into his communicator: "Madge, get Paula Paris on the wire."

"*Requiescat in pace,*" sighed Ellery. "Anybody know the dope on the next train to New York?"

Lew was racing about, declaiming to the ceiling. "Wham goes the big idea. Conflict—huh! Feud! Build up a natural for over twenty years and then they go into a clinch and kill the whole thing. They can't do this to me!"

The telephone rang. "Paula, Jacques Butcher. Is it true what Sam Vix says you say about Jack and Blythe?"

"They agreed to forgive and forget Wednesday night," answered Paula. "I heard it late yesterday. It seems Jack saw the light Saturday night at the Horseshoe Club after that fuss over Park, the actor, and he's been brooding over his own cussedness ever since. Seems to be true love, Mr. Butcher. They're rushing plans for the wedding."

"What happened?"

"Your guess is as good as mine."

"Well, I'm counting on you to give it a royal send-off in your column, Paula."

"Don't worry, Mr. Butcher," cooed Paula. "I shall."

Lew glared. "Is it on the level?"

And Ellery said: "Did she—did she mention me?"

"Yes to you, no to you." The Boy Wonder sat back comfortably. "Now, boys, what's the panic about?"

"I'm dying," howled Lew, "and he cracks wise!"

"It's a cinch," argued the publicity man, "this marriage knocks the feud for a loop, Butch. Where's your publicity build-up now? If they had to get hitched, blast it, why couldn't they wait till the picture was released?"

"Look," said the producer patiently, getting to his feet and beginning to walk around. "What's our story? The story of four people in a romantic conflict. Jack and Blythe as the central figures. Why?"

"Because they're crazy," yelled Lew. "This proves it."

"Because, you simpleton, they're deeply in love. You're doing a love story, gentlemen, although neither of you seems aware of it. They love, they break off, they become bitter enemies, and after twenty years they suddenly fall into a clinch."

"It's illogical," complained Ellery.

"And yet," smiled the Boy Wonder, "it's just happened. Don't you see what you've got? The natural wind-up of your picture! It follows real life like a photostat. After a generation of clawing at each other's throats, *they've made up.*"

"Yes, but why?"

"How should I know the motivation? That's your job, and Lew's. You're writers, aren't you? What's the gag? What's the answer to this romantic mystery? What do you think you men are being paid for?"

"Wow," said Vix, staring.

"As for you, Sam, you've got an even bigger publicity angle now than the feud."

"They've made up," said Vix reverently.

"Yes," snapped Butcher, "and every movie fan within arm's-length of a newspaper or fan mag will wonder why the hell they did. There's your line, Sam—crack down on it!"

The publicity man slapped the desk. "Sure—why did they clinch after twenty years' scrapping around? *See the picture and find out!*"

"Now you've got it. You talk about holding up their marriage until the picture's released. Nuts! They're going to be spliced right away, and to the tune of the loudest ballyhoo you've ever blasted out of this studio."

"Leave it to me," said Vix softly, rubbing his hands.

"We'll make it a super-marriage. Shoot the works. Brass bands, high hats, press associations. . . . It's a colossal break for the production."

"Wait," whispered Lew. "I've got an idea." He rubbed his nose viciously.

"Yes?"

"Everybody out here puts on the dog the same way when they take the sentence. We've got to do it different. The preacher, the ceremony don't mean nothin'; it's the build-up that gets the headlines. Why not put reverse English on the marriage?"

"Spill it, you tantalizing slug!"

"Here's the gag. Offer 'em the use of Reed Island for the honey-moon."

"Reed Island?" frowned Ellery.

"I've got a place there," explained Butcher. "It's just a hunk of rock in the Pacific—southwest of Catalina—fishing village there. Go on, Lew."

"That's it!" cried Lew. "You can have 'em flown down. Just the two of 'em—turtle-doves flying off into the setting sun, to be alone with lo-o-ove. BUT—before they take off, what happens? They're hitched right on the field! We can use old Doc Erminius, the Marryin' Parson. You'll have a million people at the airport. There's more room on a flying field than in a church."

"Hmm," said the Boy Wonder. "It has its merits."

"Hell, I'll fly 'em down in my own crate," grinned Lew. "I've always thought I'd look swell in a g-string and a bow-and-arrow. Or Sam here could do it."

"Say," chuckled Vix, "the screwball's got something. Only I got a better idea. How about getting *Ty Royle* to pilot them? Son Forgives Father, Plays Cupid to Famous Film Duo. He can fly like a fool, and that's a sweet ship he's got."

"That's it," said the Boy Wonder thoughtfully. "We can really go to town on a stunt like that. Dignified, too. They want to be alone. Going to spend their honeymoon on famous producer's hideaway estate in lonely Pacific, far from the maddening crowd. Newspapers, for God's sake stay away. . . . Yes, they won't! Reed Island will look like Broadway during the Lindy reception. Lew, it's in."

Lew seized a bottle. "To the bride!"

"Lemme out of here," muttered Vix, and he scrambled out.

"Pardon the small still voice," said Ellery, "but aren't you boys being a little optimistic? Suppose our friends the lovebirds refuse to be exploited? Suppose Ty Royle frowns on his eminent father's hatchet-burying ritual?"

"Leave the details to me," said Butcher soothingly. "It's my job to worry. Yours is to whip that story into shape. I want an adaptation okayed by the time they get back; if possible, the first sequence of the script ready. Get going."

"You're the boss," grinned Ellery. "Coming, Lew?"

Lew waved the bottle. "Can't you see I'm celebratin' the nup-chu-als?"

So Ellery set out on his quest alone.

After a few telephone calls he headed his rented coupé towards Beverly Hills. He found the Royle estate near the grounds of the Los Angeles Country Club—an enormous castellated pile in the mediaeval English manner, faithful even unto the moat.

The portals gaped, and flunkies seemed nonexistent; so Ellery followed his ears and soon came to an upper hall from which the raucous noises of a small but brisk riot were emanating. There he found the missing servants, grouped at a door in various attitudes of excited and pleasurable eavesdropping.

Ellery tapped an emaciated English gentleman on the shoulder.

"Since this seems to be a public performance," he drawled, "do you think there would be any objection to my going in?"

A man gasped, and the Englishman colored, and they all backed guiltily away. "I beg pawdon. Mr. Royle—"

"Ah, Louderback," said Ellery. "You *are* Louderback?"

"I am, sir," said Louderback stiffly.

"I am happy to note," said Ellery, "that your mastiff quality of loyalty is leavened by the human trait of curiosity. Louderback, stand aside."

Ellery entered a baronial room, prepared for anything. Nevertheless, he was slightly startled. Bonnie Stuart sat campfire fashion on top of a grand piano, gazing tragically into her mother's calm face. On the other side of the room Jack Royle sat sipping a cocktail while his son raced up and down the hearthstone flapping his arms like an agitated penguin.

"—won't stand for it," moaned Bonnie to her mother.

"Darling, *you* won't stand for it?"

"—hell of a note," said Ty. "Dad, are you out of your mind? It's—it's treason!"

"Just coming to my senses, Ty. Blythe, I love you."

"I love you, Jack."

"Mother!"

"Dad!"

"Oh, it's impossible!"

"—even make me set *foot* in this house," cried Bonnie. Blythe rose from the piano bench and drifted dreamy-eyed towards her fiancé. Bonnie jumped down and began to follow her. "Even that's a concession. Oh, mother darling. But I wouldn't, only Clotilde said you'd come *here* to visit that—that man, and—"

"Do you have to marry her?" pleaded Ty. "After so many years? Look at all the women you could have had!"

"Blythe dear." Jack Royle rose, too, and his son began a second chase. Ellery, watching unobserved and wide-eyed, thought they would soon need some one to direct traffic. They were weaving in and out without hand-signals, and it was a miracle no collisions occurred.

"—old enough to lead my own life, Ty!"

"Of all the women in the world—"

"The only one for me." Jack took Blythe in his arms. "Two against the world, eh, darling?"

"Jack, I'm so happy."

"Oh, my God."

"—after all the things you *said* about him, mother, I should think you'd be *ashamed*—"

"Bonnie, Bonnie. We've made up our minds. We've been fools—"

"Been?" Bonnie appealed to the beamed ceiling. "Fools, fools!"

"Who's a fool?"

"Oh, so the shoe fits!"

"You keep out of this!"

"She's my mother, and I love her, and I *won't* see her throw her life away on the father of a useless, pretty-faced, contemptible *Turk!*"

"*You* should talk, with your weakness for Argentine polo-players!"

"Ty Royle, I'll slap that hateful face of yours again!"

"Try it and I swear I'll tan your beautiful hide—yes, and where you sit, too!"

"Ty—"

"Bonnie, sweet child—"

"Oh, hello, Queen," said Jack Royle. "Have a ringside seat. Ty, you've got to cut this out. I'm old enough to know what I'm doing. Blythe and I were made for each other—"

"Page ninety-five of the script," growled Ty. "We're shooting the clinch tomorrow. For the love of Pete, dad!"

"Who *is* that man?" murmured Blythe, glancing at Ellery. "Now, Bonnie, I think you've said enough. And you need some lipstick."

"Hang the lipstick! Oh, mother, mother, how *can* you?"

"Jack darling, a Martini. Extra dry. I'm parched."

"Mr. Queen," wailed Bonnie, "isn't this *disgraceful?* They're actually making up! Mother, I simply will not allow it. Do you hear? If you insist on going through with this impossible marriage—"

"Whose marriage is this, anyway?" giggled Blythe.

"I'll—I'll disown you, that's what I'll do. I *won't* have this leering, pop-eyed, celluloid stuffed shirt for a step-brother!"

"Disown *me?* Bonnie, you silly child."

"That's the only sane thing I've ever heard this blondined, arrow-chinned, lopsided female Gorgonzola say!" shouted Ty to his father. "Me, too. If you go through with this we're quits, dad. . . . Oh, Queen; sorry. You *are* Queen, aren't you? Help yourself to a drink. Come on, dad, wake up. It's only a bad dream."

"Ty, chuck it," said Jack Royle crisply. "Cigars in the humidor, Queen. It's settled, Ty, and if you don't like it I'm afraid you'll have to lump it."

"Then I lump it!"

"Mother," said Bonnie hollowly, "are you going to leave this hateful house with me this minute, or aren't you?"

"No, dear," said Blythe sweetly. "Now run along, like a sweet baby, and keep that appointment with Zara. Your hair's a fright."

"Is it?" asked Bonnie, startled. Then she said in a tragic voice: "Mother, this is the *end.* Goodbye, and I hope he doesn't beat you, although I know he will. Remember, you'll always be able to come back to me, because I *really* love you. Oh, mother!" And, bursting into tears, Bonnie made blindly for the door.

"Now, it's Sidecars," said Ty bitterly, "but after a year with *her* it'll be absinthe and opium. Dad, goodbye."

Thus it came about that the prince and princess of the royal families endeavored to make their dramatic exits simultaneously, and in so endeavoring bumped their royal young heads royally at the door.

"Lout!" said Bonnie through the tears.

"Why don't you watch where you're going?"

"Such a gentleman. Where did you get your manners—from Jem Royle, the celebrated horse-thief of Sussex?"

"Well, this is my house, and you'll oblige me by getting out of it as quickly as those Number Eights of yours can carry you," said Ty coldly.

"*Your* house! I thought you'd just renounced it forever. As a matter of fact, Tyler Royle, you're probably behind this absurd idea of mother's. You've manipulated it some way, you—you Machiavelli!"

"I? I'd rather see my dad playing off-stage voice at Minsky's than tied up to your family! If you ask me, the whole thing is *your* doing."

"Mine? Ha, ha! And why should I engineer it, please?"

"Because you and Blythe are on the skids. While in our last picture—"

"Yes, I read those rave exhibitor reports in the *Motion Picture Herald*. And weren't those *Variety* box-office figures encouraging!"

"Ah, I see you're one of the Royle public."

"What public?"

"Mugger!"

"Camera hog!"

At this breathless moment, as Ty and Bonnie glared sadistically at each other in the doorway, and Jack and Blythe wrapped their famous arms defiantly about each other near the fireplace, and Mr. Queen sighed over a hooker of aged brandy, Louderback coughed and marched stately in bearing a salver.

"Beg pawdon," said Louderback, regarding the Fragonard on the opposite wall. "A French person has just delivered this letter for Miss Blythe Stuart. The person says it has just arrived at Miss Stuart's domicile in the last post, and that it is marked 'important.'"

"Clotilde!" cried Bonnie, reaching for the envelope on the salver. "Delivering your mail *here?* Mother, haven't you any shame?"

"Bonnie, my child," said Blythe calmly, taking the envelope. "Since when do you read your mother's mail? I thought you were leaving me forever."

"And you, Ty," chuckled Jack Royle, sauntering over. "Have you changed your mind, too?"

Blythe Stuart said: "Oh," faintly.

She was staring at the contents of the envelope. There were two pieces of colored pasteboard in her hand, and with the other she was shaking the envelope, but nothing else came out.

She said: "Oh," again, even more faintly, and turned her back.

Mr. Queen, forgotten, approached quietly and peeped. The two pieces of pasteboard were, as far as he could see, ordinary playing-cards. One was a deuce of clubs, the other a ten of spades. As Blythe turned the cards slowly over he saw that their backs were blue and were decorated with a golden horseshoe.

"What's the matter, mother?" cried Bonnie.

Blythe turned around. She was smiling. "Nothing, silly. Somebody's idea of a joke. Are you really so concerned about your poor old mummy, whom you've just renounced forever?"

"Oh, mother, don't be tedious," said Bonnie, tossing her golden curls; and with a sniff at Mr. Tyler Royle she flounced out.

"See you later, dad," said Ty glumly, and he followed.

"That's that," said Jack with relief. He took Blythe in his arms. "It wasn't so bad, was it, darling? Those crazy kids! Kiss me."

"Jack! We've quite forgotten Mr. Queen." Blythe turned her magnificent smile on Ellery. "What must you think of us, Mr. Queen! And I don't believe we've been introduced. But Jack has mentioned you, and so has Butch—"

"Sorry," said the actor. "My dear, this is Ellery Queen, who's going to work with Lew Bascom on our picture. Well, what do you think of us, Queen? A little *meshugeh,* eh?"

"I think," smiled Ellery, "that you lead horribly interesting lives. Queer idea of humor. May I see them, Miss Stuart?"

"Really, it's nothing—" began Blythe, but somehow the cards and envelope managed to pass from her hand to Mr. Queen's; and before she could protest he was examining all three intently.

"The Horseshoe Club, of course," murmured Ellery. "I noticed that distinctive design on their cards the other night. And your practical joker has been very careful about the envelope. Address block-lettered by pen in that scratchy, wishy-washy blue that's so characteristic of American post-offices. Postmarked this morning. Hmm. Is this the first envelope of its kind you've received, Miss Stuart?"

"You don't think—" began Jack Royle, glancing at Blythe.

"I told you. . . ." Blythe tossed her head; Ellery saw where Bonnie had acquired the habit. "Really, Mr. Queen, it's nothing at all. People in our profession are always getting the funniest things in our fan-mail."

"But you *have* received others?"

Blythe frowned at him. He was smiling. She shrugged and went over to the piano; and as she returned with her bag she opened it and extracted another envelope.

"Blythe, there's something behind this," muttered Royle.

"Oh, Jack, it's such a fuss about nothing. I can't understand why you should be so interested, Mr. Queen. I received the first one this past Tuesday, the day after we signed the contracts."

Ellery eagerly examined it. It was identical with the one Clotilde had just brought, even to the color of the ink. It was postmarked Monday night and like the second envelope had been stamped by the Hollywood post-office. Inside were two playing-cards with the horseshoe-backed design: the knave and seven of spades.

"Puzzles and tricks amuse me," said Ellery. "And since you don't ascribe any significance to these doojiggers, surely you won't mind if I appropriate them?" He put them into his pocket. "And now," Ellery went on cheerfully, "for the real purpose of my visit. Sam Vix just got the news at the studio of your reconciliation—"

"So soon?" cried Blythe.

"But we haven't told a soul," protested Royle.

"You know Hollywood. The point is: How come?"

Jack and Blythe exchanged glances. "I suppose Butch will be on our heads soon, so we'll have to explain anyway," said the actor. "It's very simple, Queen. Blythe and I decided we've been idiots long enough. We've been in love for over twenty years and it's only pride that's kept us apart. That's all."

"When I think of all those beautiful years," sighed Blythe. "Darling, we have messed up our lives, haven't we?"

"But this isn't good story material," cried Ellery. "I've got to wangle a reason for your burying the hatchet. Plot, good people, plot! Where's the complication? Who's the other man, or woman? You can't leave it at just a temperamental spat!"

"Oh, yes, we can," grinned Royle. "Ah, there's the phone. . . . Yes, Butch, it's all true. Whoa! Wait a minute. . . . Oh! Thanks, Butch. I'm a little overwhelmed. Wait, Blythe wants to talk to you, too. . . ."

Foiled, Mr. Queen departed.

* * *

Mr. Queen emerged from the gloomy great-hall of the Royles' Eliza-
bethan castle and spied, to his astonishment, young Mr. Royle and
young Miss Stuart sitting on the drawbridge swinging their legs over
the waters of the moat. Like old friends! Well, not quite. He heard Mr.
Royle growl deep in his throat and for an instant Mr. Queen felt the
impulse to leap forward, thinking that Mr. Royle contemplated drown-
ing his lovely companion among the lilies below.

But then he stopped. Mr. Royle's growl was apparently animated
more by disgust with himself than with Miss Stuart.

"I'm a sucker to do this," the growl said, "but I can't run out on the
old man. He's all I've got. Louderback's prissy, and the agent only
thinks of money, and if not for me he'd have been like old Park long
ago."

"Yes, indeed," said Bonnie, gazing into the water.

"What d'ye mean? He's got more talent in his left eyebrow than all
the rest of those guys in their whole bodies. I mean he's so impracti-
cal—he tosses away all this dough."

"And you," murmured Bonnie, "you're such a miser. Of course.
You've got *millions*."

"Leave me out of this," said Ty, reddening. "I mean, he needs me.
That's why I've agreed."

"You don't have to explain to *me*," said Bonnie coldly. "I'm not
interested in you, or your father, or anything about either of you. . . .
The only reason *I've* agreed is that I don't want to hurt mother. I
couldn't desert her."

"Who's explaining now?" jeered Ty.

Bonnie bit her lip. "I don't know why I'm sitting here talking to
you. I detest you, and—"

"You've got a run in your stocking," said Ty.

Bonnie jerked her left leg up and tucked it under her. "You nasty
thing! You would notice such things."

"I'm sorry I said that about—I mean, about your Number Eights,"
mumbled Ty. "You've really got pretty fair legs, and your feet are small
for such a big girl." He threw a pebble into the moat, gazing at the

resulting ripples with enormous interest. "Nice figure, too—of sorts, I mean."

Bonnie gaped at him—Ellery noticed how the roses faded from her cheeks, and how suddenly little-girlish and shy she became. He noticed, too, that she furtively wet the tip of one finger and ran it over the run on the tucked-in leg: and that she looked desperately at her bag, as if she wanted more than anything else in the world to open it and take out a mirror and examine her lips—*did* they need lipstick?—and poke at her honey-gold hair and generally act like a normal female.

"Nice figure," muttered young Mr. Royle again, casting another stone.

"Well!" gasped Bonnie. And her hand did dart to her hair and begin poking with those expert pokings so meaningless to the male eye.

"So," continued the young man irrelevantly, "we'll be friends. Until the wedding, I mean? Hey?"

Mr. Queen at this psychological moment struggled to suppress a cough. But the cough insisted on erupting.

They both jumped as if he had shot off a revolver. Ty got red all over his face and scrambled to his feet. Bonnie looked guilty and then bit her lip and then opened her bag and then closed it and then said icily: "That's not the bargain. Oh, hello, Mr. Queen. I'd sooner get chummy with a polecat. No dice, my fine-feathered friend. I know *your* intentions with women. I just won't fight with you in public until mother and your father are married."

"Hello, Queen. Say, did you ever see a more disagreeable woman in your life?" Ty was busy brushing himself off. "Not a kind word in several million. All right, have it your way. I was just thinking of dad, that's all."

"And I wouldn't do a thing like this for any one else in the world but mother. Help me up, please, Mr. Queen."

"Here, I'll—"

"Mr. Queen?" cooed Bonnie.

Mr. Queen silently helped her up. Ty worked his powerful shoulders up and down several times, like a pugilist loosening his muscles. He glared at her.

"All right, damn it," growled Ty. "Till the wedding."

"You're *so* chivalrous, you great big beautiful man."

"Can I help it if I was born handsome?" yelled Ty.

And they stalked off in opposite directions.

Mr. Ellery Queen gazed after them, mouth open. It was all too much for his simple brain.

5

GONE WITH THE WIND

Paula Paris's column gave the news to a palpitating world on Saturday morning, and on Saturday afternoon the Magna Studios doubled the guards at the main gate. The hounds were baying outside Jack Royle's mansion in Beverly Hills; Blythe had shut herself up in her mosque of a house in Glendale, its door defended by the loose-chested, tight-lipped Clotilde; and Ty and Bonnie, playing their strange rôles, granted a joint interview to the puzzled press in which they said nice things about each other and were photographed smiling into each other's eyes.

"It's all set," said Sam Vix to Ellery at the end of a furious day. He wiped his face. "But, boy, oh, boy—tomorrow!"

"Isn't Bonnie going along?" asked Ellery.

"She wanted to, but I discouraged her. I was afraid that when Ty flew her back from Reed Island, they'd strangle each other in midair."

"It's wonderful how cooperative Jack and Blythe have been," beamed the Boy Wonder. "And with Ty piloting 'em—is that a story, Sam?"

"Sweet mama," grinned Lew Bascom. "Gimme that bottle."

"Boys will handle the jamboree tomorrow at the field, Butch," said the publicity man. "I'm hopping off for Reed Island to direct the preparations for the reception. See you tomorrow night."

"Not me," said Butcher hastily. "I hate these Hollywood shindigs. I've told Jack and Blythe my doctor advised a rest, and Bonnie understands. Driving out to Palm Springs tomorrow morning for a day in the sun. Conference Monday morning."

At noon on Sunday Ellery and Lew Bascom drove out to the airport in Ellery's coupé. Los Feliz Boulevard was jammed with cars crawling bumper to bumper. They wasted an hour getting to the turn-off at Riverside and another along the Los Angeles River drive through Griffith Park to the field. After fifteen minutes of trying to park his car, Ellery abandoned it and they shouldered their way through the mob.

"Too late," groaned Lew. "There's Erminius doing his stuff!"

Ty's brilliant red-and-gold cabin monoplane, gleaming in the sun, was surrounded by a cordon of cursing police. The Royles and the Stuarts, arms locked about one another, bowed and smiled in the vortex of a maelstrom of photographers, radio men, and friends screaming above the blare of a brass band. Dr. Erminius, his sleek black whiskers flowing fluently in the wind, beamed on every one over his prayer-book and sidled closer to the crowded spot on which the cameras were trained.

"Swell work, Doc!" shouted some one.

"Boy, was that a ceremony?"

"Neat, neat. How about a snifter, Doc Erminius?"

"He'll never marry *me!*"

"It's like the Judgment Day," grinned Lew. "Hey, lemme through here! Come on, Queen. Jack! Blythe!"

The band stopped playing *Here Comes the Bride* and swung into *California, Here I Come.*

"Lew! Mr. Queen! It's all right, officer!"

"Bonnie—Bonnie Stuart! This way, please. Smile at Ty!"

"Won't you say a few words to the radio audience, Jack?"

"Dr. Erminius, how about a few shots?"

"Yes, my son," said the good man hastily, and stepped in front of Jack Royle.

"Jack! Blythe! Let's take a shot of clasped hands showing those wedding rings!"

"Get those people away from that plane, damn it!"

"Miss Blythe! Miss Blythe!" shrieked a feminine voice, and a primly attired French lady of middle age elbowed her way through to the wall of police, waving an envelope frantically.

"Clotilde!" screamed Blythe. She was radiant, her arms full of flowers; her hat askew on her head. She ran over; and as she saw the envelope she gasped aloud, going pale. Then she snatched it from Clotilde's hand over a policeman's shoulder and tore it open. Ellery saw her close her eyes, crumple the envelope convulsively. She hurled it away.

Then she put on a smile and returned to the group before the plane.

Ellery picked his way through the fruit and flower baskets littering the ground and managed to pick up the envelope unnoticed. It was another of the post-office-written envelopes, this time sent by special delivery. Inside were the torn halves of a horseshoe-backed playing-card, the eight of spades.

Torn in half. Blythe had not torn it, Ellery was certain. Queer. . . . He frowned and pocketed the envelope, looking about. The French-woman had vanished in the mob.

"Ty! Kiss Bonnie for the newsreel!"

"Jack! Jack! Go into a clinch with the blushing bride!"

"What's this?" yelled some one, holding aloft a handsome wicker hamper.

"Somebody sent it!" roared Jack Royle.

"Open it!"

Bonnie straightened up with two enormous thermos bottles from the hamper. "Look what I found, people!"

"Sidecars!" bellowed Jack, unscrewing the cap of one of the bottles and sniffing. "Thanks, anonymous friend. How'd you know my weakness?"

"And mine? Martinis!" screamed Blythe over the other bottle. "Isn't that the loveliest going-away gift!"

"Toast to the bride and groom!"

The thermos bottles were hurled from hand to hand; for a few moments they were all laughing and struggling for a drink. Lew battled desperately with a large stout lady, rescued both bottles, and poured out another round in a nest of paper-cups which appeared from somewhere magically.

"Hey, save some for us," growled Jack.

"Can't you get drunk on love?"

"An old buck like you—d'ye need a *stimulant?*"

"Love—Marches—ON!"

"I said save some!" howled Jack, laughing.

Lew reluctantly dropped the thermos bottles into the hamper, screwing on the caps. The hamper lay beside a pile of luggage near the plane.

Lew and Ellery were squeezed, pummeled, pushed, and mauled, stumbling over the luggage. Ellery sat down on the hamper and sighed: "No wonder Butch went to Palm Springs."

"Who swiped my helmet?" yelled Ty Royle. "Mac! Rev 'em while I get another!" And he darted into the crowd, fighting towards the nearby hangar.

"What's going on here, the Revolution?" panted a voice. Ellery, trying to save his hat from being crushed, turned to find Alan Clark, his agent, grinning down at him.

"Just a quiet Sunday in Hollywood, Alan. They're almost ready to take off."

"I gotta kiss the bride, for gossakes," shouted Lew frantically. He grabbed at Blythe, caught her, and bussed her heartily while Jack Royle, grinning, began to toss things into the cabin of the plane. Bonnie, heart-stopping in a knee-length leopard coat and Russian leopard hat, was obviously his next victim, but just then a man ran up.

"Miss Bonnie Stuart! Mr. Tyler Royle wants to see you in the hangar."

Bonnie made a face, smiled for the benefit of the staring public, and slipped after him.

Bonnie looked around inside the hangar. It seemed empty. She turned to question the man who had brought Ty's message, but he was gone.

"Ty?" she called, puzzled. Her voice echoed from the high roof.

"Here I am!" She followed the sound of Ty's voice and found him behind a tarpaulined biplane, rummaging in a steel locker.

Ty stared at her. "What do *you* want, pest?"

"What do *I* want! What do *you* want?"

"Me? Not a thing—from you."

"Look here, Ty Royle, I've stood enough from you today without playing puss-in-the-corner. You just sent a messenger to me. What do you want?"

"I sent a messenger? The hell I did."

"Ty Royle, don't stand there and be cute!"

Ty clenched his hands. "Oh, God, if only you weren't a woman."

"You seemed thankful enough just now that I was a woman," said Bonnie coldly. "That was quite a kiss you gave me."

"The cameraman asked for it!"

"Since when do you follow a cameraman's orders?"

"Listen!" yelled Ty. "I wouldn't kiss you of my own free will if I hadn't seen a woman for five years. Your lips tasted like two hunks of rouged rubber. How your leading men can keep kissing you in front of the camera. . . . They ought to get medals for exceptional heroism in line of duty!"

Bonnie went white. "You—You—" she began in a fury.

Some one coughed behind them. They both turned around. They both blinked.

A tall figure in heavy flying clothes, wearing a helmet and goggles, hands gloved in fur, stood there widelegged and still. One hand pointed a revolver at them.

"All right, I'll bite," said Ty. "What's the gag?"

The revolver waved a little, with an unmistakable meaning: Silence. Ty and Bonnie drew sharp breaths simultaneously.

The figure sent a chair skittering across the hangar floor. The revolver pointed to Ty, to the chair. Ty sat down in the chair. Bonnie stood very still.

A bundle of ropes, cut in short lengths, came flying through the air from the tall figure and struck Bonnie's legs. The revolver pointed to Ty.

Ty jumped out of the chair, snarling. The revolver covered him instantly, trained on his chest.

"Ty," said Bonnie. "Please. Don't."

"You can't hope to get away with this stunt," said Ty in a thick voice. "What do you want, money? Here—"

But the weapon's weaving eye stopped him. Bonnie quickly stooped, picked up the ropes, and began to bind Ty to the back and legs of the chair.

"I see," said Ty bitterly. "I see the whole thing now. One of your little jokes. This time, by God, you've gone too far. I'll put you in clink for this."

"That revolver's no joke," whispered Bonnie, "and I may play rough, but not with guns. Can't you see he means business? I won't bind you tightly—"

The revolver poked her between the shoulder-blades. Bonnie bit her lip and bound Ty tightly. A prepared gag materialized in one gloved hand. She gagged Ty.

Things blurred. It was absurd—this deadly silence, this tongueless figure, the menace of the revolver. She opened her mouth and screamed. Only the echo answered.

The figure was upon her instantly, however. Glove over her mouth, she was forced into another chair. She fought back, kicking, biting. But soon she was strapped to the chair, as gagged and helpless as Ty; and the figure was stooping over Ty, tightening his bonds, adding others.

And then, still without a word, the figure pocketed the revolver, raised one arm in a mocking salute, and darted out of sight behind the tarpaulined biplane.

Ty's eyes were savage above the gag; he struggled against the ropes, rocking the chair. But he succeeded only in upsetting himself. He fell backwards, striking his head against the stone floor with a meaty *thunk!* that turned Bonnie's stomach.

He lay still, his eyes closed.

"Here he comes!" shouted Jack, his arm about Blythe as they stood on the movable steps of the plane. "Ty! Come on!"

"Where's Bonnie?" screamed Blythe. "Bon-NIE!"

"Crowd's got her. Ty!"

The tall goggled figure shoved his way through the mob and began to toss the remaining luggage into the cabin. Ellery stood up, helpfully handing him the hamper. He waved Blythe and Jack into the plane, raised the hamper in a farewell to the crowd, and vaulted into the cabin. The door slapped shut.

"Happy landings!" roared Lew.

Blythe and Jack pressed their faces to one of the windows, and the band struck up the *Wedding March* from *Lohengrin*.

Everybody sang.

Bonnie looked frantically about. And then she caught her breath. Through the hangar window nearest her she saw the tall goggled figure running towards Ty's plane; and for the first time Bonnie realized that the figure was dressed in a flying suit identical with Ty's. Jack ... Blythe ... waving, shouting ... The brassy sounds of the band came faintly through the hangar walls.

And then, before her distended eyes, the red-and-gold plane began to move, taxiing down the field, rising ... rising ...

The last thing Bonnie saw before everything went black was her mother's handkerchief signalling a farewell in the cabin window.

Bonnie opened her eyes aeons later to a blank world; slowly it filled in. She was lying on her side, on the floor. A few feet away lay Ty, looking very pale, looking ... dead. Ty!

She stirred, and thousands of needles began to shoot into her numb flesh. With the pain came full awareness. Blythe ... Blythe was gone.

She had fallen sidewise when she fainted. How long ago? What—what time was it?

Blythe. Blythe was gone. Like smoke in thin air.

In her fall the gag had been dislodged from her mouth.

And Ty was dead.

Mother. . . .

Bonnie screamed. Her own screams came screaming back at her, lying on the cold floor of the hangar behind the concealing plane.

Ty moaned.

Bonnie inched her way painfully the few feet across the floor towards him, dragging the chair to which she was bound. He opened his bloodshot eyes.

"Ty," she gasped. "They've been kidnapped! Jack—my mother. . . . That man—he flew them off the field, pretending to be you!"

Ty closed his eyes. When he opened them again Bonnie was shocked by their unnatural red color. The gag over his lips worked spasmodically, as if he were trying to speak. She could see the cords of his neck distend.

She bared her teeth, face pressed to his, gnawing at his gag like a mouse, tugging, worrying it. His cheek felt cold.

"Bonnie." His voice was unrecognizable. "Loosen these ropes."

For an instant their breaths mingled and their eyes locked. Then Bonnie looked away and Ty turned over, and with a little cry she bent her head to his bound, straining hands.

Luckily Ellery and his two companions had not left the field. Ellery had looked once at the thousands milling about the parked cars and wisely suggested procrastination. So he and Lew and Alan Clark went over to the airport restaurant for sandwiches and coffee.

They were roused out of a listless discussion of the picture story by a commotion outside, and near one of the hangars they came upon an anthill of officials and pilots and mechanics and police. They were swarming about Ty, who was rubbing his skinned hands, and Bonnie, who was seated with folded hands, paler than her own handkerchief, staring numbly at all the busy ants without seeing them.

"My father's in that plane," said Ty. There was a purplish lump on the back of his head; he looked ill. "Queen! Thank God there's one face I recognize. And Lew! Get Butch. Call Reed Island. Do something, somebody!"

"No point in calling Reed Island first," said Ellery to Lew. "That's the one place this chap *didn't* take them to. I wonder if . . . "

"Took mother," said Bonnie simply. A female attendant tried to lure her away, but she shook her head.

Ellery rang Information, then put in a call to Tolland Stuart's estate. A man with a dry, peevish voice answered after a long time.

"Is this Mr. Tolland Stuart?"

It seemed to Ellery that the voice was instantly cautious. "No, this is Dr. Junius. Who's calling Mr. Stuart?"

Ellery explained what had happened and asked if Ty's monoplane had passed near the Chocolate Mountain estate. But Tolland Stuart's physician crushed that possibility.

"Not a plane near here all day. By the way, isn't it possible that Mr. Royle and Miss Stuart merely took that way of escaping the crowds? Perhaps—it would be natural—they wanted a really private honeymoon."

"And hired some one to tie up Ty Royle and Bonnie Stuart and kidnap the plane?" said Ellery dryly. "I hardly think so, Doctor."

"Well, let me know when you get word," said Dr. Junius. "Mr. Stuart went rabbit-hunting this morning and hasn't got back yet."

Ellery thanked him, disconnected, and called Palm Springs. But Jacques Butcher could not be located. So Ellery left a message and telephoned Reed Island. Sam Vix was not about—he had flown off somewhere: Ellery could not clearly get his destination.

"Then Mr. Royle's plane hasn't landed on Reed Island?"

"No. We've been waiting. Is something the matter? They should have been here by this time."

Ellery sighed and hung up.

The police appeared, county men; swarms of newspaper reporters descended, a plague of locusts. In a short time the field was more blackly populated than at the take-off, and it was necessary to summon police reserves. Meanwhile, searching planes from the municipal airport and the nearest Army field were darkening the sky, streaming southwestward on the probable route of the red-and-gold monoplane.

The afternoon lengthened; toward sunset a small two-seater skimmed in from the west and the Boy Wonder leaped to the ground from the cockpit and ran for the hangar.

He put his arms about Bonnie and she sobbed against his chest while Ty paced up and down consuming cigaret after cigaret.

"Here it is!" shouted an airport official, dashing up. "An Army scout has just sighted a red-and-gold monoplane on a barren plateau in the Chocolate Mountains! No sign of life."

"A wreck?" asked Ty harshly.

"No. It's just grounded there."

"That's strange," muttered Ellery, but he said nothing more as he saw the expression on Bonnie's face. He had seen expressions like that on the faces of condemned criminals reprieved at the eleventh hour.

And so more planes were commandeered, and a small fleet rose from the airport in the dusk and preened their wings in the setting sun.

And soon, in the darkness, they were feeling their way over the San Bernardino Mountains, guided by radio. Then they followed a brightness in the hills to the south, which grew into flares on a flat, deserted plateau.

When they landed Army men challenged them with drawn revolvers. There seemed a curious diffidence in their manner, as if they were indisposed to talk in the evening under the white stars in the cold pale light of the flares.

Also see page 58

"My father—" began Ty, breaking into a run. His red-and-gold plane rested quietly on the plateau, surrounded by men.

"My mother—" said Bonnie, stumbling after him.

A helmeted officer said something in a low voice to Jacques Butcher, and he made a face and instantly smiled in the most peculiar way; and he beckoned to Ellery and Lew and called out to Bonnie: "Bonnie. Just a minute."

And Bonnie stopped, her face turned sidewise in the ghostly light, looking frightened and yet trying not to look frightened; and Ty stopped, too, very abruptly, as if he had come up to a high stone wall.

And Ellery and Jacques Butcher entered the cabin of Ty's plane, and some one shut the door behind them.

Outside, Ty and Bonnie stood a few feet apart, two rigid poles in a mass of stirring humanity. Neither said anything, and both kept looking at the closed door of the monoplane. And no one came near them.

The sky was so near, thought Bonnie, so close here in the mountains at night.

The cabin door opened and Jacques Butcher came out with a strong heavy step, like a diver walking on the bottom of the sea. And he went up to Ty and Bonnie and stood between them and put his right arm about Bonnie's shoulder and his left arm about Ty's, and he said in a voice that hissed against the silence of the plateau:

"The pilot is missing, Bonnie. Ty. What can I say? Jack and Blythe are in that plane. . . ."

"In the plane," said Bonnie, taking a half-step forward. And she stopped. "Inside?" she asked in a small-child, wondering voice. "Why don't they . . . come . . . out?"

Ty turned and walked off. Then he stopped, too, his back dark and unmoving against the stars.

"Bonnie. Darling," said Butcher thickly.

"Butch." Bonnie sighed. "They're—they're not . . . ?"

"They're both dead."

The sky was so close.

PART TWO

6

CHOCOLATE MOUNTAINS

The sky was so close. Because it was falling down. Down the chute of a trillion miles. Down through the pinhole stars. Down to the gorse-covered plateau. Down on Bonnie's head.

She pressed her palms to her eyes. "I don't believe it. I don't believe it."

"Bonnie," said Jacques Butcher.

"But it can't be. Not Blythe. Not mother."

"Bonnie. Darling. Please."

"She always said she'd never grow old. She always said she'd live a million, million years."

"Bonnie, let me take you away from here."

"She didn't want to die. She was afraid of death. Sometimes in the middle of the night she'd start to cry in her sleep, and I'd crawl into bed with her and she'd snuggle up to me like a baby."

"I'll get one of these Army pilots to fly you back to Los Angeles—"

Bonnie dropped her hands. "It's a horrid joke of some kind," she said slowly. "You're all in a conspiracy."

Tyler Royle came stalking back, his face blank against the pale background of the flares.

As he passed he said: "Come on, Bonnie," as if only he and Bonnie existed in a dark dead world.

And Bonnie turned from Butch and followed Ty with something of the otherworldly stiffness of a Zombie.

Lew Bascom came up to Butcher, who was standing still, and said hoarsely: "For gossakes, how do you get outa here?"

"You grow a pair of wings."

"Nah," said Lew. "I'm—pooped." He stuck his fat face out over the gorse and made a sickish, retching sound. "Butch, I gotta get off this damn table-top. I need a drink. I need a lot o' drinks."

"Don't bother me."

"I never could stand a stiff. Are they—are they—"

Butcher walked away. Ty and Bonnie seemed to be floating in the weird aura of mingled flarelight and starshine. They merged with and were lost in the black figures about the resting plane.

Lew sank to the harsh grass, clutching his belly and shivering in the wind. After a moment he struggled to his feet and waddled towards an Army plane, its propeller roaring for a take-off.

"You gettin' outa here?" he shrieked.

The pilot nodded, and Lew scrambled into the rear cockpit. His hat flew off in the backwash of air. He sank low in the cockpit, trembling. The plane trundled off.

In the red-and-gold monoplane a man in flying togs was saying: "Hijacked by a pilot who made pretty sure he wouldn't be recognized—and then this. It looks funny, Mr. Queen."

"Funny?" scowled Ellery. "The Greeks had another word for it, Lieutenant."

John Royle and Blythe Stuart half-sat, half-lay in upholstered swivel chairs in the cabin, across the aisle from each other. Their luggage, baskets of flowers, the wicker hamper were in the aisle between them. The lid of the hamper stood open. On the floor under Royle's slack left hand lay the half-eaten remains of a ham sandwich. One of the thermos bottles from the hamper stood beside it. The empty cap-cup of the bottle was wedged between his thighs. His handsome features were composed. He looked as if he had fallen asleep.

The second thermos bottle had obviously fallen from Blythe's right hand: it lay, mouth tilted up, among the bruised blossoms of a rose-basket beside her. A wad of crumpled waxed paper, the wrappings of a consumed sandwich, was in her lap. The cup of the other thermos bottle had fallen to the floor between her feet. And she, too, eyes closed, serene of face, seemed asleep.

"It's awfully queer," remarked the Lieutenant, studying the still cold faces, "that they should both pop off around the same time."

"Nothing queer about it."

"They haven't been shot or stabbed or strangled; you can see that. Not a sign of violence. That's why I say . . . Only double heart-failure isn't—well, it's quite a coincidence."

"You could say," retorted Ellery, "that a man whose skull had been bashed into turkey-hash with a sledge-hammer died of heart-failure, too. Look here, Lieutenant."

He stooped over Royle's body and with his thumb pressed back the lid of the right eye. The pupil was almost invisible; it had contracted to a dot.

Ellery stepped across the littered aisle and opened Blythe Stuart's right eye.

"Highly constricted pupils," he shrugged. "And notice that pervasive pallor—cyanosis. They both died of morphine poisoning."

"Jack Royle and Blythe Stuart *murdered?*" The Lieutenant stared. "Wow!"

"Murdered." Bonnie Stuart stood in the cabin doorway. "No. Oh, no!"

She flung herself upon her mother's body, sobbing. Ty Royle came in then, looked down at his father. After a moment his hand felt for the cabin wall. But he did not take his eyes from that calm marble face.

Bonnie suddenly sat up, glaring at her hands where they had touched her mother's body. Although there was no mark on her white flesh, Ellery and the Lieutenant knew what she was staring at. She was staring at the invisible stain, the impalpable taint, the cold outer-space enamel of death.

"Oh, no," whispered Bonnie with loathing.

Ty said: "Bonnie," futilely, and took an awkward step across the aisle towards her.

But Bonnie sprang to her feet and screamed: "Oh, no!" and, standing there, tall and distraught, her cheeks pure gray, her breast surging, she swayed and began to fold up like the bellows of an accordion. And as she crumpled in upon herself her eyes turned completely over in their sockets.

Ty caught her as she fell.

Icy bristles of mountain wind curried the plateau. Butch took Bonnie from Ty's arms, carried her through the whipping grass to an Army plane, and threw a borrowed fur coat over her.

"Well, what are we waiting for?" said Ty in a cracked voice. "Death by freezing?"

And the Lieutenant said: "Take it easy, Mr. Royle."

"What are we waiting for?" shouted Ty. "Damn it, there's a murderer loose around here! Why doesn't somebody start tracking the scum down?"

"Take it easy, Mr. Royle," said the Lieutenant again, and he dived into a plane.

Ty began to thrash around in the knee-high grass, trampling swatches of it down in blind parabolas.

Ellery said to a pilot: "Just where are we?"

"On the north tip of the Chocolate Mountains."

He borrowed a flashlight and began to examine the terrain near the red-and-gold monoplane. But if the mysterious aviator who had borne Jack Royle and Blythe Stuart through the circumambient ether to their deaths had left tracks in making his escape from the grounded plane, the tracks had long since been obliterated by the milling feet of the Army men. Ellery wandered farther afield, skirting the rim of the plateau.

He soon saw, in the powerful beam of the electric torch, that the task of finding the unknown pilot's trail quickly was almost a hopeless one. Hundreds of trails led from the plateau down through scrub pine to the lowlands—chiefly horse-trails, as he saw from the many droppings and steel-shoe signs. To the east, as he recalled the topography, lay Black Butte; to the northwest the southern range of the San Bernardino Mountains; to the west the valley through which ran the Southern Pacific Railroad, and beyond it the Salton Sea and the San Jacinto range. The fleeing pilot could have escaped in any of the three directions, through sparsely settled country. It would take days by experienced trackers to find his trail, and by that time it would be stone-cold.

Ellery returned to the red-and-gold plane. The Lieutenant was there again. "It's a hell of a mess. We've made three-way contact by radiophone with the authorities. There's a mob of 'em on their way up."

"What's the trouble?"

"This end of the Chocolate Mountains just laps over into Riverside County—most of it lies in Imperial County to the south. The plane in coming here passed over Los Angeles County, of course, and probably the southeast tip of San Bernardino County. That makes three different counties in which these people may have died."

"So the assorted gentlemen of the law are fighting," nodded Ellery grimly, "for the right to sink their teeth into this juicy case?"

"Well, it's their oyster—let 'em scramble for it. My responsibility ends when some one shows up to claim jurisdiction."

Butcher said curtly: "I don't know about your legal responsibility, Lieutenant, but something's got to be done about Miss Stuart. She's in a bad way."

"I suppose we *could* fly you folks back to the municipal airport, but—"

"What's the trouble?" asked Ty Royle in a high-pitched voice. Ellery felt uncomfortable at the sight of his haggard face. His lips were blue and he was shivering with a cold not caused by the wind.

"Bonnie's collapsed, Ty. She's got to have a doctor."

"Well, sure," said Ty abstractedly. "Sure. I'll fly her down myself. My plane—" But then he stopped.

"Sorry," said the Lieutenant. "That's the one thing that doesn't leave this place till the police get here."

"I suppose so," mumbled Ty. "I guess so." He yelled suddenly: "Damn it to hell!"

"Here," said Ellery grabbing his arm. "You're not far from collapse yourself. Lieutenant, have you any notion how far Tolland Stuart's place is from here? It's supposed to be on a butte in the Chocolate Mountains, somewhere below in Imperial County."

"It's only a few minutes south by air."

"Then that's where we'll take her," rasped Butcher. "If you'll be good enough to place a plane at our disposal—"

"But I don't know if I ought to."

"We'll be at Tolland Stuart's when they want us. You said yourself it's only a few minutes' hop from here."

The Lieutenant looked unhappy. Then he shrugged and shouted: "Garms! Turn 'em over."

A pilot saluted and climbed into a big Army transport. The motors began to spit and snarl. They all broke into a run.

"Where's Lew?" shouted Ellery above the din.

"He couldn't take it," Butcher shouted back. "Flew back to L.A. with one of the Army pilots."

A few minutes later they were in the air headed southeast.

The brightness on the plateau dwindled to a pale blob, then to a pinpoint, and finally blinked out altogether. Butcher held Bonnie, whose eyes were closed, tightly to his chest. Ty sat alone, forward, buried to the nose in his thin coat; he seemed to be dozing. But once Ellery caught the wild shine of his eyes.

Ellery shivered and turned to peer down at the black wrinkled face of the mountain slipping by below.

In less than ten minutes the transport was wheeling over a luminous rectangle lying flat among the crags. To Ellery it seemed no larger than a postage stamp, and he began uncomfortably to think of his own immortal soul.

As he clutched the arms of his seat he saw dimly a massive pile of stone and wood beyond the lighted field. Then they were rushing down the little landing-place, bound, he could swear, for a head-on collision with a hangar.

Miraculously, however, the plane bumped and hopped to a safe stop; and Ellery opened his eyes.

A tall emaciated man was standing outside the hangar, shading his eyes from the glare of the arcs, staring at the plane. It seemed to Ellery that there was something peculiar about the man's rigidity—as if the plane were some Medusa-like monster and he had been petrified by the mere sight of it.

Then the man relaxed and ran forward, waving his arms.

Ellery shook his head impatiently at the mercurial quality of his imagination. He tapped Ty on the shoulder and said gently: "Come on, Ty." Ty started. "We're here."

Ty got up. "How is she?" Butcher shook his head. "Here. I'll—I'll give you a hand."

Between them they managed to haul Bonnie out of the plane. Her body was flaccid, as if all her bones had melted; and her eyes were open, ignoring Butcher, ignoring Ty, fixed on space with a rather terrifying blankness.

Ellery stopped to talk to the pilot. When he jumped to the ground a moment later he heard the tall thin man exclaiming in a distressed voice. "But that's not possible. Perfectly ghastly. When did it happen?"

"We can talk later," said Butch shortly. "Miss Stuart needs your professional attention now, Dr. Junius."

"Appalling," said the doctor. "And the poor child; all broken up. Naturally! This way, please."

The Army transport took to the air again as they passed the hangar, in which Ellery noted a small, stubby, powerful-looking plane, and entered a tree-canopied path leading to the dark mansion beyond. The transport circled the field once, raising echoes from the surrounding mountain walls, and then darted off towards the northwest.

"Careful. The path is rough." Dr. Junius swept the ground with the beam of a flash. "Watch these steps." Silently pursuing, Ellery made out a wide doorway. Open. A sepia cavern lay behind. The flashlight stabbed here and there; then it went out and lights sprang on.

They stood in an enormous, damp-smelling chamber, heavily raftered, with bulky oak furniture, a stone mat-strewn floor, and an immense dark fireplace.

"The settee," said Dr. Junius briskly, running back to shut the door. Except for one penetrating glance in Ellery's direction, the doctor paid no attention to him.

The man's skin was yellowed and bland, so tightly drawn over his bones that it could not wrinkle. The eyes were clever and unfriendly. The figure was stooped, even thinner than Ellery had thought at first sight. He wore a pair of shapeless grimy slacks tucked into high, laced, lumberman's shoes, and a mildew-green smoking-jacket glazed with age. Everything about the man was old—a creature who had grown old by a process of dehydration. There was something cringing about him, too, and watchful, as if he were constantly on the dodge from blows.

Ty and Butch laid Bonnie gently down on the settee.

"We weren't expecting visitors," whined Dr. Junius. "Mr. Royle, would you be good enough to start the fire?"

He scurried away, vanishing down a small side-hall, while Ty struck a match and applied it to the paper and kindling beneath the large logs in the fireplace. Butch rubbed his freezing hands, staring sombrely down at Bonnie's white face. She moaned as the fire blazed up with a great snapping and crackling.

Dr. Junius came hurrying back with an armful of blankets and a small green-black bag, its handle hanging by one link.

"Now if you gentlemen will clear out. Would one of you be kind enough to watch the coffee? Kitchen is at the end of that hall. Brandy, too, in the pantry."

"Where," asked Ellery, "is Mr. Tolland Stuart?"

Dr. Junius, on his bony knees before the settee tucking Bonnie's tossing figure into the blankets, looked up with a startled, ingratiating smile. "You're the gentleman who phoned me a few hours ago from the

Griffith Park airport, aren't you? Voice has a distinctive ring. Hurry, please, Mr. Queen. We can discuss Mr. Stuart's eccentricities later."

The three men went wearily down the hall and, passing through a swinging door, found themselves in a gigantic kitchen, badly illuminated by a single small electric bulb. A pot of coffee bubbled on an old-fashioned range.

Ty sank into a chair at the worktable and rested his head on his arms. Butch blundered about until he found the pantry, and emerged with a dusty bottle of cognac.

"Drink this, Ty."

"Please. Let me alone."

"Drink it."

Ty obeyed tiredly. The Boy Wonder took the bottle and another glass and went out. He returned empty-handed, and for some time they sat around in silence. Ellery turned off the light under the coffee. The house seemed unnaturally quiet.

Dr. Junius bobbed in.

"How is she?" asked Butch hoarsely.

"Nothing to be alarmed about. She's had a bad shock, but she's coming around."

He ran out with the coffee. Ellery went to the pantry and, for lack of anything else to do, nosed about. The first thing he spied was a case of brandy on the floor. Then he remembered the ruddy bulb on Dr. Junius's nose. He shrugged.

A long time later Dr. Junius called: "All right, gentlemen," and they trooped back to the living-room.

Bonnie was sitting up before the fire, sipping the coffee. There was color in her cheeks and, while the circles under her eyes were heavy and leaden, her eyes were sane again.

She gave Butcher one hand and whispered: "I'm sorry I've been such a fuss, Butch."

"Don't be silly," said Butch roughly. "Drink that java."

Without turning her head she said: "Ty. Ty, it's so hard to say. . . . Ty, I'm sorry."

"For me?" Ty laughed, and Dr. Junius looked alarmed. "I'm sorry, too. For you. For dad. For your mother. For the whole God-damned world." He shut off the laugh in the middle of its highest note and flung himself full length on the mat before the fire at Bonnie's feet, covering his face with his hands.

Bonnie looked down at him. Her lower lip began to quiver. She set the coffee-cup down blindly.

"Oh, here, don't—" began Butcher miserably.

Dr. Junius whispered: "Let them alone. There's really nothing to do for them but let the shock and hysteria wear off naturally. A good cry will do wonders for her, and the boy is fighting it off very nicely by himself."

Bonnie wept softly into her fingers and Ty lay still before the fire. The Boy Wonder cursed and began to prowl up and down, throwing epileptic shadows on the flame-lit walls.

"Once again," said Ellery. "Dr. Junius, where the hell is Tolland Stuart?"

"I suppose you find it strange." The doctor's hands were shaking, and it occurred to Ellery that Tolland Stuart's dictum against alcohol worked a special hardship on his physician. "He's upstairs behind a barricade."

"What!"

Junius smiled apologetically. "Oh, he's quite sane."

"He must have heard our plane coming down. Hasn't the man even a normal curiosity?"

"Mr. Stuart is—peculiar. He's been nursing a grudge against the world for so many years that he detests the very sight of people. And then he's a hypochondriac. And odd in other ways. I suppose you noticed the lack of central heating. He has a theory about that—that steam heat dries up your lungs. He has a theory about nearly everything."

"Very amusing," said Ellery, "but what's all this to do with the fact that his granddaughter has come calling for the first time in years? Hasn't he the decency to come downstairs to greet her?"

"Mr. Queen," said Dr. Junius, baring his false teeth in a humorless grin, "if you knew as much about Mr. Tolland Stuart as I do you wouldn't wonder at any of his vagaries." The grin became a whining snarl. "When he came back late this afternoon from his damned eternal rabbit-shooting, and I told him about your call and his daughter Blythe apparently kidnapped on her wedding day and all, he shut himself up in his room and threatened to discharge me if I disturbed him. He claims he can't stand excitement."

"Can he?"

The doctor said spitefully: "He's the healthiest man of his years I know. Damn all hypos! I have to sneak my liquor and coffee up here, go out into the woods for a smoke, and cook meat for myself when he's out hunting. He's a cunning, mean old maniac, that's what he is, and why I bury myself up here with him is more than I can understand!"

The doctor looked frightened at his own outburst; he grew pale and silent.

"Nevertheless, don't you think you might make an exception in this case? After all, a man's daughter isn't murdered every day."

"You mean go up those stairs and into his bedroom, when he's expressly forbidden it?"

"Something like that."

Dr. Junius threw up his hands. "Not I, Mr. Queen, not I. I want to live out the few remaining years of my life with a whole skin."

"Pshaw, he has you buffaloed."

"Well, you're welcome to try, if you don't mind risking a load of buckshot. He always keeps a shotgun by his bed."

Ellery said abruptly: "Ridiculous!"

The doctor made a weary gesture of invitation towards the oak staircase and trudged down the hall to the kitchen—and his cache of brandy—with sloping shoulders.

Ellery went to the foot of the staircase and shouted: "Mr. Stuart!"

Ty raised his head. "Grandfather," said Bonnie limply. "I'd forgotten about *him*. Oh, Butch, we'll have to tell him!"

"Mr. Stuart?" called Ellery again, almost angrily. Then he said: "Damn it, I'm going up."

Dr. Junius reappeared, his ruddy nose a little ruddier. "Wait, please.

If you insist on being foolhardy, I'll go up with you. But it won't do you any good, I warn you."

He joined Ellery and together they began to ascend the stairs into the thickening shadows above.

And just then a low humming mutter came to their ears, growing louder with each passing moment, until it became raw thunder. They stopped short halfway up the stairs.

"A plane!" cried Dr. Junius. "Is it coming here?"

The thunder grew. It was a plane, unquestionably, and it was circling Tolland Stuart's eyrie.

"This is the last straw," moaned the doctor. "He'll be unbearable for a week. Stay here, please. I'll go out."

And without waiting for an answer he hurried down the stairs and out into the darkness.

Ellery remained uncertainly on the staircase for an instant. Then he slowly descended.

Bonnie said: "I can't understand grandfather. Is he ill? Why doesn't he come down?"

No one answered. The only sounds came from the fire. The thunder had died.

And then Dr. Junius reappeared, wringing his hands. "He'll kill me! Why did you all have to come here?"

A large man in an overcoat and fedora marched in, blinking in the firelight. He blinked at each of them, one by one.

Ellery smiled. "It seems we meet again, Inspector Glücke."

7
THE OLD MAN

Inspector Glücke grunted and went to the fire, shedding his coat and rubbing his great red hands together. A man in flying togs followed him, and Dr. Junius hastily shut the outer door against a rising wind. The aviator sat quietly down in a corner. He said nothing, and Inspector Glücke did not introduce him.

"Let's get you people straight now," said Glücke, contracting his black brows. "You're Miss Stuart, I suppose, and you're Mr. Royle? You must be Butcher."

Ty scrambled to his feet. "Well?" he said eagerly. "Have you found him?"

Bonnie cried: "Who is he?"

"No, now, all in good time. I'm half-frozen, and we've got a long wait, because the pilot says there's a storm coming up. Where's the old man?"

"Upstairs sulking," said Ellery. "You don't seem very glad to see me, old friend. And how did you horn into this case?"

Glücke grinned. "What d'ye mean? They were Angelenos, weren't they? Say, this fire feels swell."

"I take it you simply jumped in feet first and usurped the authority to handle the case?"

"Now don't start anything, Queen. When we got the flash at Headquarters that Mr. Royle and Miss Stuart had been found dead—we already knew they'd been snatched—I got me a plane and flew up to that plateau. I beat the Riverside and San Bernardino County men by a hair. If you ask me, they were tickled to death to have L.A. step in and take over. It's too big for them."

"But not for you, eh?" murmured Ellery.

"Oh, it's simple enough," said the Inspector.

"Then you *have* found him!" cried Ty and Bonnie together.

"Not yet. But when we do, there's our man, and that's the end of it."

"When you find him?" said Ellery dryly. "Don't you mean 'if'?"

"Maybe, maybe." Glücke smiled. "Anyway, it's no case for you, Queen. Just a plain, everyday manhunt."

"How sure are you," said Ellery, lighting a cigaret, "that it *was* a man?"

"You're not suggesting it was a woman?" said the Inspector derisively.

"I'm suggesting the possibility. Miss Stuart, you and Mr. Royle saw that pilot in good light. Was it a man or woman?"

"Man," said Ty. "Don't be foolish. He was a man!"

"I don't know," sighed Bonnie, trying to concentrate. "You couldn't really tell. Those flying togs were a man's, but then a woman could have worn them. And you couldn't see hair, or eyes, or even face. The goggles concealed the upper part of the face and the lower part was hidden by the turned-up collar."

"He walked like a man," cried Ty. "He was too tall for a woman."

A spirited note crept into Bonnie's voice. "Nonsense. Hollywood is full of impersonators of both sexes. And I'll bet I'm as tall as that . . . creature was."

"And nobody," put in Ellery, "heard the creature's voice, for the excellent reason that the creature took remarkable care not to speak. If it were a man, why the silence? He could have disguised his voice."

"Now listen, Queen," said Glücke plaintively, "stop throwing monkey-wrenches. All right, we don't know whether it was a man or a woman. But, man or woman, we've got the height and build—"

"Have you? Heels can be built up, and those flying suits are bulky and deceptive. No, there's only one thing you can be sure of."

"What's that?"

"That the pilot can fly an airplane."

Glücke growled deep in his throat. Dr. Junius coughed in the silence. "I don't want to seem inhospitable, but . . . I mean, don't you think it would be wise to take off now, before the storm breaks, Inspector?"

"Huh?" The Inspector turned cold eyes on Dr. Junius.

"I said—"

"I heard what you said." Glücke stared hard at the doctor's saffron face. "What's the matter with you? Nervous?"

"No. Certainly not," said the doctor, backing away.

"Who are you, anyway? What are you doing here?"

"My name is Junius, and I'm a medical doctor. I live here with Mr. Stuart."

"Where'd you come from? Did you know Blythe Stuart and Jack Royle?"

"No, indeed. I mean—I've seen Mr. Royle in Hollywood at times and Miss Blythe Stuart used to come here. . . . But I haven't seen her for several years."

"How long have you been here?"

"Ten years. Mr. Stuart hired me to take care of him. At a very nice yearly retainer, I must say, and my own practice wasn't terribly—"

"Where'd you come from? I didn't hear you say."

"Buenavista, Colorado."

"Police record?"

Dr. Junius drew himself up. "My dear sir!"

Glücke looked him over. "No harm done," he said mildly. The doctor stepped back, wiping his face. "Now here's what we've found. You were right, Queen, about the cause of death. The coroner of Riverside County flew up there with his sheriff, examined the bodies—"

Bonnie grew pale again. Butcher said sharply: "Dr. Junius is right.

We ought to clear out of here and get these kids home. You can talk to them tomorrow."

"It's all right," said Bonnie in a low voice. "I'm all right, Butch."

"As far as I'm concerned," growled Ty, "the sooner you get started the better I'll like it. Do you think I could sleep and eat and laugh and work while my father's murderer is breathing free air somewhere?"

The Inspector went on, quite as if nobody had spoken: "Well, as I was saying, preliminary examination showed they both died of very large doses of morphine."

"In the thermos bottles?" asked Ellery.

"Yes. The drinks were loaded with the stuff. The Doc couldn't be sure without a chemical analysis, but he says there must easily have been five grains to each cocktail drink. I'm having Bronson, our chemist, analyze what's left in the bottles as soon as he can lay his hands on them."

"But I don't understand," frowned Bonnie. "We all drank from the bottles just before the take-off. Why weren't we poisoned, too?"

"If you weren't, it's because the drinks were okay at that time. Does anybody remember exactly what happened to that hamper?"

"I do," said Ellery. "I was shoved about by the crowd and was forced to sit down on the hamper immediately after the last round, when the bottles were put back. And I had my eye on that hamper every instant between the time the bottles were stowed away and the time I sat down on the hamper."

"That's a break. Did you sit on the hamper till this disguised pilot hijacked the plane?"

also see page 63!

"Better than that," said Ellery wryly. "I actually got up and handed it to him with my own hands as he got into the plane."

"So that means the drinks were poisoned inside. We've got a clear line there." Glücke looked pleased. "He swiped the plane, poisoned the drinks in the plane as he was stowing away the hamper, took off, waited for Jack and Blythe to drink—stuff's practically tasteless, the coroner said, in booze—and when they passed out he just set the plane down on that plateau and beat it. No fuss, no bother, no trouble at all. Damned neat, and damned cold-blooded."

The pilot's predicted storm broke. A thousand demons howled, and

And: See page 80!!

the wind lashed at the butte, pounding the old house, banging shutters and rattling windows. Suddenly lightning crashed about the exposed mountain-top and thunder roared.

Nobody spoke. Dr. Junius shambled forward to throw another log on the fire.

The thunder rolled and rolled as if it would never stop. Ellery listened uneasily. It seemed to him that he had detected the faintest undertone in the thunder. He glanced about, but none of his companions seemed conscious of it.

The thunder ceased for a moment, and Glücke said: "We've got the whole State looking for that pilot. It's only a question of time before we catch up with the guy."

"But this rain," cried Ty. "It will wipe out his trail from the plateau!"

"I know, I know, Mr. Royle," said Glücke soothingly. "Don't fret yourself. We'll collar him. Now I want you young people to tell me something about your parents. There must be a clue somewhere in their background."

Ellery took his hat and coat from the chair near the front door where he had dropped them and, unobserved, slipped down the hallway to the kitchen and out the kitchen door into the open.

The trees about the side of the house were bent over in the gale, and a downpour that seemed solid rather than liquid drenched him the instant he set foot on the spongy earth. Nevertheless he lowered his head to the wind, clutching his hat, and aided by an occasional lightning-flash fought his way toward the distant glow of the landing-field.

He stumbled onto the field and stopped, gasping for breath. A commercial plane, apparently the one which had conveyed Glücke to Tolland Stuart's mountain home, strained within the hangar beside the small stubby ship; the hangar doors stood open to the wind.

Ellery shook his head impatiently, straining to see the length of the field in the badly flickering arc-lights. But the field was empty of life.

He waited for the next flash of lightning and then eagerly searched the tossing skies overhead. But if there was anything up there, it was lost in the swollen black clouds.

So it had been his imagination after all. He could have sworn he had heard the motors of an airplane through the thunder. He retraced his steps.

And then, just as he was about to break from under the trees in a dash back to the house, he saw a man.

The man was crouching in the lee of the house, to the rear, a black hunched-over figure. The friendly lightning blazed again, and Ellery saw him raise his head.

It was an old face with a ragged growth of gray beard and mustache, a deeply engraved skin, and slack blubbering lips; and it was the face of one who looks upon death, or worse. Ellery was struck by that expression of pure, stripped terror. It was as if the old man had suddenly found himself cornered against an unscalable wall by a horde of the ghastliest denizens of his worst nightmare.

In the aftermath of darkness Ellery barely made out the stooped figure creeping miserably along the side of the house to vanish somewhere behind it.

The rain hissed down, and Ellery stood still, oblivious to it, staring into the darkness. What was Mr. Tolland Stuart doing out in the storm raging about his mountain retreat at a moment when he was supposed to be shivering behind the barred door of his bedroom?

Why, indeed, only a few hours after the murder of his only child in an airplane, should he be crawling about his estate with a flyer's helmet stuck ludicrously on his head?

Ellery found the Inspector straddle-legged across the fire. He was saying: "Not much help. . . . Oh, Queen."

Ellery dashed the rain from his hat and spread his coat before the flames. "I thought I heard something on the landing-field."

"Another plane?" groaned Dr. Junius.

"It was my imagination."

Glücke frowned. "Well, we're not getting anywhere. Then aside from this down-and-outer Park you mention, Mr. Royle, you'd say your father had no enemies?"

"None I know of."

"I'd quite forgotten that little flare-up at the Horseshoe Club a couple of weeks ago," said Ellery slowly.

"Nothing to it. The man was just peeved about being found out. It's not going to be as easy as all that."

"The man's cracked," said Ty shortly. "A crackpot will do anything."

"Well, we'll check up on him. Only if he's the one, why did he kill Miss Stuart's mother as well as your father? He couldn't have had anything against *her*."

"He could have held her responsible for the whole situation," snapped Ty. "An irrational man would react that way."

"Maybe." Glücke looked at his fingernails. "By the way. It seems to me there's been a lot of talk about your two families sort of—well, not getting along."

The fire crackled, and outside the thunder and lightning went out in a spectacular finale. The rain fell to a steady patter.

The pilot got up and said: "I'll take a look at my crate, Inspector," and went out.

And then the Boy Wonder mumbled: "Nonsense."

"Did I say something wrong?" inquired Glücke innocently.

"Didn't Jack and Blythe make up? You couldn't want better proof than their reconciliation and marriage."

"But how about these two?" said Glücke. There was another silence. "Hey?" said Glücke.

Bonnie stared straight at the lowest button of the Inspector's jacket. And Ty turned his back to look at the fire.

"There's no sense smearing it, Butch. We've hated each other's guts since we were kids. We were brought up on hate. When a thing like that is fed to you morning, noon, and night from your nursery days it gets into your blood."

"You feel the same way, huh, Miss Stuart?"

Bonnie licked her dry lips. "Yes."

"But that doesn't mean," said Ty slowly, turning around, "that one of us committed those murders. Or do you think it does, Inspector Glücke?"

"But he *couldn't* think a horrible thing like that!" cried Bonnie.

"How do I know," said Glücke, "that story about the hold-up at the hangar in Griffith Park airport is on the level?"

"But we've got each other as witnesses!"

"Even if we didn't," growled Ty, "do you think I would poison my own father to revenge myself on Bonnie Stuart's mother? Or that Bonnie Stuart would murder her own mother to get even with my father? You're crazy."

"I don't know anything," said the Inspector blandly, "about anything. You might be interested to learn that the Homicide Detail's turned up the boy who brought Miss Stuart the message before the take-off. I got the news by radiophone while I was examining your plane on the plateau."

"What's he got to say for himself?"

"He says he was stopped near the hangar—he's a page, or steward, or something, at the municipal field—by a tall thin man bundled up in flying clothes, wearing goggles." The Inspector's tone was amiable, but he kept glancing from Bonnie to Ty and back again. "This man held up a piece of paper with typewriting on it in front of the kid's nose. The paper said for him to tell Miss Stuart Mr. Royle wanted her in the hangar."

"The come-on," muttered Ty. "That was the pilot, all right. What a clumsy trick!"

"Which worked nevertheless," remarked Ellery. "You're positive the boy's on the level, Inspector?"

"The airport people give him a clean bill."

"How about the typewritten note?"

"The kid never got his hands on it. It was just shown to him. Then the disguised pilot faded into the crowd, the kid says, taking the paper with him."

Bonnie rose, looking incensed. "Then how can you believe one of us had a hand in those horrible crimes?"

"I'm not saying you had," smiled Glücke. "I'm saying you could have had."

"But if we were held up and tied!"

"Suppose one of you hired that tall fellow to fake the hold-up—to make you look innocent?"

"Oh, my God," said Butch, throwing up his hands.

"You're a fool," said Ty curtly. He sat down on the settee and cupped his face in his hands.

Inspector Glücke smiled again and, going to his coat, fished in one of the pockets. He came back to the fire with a large manila envelope and slowly unwound the waxed red string.

"What's that?" demanded Ellery.

Glücke's big hand dipped into the envelope and came out with something round, thin, and blue. He held it up.

"Ever see one of these before?" he asked of no one in particular.

They crowded about him, Dr. Junius nosing with the rest. It was a blue chip, incised with a golden horseshoe.

"The Horseshoe Club," exclaimed Bonnie and Ty together. In their eagerness they bumped against each other. For a moment they were pressed together; then they drew apart.

"Comes from Jack Royle's pocket," said the Inspector. "It's not important." Nevertheless, Ellery noted the careful manner in which he handled it, holding it between thumb and forefinger on the thin edge of the disc, as if he were afraid of smudging a possible fingerprint.

He dropped the plaque back into the envelope and pulled out something else—a sheaf of ragged pieces of paper held together by a paper-clip.

"This clip is mine," he explained. "I found these torn scraps in Royle's pocket, too."

Ellery seized them. Separating the scraps, he spread them on the settee. It took only a few minutes to assemble the pieces. Reassembled, they constituted five small rectangles of linen memorandum paper, with the words: THE HORSESHOE CLUB, engraved in blue over a tiny golden horseshoe at the top of each sheet.

Each sheet bore a date; the dates covered roughly a period of a month, the last date being the second of the current month. In the same-colored ink, boldly scrawled, were the letters IOU, a figure preceded by a dollar-sign, and the signature *John Royle*. Each IOU noted a different sum. With a frown Ellery totaled them. They came to exactly $110,000.

"Know anything about these things?" asked the Inspector.

Ty studied them incredulously. He seemed baffled by the signature.

"What's the matter?" asked Ellery quickly. "Isn't that your father's signature?"

"That's just the trouble," murmured Ty. "It is."

"All five?"

"Yes."

"What d'ye mean trouble?" demanded Glücke. "Didn't you know about these debts?"

"No. At least I didn't know dad had got in so deep with Alessandro. A hundred and ten thousand dollars!" He plunged his hands into his pockets and began to walk up and down. "He was always a reckless gambler, but this—"

"You mean to say he was that broke and his own son didn't know it?"

"We rarely discussed money matters. I led my life and—" he sat slowly down on the settee, "he led his."

He fell into a deep inspection of the fire. Glücke gathered the scraps together, clipped them, and in silence stowed them away in the manila envelope.

Some one coughed. Ellery turned around. It was Dr. Junius. He had quite forgotten Dr. Junius.

Dr. Junius said nervously: "The rain's stopped, I think. You ought to be able to fly out safely now."

"Oh, it's you again, Doctor," said the Inspector. "You *are* in a fret to get rid of us, aren't you?"

"No, no," said the doctor hastily. "I was just thinking of Miss Stuart. She must have a night's rest."

"And that reminds me." Glücke looked at the staircase. "While I'm here I think I'll have a talk with the old man."

"Dr. Junius doesn't think that would be wise," said Ellery dryly. "Are you impervious to buckshot? Tolland Stuart keeps a shotgun by his bed."

"Oh, he does, does he?" said Glücke. And he strode towards the staircase.

"Be careful, Inspector!" cried Junius, running after. "He doesn't even know his daughter's dead."

"Go on," said Glücke grimly. "That shy kind have a cute habit of listening at keyholes and at the top of stairs."

He strode on. Ellery, remembering the fact of the old man in the downpour outside the house, silently applauded Glücke's shrewdness. That livid old man had known the facts of death; there was no question about that.

He followed the two men up the stairs.

The light of the downstairs chamber faded as they ascended, and by the time they reached the landing upstairs they were in iced and murky darkness.

Glücke stumbled on the top step. "Aren't there any lights in this blasted morgue?" Dr. Junius brushed hurriedly and sure-footedly by.

"Just a moment," he whined. "The switch is—"

"Wait," said the Inspector. Ellery waited. But, strain as he might, Ellery heard nothing but the hiss of the fire downstairs and the murmur of Butcher's voice soothing Bonnie.

"What's the matter?"

"Thought I heard some one scramble away. But I guess I was wrong. This place could drive a man nuts."

"I don't think you were wrong," said Ellery. "Our aged friend has probably been ensconced up here for some time, eavesdropping, as you suggested."

"Switch those lights on, Junius," growled Glücke, "and let's have a look at the old turkey."

The magic of sudden light after darkness materialized a wide draughty hall, thickly carpeted and hung with what seemed to Ellery a veritable gallery of old masters—lovely pictures with the rich brown patina of the Dutch period and uniformly framed in a dust no less rich and brown. There were many doors, and all were closed, and of Tolland Stuart no sign.

"Mr. Stuart!" cried Junius. There was no answer. He turned to the Inspector piteously. "There you are, Inspector. Can't you come back tomorrow? He's probably in an awful state."

"I can, but I won't," said the Inspector. "Which one is his cave?"

The doctor made a despairing gesture and, crying out: "He'll probably shoot us all!" led the way to a double door at the farthest point in the corridor. Trembling, he knocked.

An old man's voice quavered: "Keep out!" and Ellery heard scuttling sounds, as if the possessor of the voice had scrambled away from the other side of the door.

Dr. Junius yelped and fled.

Glücke chuckled: "The old guy must have something at that. Chicken-hearted mummy!" And he thundered: "Come on, open up there, Mr. Stuart!"

"Who is it?"

"The police."

"Go away. Get off my grounds. I'll have no truck with police!" The quaver was a scream now, with a curious lisping quality to the syllables which could only be effected by a toothless mouth.

"Do you know, Mr. Stuart," shouted the Inspector sternly, "that your daughter Blythe has been murdered?"

"I heard 'em. I heard you! Get out, I say!"

Bonnie came running up the hall towards them, crying: "Grandfather!"

Dr. Junius sidled after, pleading: "Please, Miss Stuart. Not now. He isn't—pleasant. He'll upset you."

"Grandfather," sobbed Bonnie, pounding on the door. "Let me in. It's Bonnie. Mother—she's dead. She's been killed, I tell you. There's only us now. Please!"

"Mr. Stuart, sir," whined Dr. Junius, "it's your granddaughter, Bonnie Stuart. She needs you, sir. Won't you open the door, talk to her, comfort her?"

There was no reply.

"Mr. Stuart, sir. This is Dr. Junius. Please!"

Then the cracked, lisping voice came. "Go away, all of you. No police. Bonnie, not—not now. There's death among you. Death! Death. . . ." And the shriek was choked off on its ascending note, and they distinctly heard the thud of a body.

Bonnie bit her fingers, staring at the panels. Butcher came running up. Glücke said gently: "Stand aside, Miss Stuart. We'll have to break the door in. Get out of the way, Junius."

And Ty came up, too, and watched them from narrowed eyes as he stood quietly at the other end of the hall.

The Inspector hurled himself at the juncture of the two doors. Something snapped inside; the doors flew open. For a moment he stood still, breathing hard. The moment seemed interminable, with the infinitude of some arrested moments.

The room was vast, and gloomy, and filled with solid pieces like the great chamber downstairs; and the four-poster English bed of hand-carved antique oak, with its red frustian tester, was disheveled; and, surely enough, there stood a heavy shotgun by its side, handy to a reaching arm. And on the floor, before them, lay the crumpled body of the old man Ellery had glimpsed outdoors, clad in flannel pajamas and a woolen robe, thick socks, and carpet slippers over his bony feet. The only light came from a brown mica lamp near the bed; the fireplace was dark.

Dr. Junius hurried forward to drop on his knees beside the motion-less figure.

"He's fainted. Fear—venom—temper; I don't know what. But his pulse is good; nothing to worry about. Please go now. It's useless to try to talk to him tonight."

He got to his feet, and stooped, and with a surprising strength for a man of his sparse physique and evident years, lifted the old man's body and bore him in his arms to the bed.

"He's probably shamming," said Inspector Glücke disgustedly. "Crusty old termite! Come on, folks, we'll be riding the air back to Los Angeles."

8

TWO FOR NOTHING

Where to?" asked the pilot.

"Municipal airport, L.A."

The plane was not large, and they sat about in a cramped silence while the pilot nosed his ship sharply northwestward. He sought altitude; and soon they were flying high above a black valley, splitting the breeze to a hairline above and between the San Bernardino and San Jacinto ranges.

"What's happened to my plane?" asked Ty, his face against a drizzle-misted window.

"It's probably in Los Angeles by this time," replied the Inspector. He paused. "Of course, we couldn't leave them . . . it there."

Bonnie stirred on Butcher's motionless shoulder. "I was in a morgue once. It was a movie set. But even in make-believe . . . It was cold. Mother didn't like—" She closed her eyes. "Give me a cigaret, Butch."

He lit one for her and stuck it between her lips.

"Thanks." She opened her eyes. "I suppose you all think I've been acting like such a baby. But it's just that it's been . . . a shock. It's even worse, now that I can think again. . . . Mother gone. It just isn't possible."

Without turning, Ty said harshly: "We all know how you feel."

"Oh? Sorry."

Ellery stared out at the stormy dark. A cluster of lights far below and ahead began to mushroom, resembling loose diamonds strewn on a black velvet cushion.

"Riverside," said the Inspector. "We'll pass over it soon, and after that it's not far to the airport."

They watched the cluster glow and grow and shrink and fade and disappear.

Ty suddenly got up. He blundered blindly up the aisle. Then he came back. "Why?" he said.

"Why, what?" asked the Inspector, surprised.

"Why was dad knocked off? Why were they both knocked off?"

"If we knew that, son, it wouldn't be much of a case. Sit down."

"It doesn't make sense. Were they robbed? He had a thousand dollars in cash on him. I gave it to him only this morning as a sort—sort of wedding gift. Or—Bonnie! Was your mother carrying much money?"

"Don't talk to me," said Bonnie.

"It's not that," said Glücke. "Their personal belongings weren't touched."

"Then why?" cried Ty. "Why? Is he a lunatic?"

"Sit down, Ty," said the Boy Wonder wearily.

"Wait!" His bloodshot eyes narrowed. "Could it have been an accident? I mean, could it have been that only one of them was meant to be killed, that the other one was a victim of some—"

"Since you're discussing it," drawled Ellery, "Suppose you discuss it systematically."

"What do you mean?"

"I think motive is the keystone of this case."

"Yeah?" said the Inspector. "Why?"

"Simply because there doesn't seem to be any."

Glücke looked annoyed. Ty suddenly sat down and lit a cigaret. His eyes did not leave Ellery's face. "Go on. You've got an idea about this thing."

"He's a crazy galoot," growled Glücke, "but I admit he's got something besides sand in his skull."

"Well, look." Ellery put his elbows on his knees. "Let's begin in the proper place. Among the things I've observed in the past few weeks, Ty, is that your father never drank anything but Sidecars. Is that right?"

"Brandy, too. He liked brandy."

"Well, of course. A Sidecar is nothing but brandy with Cointreau and a little lemon juice added. And as for your mother, Bonnie, she seemed exclusively fond of dry Martinis."

"Yes."

"I seem to recall, in fact, that she recently made some disparaging remark about Sidecars, which would indicate she disliked them. Is that true?"

"She detested them."

"And dad couldn't stand Martinis, either," growled Ty. "So what?"

"So this. Some one—obviously the murderer; it could scarcely have been coincidence; the exact means of murder wouldn't have been left to chance—some one sends Blythe and Jack a going-away hamper and lo! inside are two thermos bottles and lo! in one of them is a quart of Sidecars and in the other an equal quantity of Martinis."

"If you mean," said Butch with a frown, "that in sending those bottles the murderer betrayed an intimate knowledge of Blythe's and Jack's liquor preferences, Ellery, I'm afraid you won't get far. Everybody in Hollywood knew that Blythe liked Martinis and Jack Sidecars."

Inspector Glücke looked pleased.

But Ellery smiled. "I didn't mean that. I'm attacking Ty's accident theory, improbable as it is, just to get it out of the way. It lends itself to logical disproof.

"For if, as seems indisputable, the donor of that hamper knew that Blythe liked Martinis and Jack Sidecars, then the dosing of *each* bottle of heavenly dew with a lethal amount of morphine means that *each* drinker—Jack, the drinker of Sidecars, Blythe, the drinker of Martinis—*was intended to be poisoned*. Had only Blythe been marked for death, only the bottle of Martinis would have been poisoned. And similarly if Jack were to be the sole victim." He sighed. "I'm afraid we're faced with no alternative. Neither your father, Ty, nor your mother, Bonnie, was intended ever to come out of that plane alive. It's the clearest case of a deliberate double-killing."

"And where does all this folderol get you?" scowled Glücke.

"I'm sure I don't know. One rarely does at this stage of the game."

"I thought," put in the Boy Wonder shortly, "you began to talk about motive."

"Oh, that." Ellery shrugged. "If the same motive applied to both of them, as seems likely, it's even more mystifying."

"But what could it be?" cried Bonnie. "Mother wouldn't have harmed a fly."

Ellery did not reply. He looked out the window at the swirling darkness.

The Inspector said suddenly: "Miss Stuart, is your father alive?"

"He died when I was an infant."

"Your mother never remarried?"

"No."

"Any . . . " The Inspector hesitated. Then he said delicately: "Did she have any . . . romantic attachments?"

"Mother?" Bonnie laughed. "Don't be absurd." And she turned her face away.

"How about your father, Royle? Your ma's dead, too, isn't she?"

"Yes."

"Well, from all I've heard," said the Inspector, clearing his throat, "your dad was sort of a lady's man. Could there be some woman floating around who had—well, who thought she had good reason to get sore when Jack Royle announced he was going to marry Blythe Stuart?"

"How should I know? I wasn't dad's nursemaid."

"Then there could be such a woman?"

"There could," snapped Ty, "but I don't think there is. Dad was no angel, but he knew women, he knew the world, and underneath he was a right guy. The few affairs I know about ended without a fuss. He never lied to his women, and they always knew exactly what they were letting themselves in for. You're a million miles wrong, Glücke.

Besides, this job was pulled by a man."

"Hmm," said the Inspector, and he slumped back. He did not seem immovably persuaded.

"I suggest," said Ellery, "we eliminate. The usual attack in theorizing about motive is to ask who stands to gain by the murder. I believe we'll make faster progress if we ask who stands to lose.

"Let's start with the principals, you, Ty, and you, Bonnie. Obviously, of every one involved you two have sustained the greatest possible loss. You've lost your sole surviving parents, to whom you were plainly tremendously attached."

Bonnie bit her lip, staring out the window. Ty crushed the burning tip of his cigaret out in his fingers.

"The studio?" Ellery shrugged. "Don't look so startled, Butch; logic knows no sentiment. The studio has suffered a large monetary loss: it has lost forever the services of two popular, money-making stars. To bring it closer home, your own unit suffers a direct and intimate loss: the big production we've been working on together will have to be abandoned."

"Wait a minute," said Glücke. "How about a studio feud? Any contract trouble with another studio, Butcher? Know anybody who wouldn't mind seeing Magna's two big stars out of pictures?"

"Oh, don't be a fool, Inspector," snapped Butch. "This is Hollywood, not mediæval Italy."

"It didn't seem likely," grunted Glücke.

"To continue," said Ellery, glancing at the Inspector with amusement. "The agency holding contracts for Jack's and Blythe's personal services—I believe it's Alan Clark's outfit—also loses.

"So that, in a sense, every one connected with Jack and Blythe personally and professionally stands to lose a great deal."

"You're a help."

"But good Lord, Ellery," protested Butch, "it stands to reason somebody gains by this crime."

"From a monetary standpoint? Well, let's see. Did Jack or Blythe leave much of an estate?"

"Mother left practically nothing," said Bonnie lifelessly. "Even her jewels were paste. She lived up to every cent she earned."

"How about Jack, Ty?"

Ty's lip curled. "What do you think? You saw those IOU's."

"How about insurance?" asked the Inspector. "Or trust funds? You Hollywood actors are always salting it away in insurance companies."

"Mother," said Bonnie tightly, "didn't believe in insurance or annuities. She didn't know the value of money at all. I was always making up shortages in her checking account."

"Dad took out a hundred-thousand-dollar policy once," said Ty. "It was in force until the second premium came due. He said to hell with it—he had to go to the racetrack that afternoon."

"But for Pete's sake," exclaimed the Inspector, "there's got to be an angle somewhere. If it wasn't gain, then revenge. Something! I'm beginning to think this guy Park better be tagged right away, at that."

"Well," said Ty coldly, "how about Alessandro and those IOU's?"

"But they turned up in your father's possession," said Ellery. "If he hadn't paid up, do you think Alessandro would have returned the IOU's?"

"I don't know anything about that," muttered Ty. "All I ask is: Where would dad get a hundred and ten thousand?"

"You're absolutely sure," said Glücke slowly, "he couldn't lay his hands on that much, huh?"

"Of course not!"

The Inspector rubbed his jaw. "Alessandro's real handle is Joe DiSangri, and he's been mixed up in a lot of monkey-business in New York. He used to be one of Al's hoods, too, way back." Then he shook his head. "But it doesn't smell like a gang kill. Poisoned drinks! If Joe DiSangri wanted to rub out a welcher, he'd use lead. It's in his blood."

"Times have changed," snarled Ty. "That's a hell of a reason to lay off the skunk! Do I have to look him up myself?"

"Oh, we'll check him."

"At any rate," said Ellery, "did Joe DiSangri, alias Alessandro, also kill Bonnie's mother because your father welched on a gambling debt?"

Bonnie said passionately: "I knew it would only lead to trouble. I knew it. Why did she have to do it?"

Ty colored and turned aside. Glücke gnawed a fingernail. And kept looking at Bonnie and Ty.

The pilot opened his door and said: "We're here."

They looked down. The field was blackly alive, heaving with people.

Bonnie blanched and groped for Butch's hand. "It . . . it looks like a—like something big and dead and a lot of little black ants running all over it."

"Bonnie, you've been a trump so far. This won't last long. Don't spoil it. Keep your chin up."

"But I can't! All those millions of staring eyes—" She held on to his hand tightly.

"Now, Miss Stuart, take it easy," said the Inspector, getting to his feet. "You've got to face it. We're here—"

"Are we?" said Ty bitterly. "I'd say we were nowhere. And that we'd got there damned fast."

"That's why I pointed out," murmured Ellery, "that when we found out why Jack and Blythe were poisoned—when we got a clear line on the motive—we'd crack this case wide open."

9

THE CLUB NINE

On Wednesday the twentieth the only completely peaceful persons in the City of Los Angeles and environs were John Royle and Blythe Stuart: they were dead.

It had been a mad three days. Reporters; cameramen, of the journalistic, artistic, and candid varieties, aging ladies of the motion picture press; State police and men of Inspector Glücke's Homicide Detail; stars; producers; directors looking for inspiration; embalmers; preachers; debtors; mortuary salesmen; lawyers; radio announcers; real estate men; thousands of glamour-struck worshipers at the shrine of the dead pair—all milled and shouted and shoved and popped in and out and made the waking hours—there were few sleeping ones—of Bonnie and Ty an animated nightmare.

"Might as well have planned services for the Bowl," cried Ty, disheveled, unshaven, purple-eyed from lack of rest. "For God's sake, somebody, can't I even send the old man out decently?"

"He was a public figure in life, Ty," said Ellery soothingly. "You couldn't expect the public to ignore him in death."

"That kind of death?"

"Any kind of death."

"They're vultures!"

"Murder brings out the worst in people. Think of what poor Bonnie's going through in Glendale."

"Yes," scowled Ty. "I guess . . . it's pretty tough on a woman." Then he said: "Queen, I've got to talk to her."

"Yes, Ty?" Ellery tried not to show surprise.

"It's terribly important."

"It's going to be hard, arranging a quiet meeting now."

"I've got to."

They met at three o'clock in the morning at an undistinguished little café tucked away in a blind alley off Melrose Street, miraculously unpursued—Ty wearing dark blue glasses and Bonnie a heavy nose-veil that revealed little more than her pale lips and chin.

Ellery and the Boy Wonder stood guard outside the booth in which they sat.

"Sorry, Bonnie," said Ty abruptly, "to bring you out at a time like this. But there's something we've got to discuss."

"Yes?" Bonnie's voice startled him; it was flat, brassy, devoid of life or feeling.

"Bonnie, you're ill."

"I'm all right."

"Queen—Butch—somebody should have told me."

"I'm all right. It's just the thought of . . . Wednesday." He saw her lips quiver beneath the veil.

Ty played with a glass of Scotch. "Bonnie . . . I've never asked a favor of you, have I?"

"You?"

"I'm . . . I suppose you'll think I'm a fool, getting sentimental this way."

"You sentimental?" Bonnie's lips curved this time.

"What I want you to do . . . " Ty put the glass down. "It's not for me. It isn't even for my dad exclusively. It's as much for your mother as for dad."

Her hands crept off the table and disappeared. "Come to the point, please."

He blurted: "I think they ought to have a double funeral."

She was silent.

"I tell you it's not for dad. It's for both of them. I've been thinking things over since Sunday. Bonnie, they were in love. Before . . . I didn't think so. I thought there was something else behind it—I don't know what. But now . . . They died together. Don't you see?"

She was silent.

"They were kept apart so many years," said Ty. "And then to be knocked off just before . . . I know I'm an idiot to be talking this way. But I can't get over the feeling that dad—yes, and your mother—would have wanted to be buried together, too."

She was silent for so long that Ty thought something had happened to her. But just as he was about to touch her in alarm, she moved. Her hands appeared and pushed the veil back from her face. And she looked and looked and looked at him out of her dark-shadowed eyes, not speaking, not changing her expression; just looking.

Then she said simply: "All right, Ty," and rose.

"Thanks!"

"It's mother I'm thinking of."

Neither said another word. They went home by different routes—Ty in Ellery's coupé to Beverly Hills, Bonnie in the Boy Wonder's limousine to Glendale.

Then the coroner released the bodies, and John Royle and Blythe Stuart were embalmed, and for several hours on Wednesday morning their magnificent mahogany caskets, sheathed in purest Anaconda copper, with eighteen-carat gold handles and $50-a-yard hand-loomed Japanese silk linings stuffed with the down of black swans, were on public display in the magnificent mortuary on Sunset Boulevard which Sam Vix, who was surreptitiously superintending the production on a 2%-commission basis, persuaded Jacques Butcher to persuade Ty Royle to beg the favor of Bonnie Stuart to select, which they did, and she did; and four women were trampled, one seriously, and sixteen women fainted, and the police had to ride into the crowd on their magnificent horses, which were all curried and glossed for the occasion; and one poorly dressed man who was obviously a Communist tried to bite the stirrup of the mounted policeman who had just run over him and was properly whacked over the head with a billy and dragged off to jail; and inside the mortuary all the glittering elect, tricked out in their most gorgeous mourning clothes—Mme. Flo's and Magnin's and L'Heureuse's had had to hire mobs of seamstresses to get the special orders out in time for the funeral—remarked how beautiful Blythe looked: "Just as if she were asleep, the darling; if she weren't under glass you'd swear she was going to *move!*" "And yet she's embalmed; it's wonderful what they can do." "Yes, and to think she's got practically *nothing* left inside. I read that they performed an autopsy, and you know what they do in autopsies." "Don't be gruesome! How should I know?" "Well, but wasn't your first husband—"—and didn't Bonnie show a too, too precious taste in dressing Blythe up in that *gorgeous* white satin evening gown with that perfectly *clever* tight bodice—"She had a beautiful bust, my dear. Do you know she once told me she never wore a *girdle?* And I know for a fact that she didn't have to wear a cup-form brassière!"— with the shirring at the waist and those *thousands* of accordion pleats— "If she could only stand up, darling, you'd see what a cunning fan effect those pleats give!"—and that one dainty orchid corsage and those *exquisite* diamond clips at the shoulder-straps—"I mean they look exquisite. Are they real, do you think, dear?" And how handsome poor old Jack looked, in his starched bosom and tails, with that cynical half-smile on his face: "Wouldn't you swear he was going to get right out of that casket and put his arm around you?" "Who put that gold statuette that Jack won in thirty-three in there with him?" "I'm sure I don't know; it does seem a little like bragging, doesn't it?" "Well, there's the Academy committee and they looked simply devastatingly pleased! "He *was* a handsome devil, though, wasn't he? My second husband knocked him down once." "Don't you think that's a little indiscreet, darling?—I mean with all these detectives around? After all, Jack was *murdered.*" "Don't be funny, Nanette! You know Llewelyn ran off to Africa or some place with that snippy extra-girl with the g-string and hips two years ago." "Well, my dear, the things I could tell you about Jack Royle—not that I'm speaking ill of the dead, but in a way Blythe's better off. She'd never have been happy with him, the way he chased every chippy in town." "Oh, my darling! I'd forgotten that you knew him well, didn't you?"

And over in Glendale, in the big seething house, Bonnie stood cold and tearless and almost as devoid of life as her mother down in Hollywood being admired by thousands; while Clotilde, whose plump cheeks and Gallic nose seemed permanently puffed out from weeping, dressed her—unresisted—in soft and striking black, even though Bonnie had often said she detested public displays of grief and typical Hollywood funerals; dressed Bonnie without assistance from Bonnie, as if in truth she were dressing a corpse.

And in Beverly Hills Ty was cursing Louderback between gulps of brandy and refusing to shave and wanting to wear slacks and a blazer, just to show the damned vultures, and Alan Clark and a hastily recruited squad of husky friends finally held him down while Louderback plied the electric razor and a doctor took the decanter away and forced Ty to swallow some luminal instead.

And then Ty and Bonnie met over the magnificent twin coffins at the mortuary, framed and bowered in gigantic banks of fresh-cut flowers until they and the corpses and the mortician's assistants and the Bishop looked like figures on a float at the annual flower festival; and neither said a single word; and the Bishop read a magnificent service against the heady-sweet background, bristling with "dear Lords" and "dear departeds," and Inspector Glücke almost wore his eyes out scanning the crowd on the fundamental theory that a murderer cannot resist visiting the funeral of his victims, and saw nothing, even though he stared very hard at Joe DiSangri Alessandro, who was present looking like a solemn little Italian banker in his morning coat and striped trousers; and Jeannine Carrel, the beautiful star with the operatic voice than whom no soprano in or out of the Metropolitan sang *Ah, Sweet Mystery of Life* more thrillingly, tearfully sang *Nearer, My God, to Thee* accompanied by the entire male chorus of Magna Studio's forthcoming super-musical production, *Swing That Thing*; and Lew Bascom did not even stagger under his share of the weight of Blythe's coffin, which was a testimonial to his stamina and capacity, since he had consumed five quarts of Scotch since Sunday night and his breath would have sent a buzzard reeling in dismay.

And among the other pallbearers present were Louis X. Selvin, executive president of Magna; an ex-Mayor; an ex-Governor; three outstanding stars (selected by Sam Vix on the basis of the latest popularity poll conducted by Paula Paris for the newspaper syndicate for which she worked); the president of the Motion Picture Academy; a Broadway producer in Hollywood making comical short subjects; Randy Round, the famous Broadway columnist, to whom no set in filmland was forbidden ground; an important official of the Hays office; and a special delegate from the Friars' Club. There was a good deal of crowding.

And somehow, aeons later, the motored processional, rich with Isotta-Fraschinis, Rolls-Royces, Cords, Lincolns, and special-bodied Duesenbergs managed to reach and penetrate the memorial park—Hollywoodese for "cemetery"—where a veritable ocean of mourners surged in eye-bursting waves, mourning, to await the interment ceremonies; and the Bishop, who seemed indefatigable, read another magnificent service while a choir of freshly scrubbed angel-faced boys in cute surplices sang magnificently, and thirty-one more women fainted, and ambulances came unobtrusively and plaintively to the scene, and one headstone was knocked over and two stone angels lost their left arms, and Jack and Blythe were lowered side by side into magnificent blue spruce-trimmed graves edged in giant fern and topped off with plaits of giant lilies; and Bonnie, disdaining the Boy Wonder's arm, stood cold, lifeless, straight of back, and watched her mother make the last slow descent, magnificently dramatic, into the earth; and Ty stood alone in his own empty dimension, with incurving shoulders and a wonderfully bitter smile, watching his father's clay make the same slow descent; and finally it was practically—not quite—over, and the only part of her costume Bonnie surrendered to posterity was her dry black lawn handkerchief, snatched from her hand by a sabled fat woman with maniacal eyes as Butcher led Bonnie back to his limousine; and Ty, observing, lost the last shred of his temper and shook his fist in the fat woman's face, to be dragged off by Lew, Ellery, and Alan Clark; and stars and stars and stars wept and wept, and the sun shone blithely over Hollywood, and everybody had a lovely time, and Sam Vix said with emotion, wiping the dampness from under his black patch, that it had all been simply—there was no other word for it—magnificent.

But once safely away from the Argus-eyed mob, Bonnie gave vent to a wild sobbing in the Boy Wonder's arms as the limousine dodged through traffic trying to escape the pursuing cars of the insatiable press.

"Oh, Butch, it was so awful. People are such pigs. It was like the Rose Bowl p-parade. It's a wonder they didn't ask me to sing over the r-radio!"

"It's over now, darling. Forget it. It's all over."

"And grandfather didn't come. Oh, I hate him! I phoned him myself this morning. He begged off. He said he was ill. He said he couldn't stand funerals, and would I try to understand. His own daughter! Oh, Butch, I'm so *miserable*."

"Forget the old buzzard, Bonnie. He's not worth your misery."

"I hope I never see him again!"

And when they got to the Glendale house Bonnie begged off and sent Butcher away and instructed Clotilde to bang the door in the face of any one, friend or foe, who so much as tapped on it. And she shut herself up in her bedroom, sniffing, and tried paradoxically to find comfort in the bulky bundles of mail Clotilde had left for her.

Ty, who had to traverse the width of Hollywood to get home to Beverly Hills, changed from open rebellion to a sulky, shut-in silence; and his escort wisely left him to Louderback's stiff ministrations and departed. He had scarcely finished his third brandy when the telephone rang.

"I'm not in," he snarled to Louderback. "To any one, d'ye hear? I'm through with this town. I'm through with every one in it. It's a phony. It's mad. It's vicious. Everybody here is phony and mad and vicious. Tell whoever it is to go to hell."

Louderback raised suffering eyes ceilingward and said into the telephone: "I'm sorry, Miss Stuart, but Mr. Royle—"

"Who?" yelled Ty. "Wait. I'll take it!"

"Ty," said Bonnie in a voice so odd a cold wave swept over him. "You've got to come over at once."

"What the devil's the matter, Bonnie?"

"Please. Hurry. It's—frightfully important."

"Give me three minutes to change my clothes."

When Ty reached Bonnie's house he found Clotilde weeping at the foot of the hall staircase.

"Clotilde, where's Miss Stuart? What's the trouble?"

Clotilde wrung her fat hands. "Oh, M'sieu' Royle, is it truly you? Of a surety Ma'm'selle has become demented! She is up the stairs demolishing! I desired to telephone M'sieu' Butch-erre, but Ma'm'selle menaces me. . . . *Elle est une tempête!*"

Ty took the stairs three at a time and found Bonnie, her mauve crêpe negligée flying, snatching things out of drawers like a madwoman. The boudoir, her mother's, looked as if it had been struck by lightning.

"They aren't here!" screamed Bonnie. "Or I can't find them, which is the same thing. Oh, I'm such a fool!"

She collapsed on her mother's bed. Her hair was bound loosely by a gold ribbon and cascaded like molten honey down her back where the sun caught it.

Ty twisted his hat in his hands, looking away. Then he looked at her again. "Bonnie, why did you call me?"

"Oh, because I suddenly remembered. . . . And then when I looked through the mail . . . "

"Why didn't you call Butch? Clotilde says you didn't want Butch. Why . . . me, Bonnie?"

She sat very still then and drew the negligée about her. And she looked away from the burn in his eyes.

Ty went to her and hauled her to her feet and put his arms about her roughly. "Shall I tell you why?"

"Ty . . . You look so strange. Don't."

"I feel strange. I don't know what I'm doing. This is the nuttiest thing of all. But seeing you there on the bed, alone, scared, like a lost kid. . . . Bonnie, why did you think of me first, when you had something important to tell some one?"

"Ty, please. Let go of me."

"We're supposed to hate each other."

She struggled away from him then, not very strongly. "Please, Ty. You can't. You . . . mustn't."

"But I don't hate you," said Ty in a wondering voice. His arms tightened. "I just found that out. I don't hate you at all. I love you."

"Ty! No!"

He held her fast and close to him with one arm, and with the other hand he tilted her chin and made her look up at him. "And you love me. You've always loved me. You know that's true."

"Ty," she whispered. "Let me go."

"Nothing doing."

Her body trembled against him in its rigidity, like a piece of glass struck a heavy blow; and then all at once the rigidity shivered away and her softness gave itself to him utterly.

They stood there clinging to each other, their eyes closed against the hard, unyielding vision of the disordered room.

A long time later Bonnie whispered: "This *is* insane. You said so yourself."

"Then I don't want ever to be sane."

"We're both weak now. We feel lost and— That horrible funeral. . . ."

"We're both ourselves now. Bonnie, if their deaths did nothing else—"

She hid her face in his coat. "It's like a dream. I felt naked. Oh, it *is* good to be close to you this way, when I know you and I, of all the people in the world, are—"

"Kiss me, Bonnie. Christ, I've wanted to . . . " His lips touched her forehead, her eyelids, her lashes.

Bonnie pushed away from him suddenly and sat down on the *chaise longue*. "How about Butch?" she said in an empty voice.

"Oh," said Ty. The hunger and the gladness drained out of his haggard face very quickly. "I forgot Butch." And then he cried angrily. "To hell with Butch! To hell with everybody. I've been deprived of you long enough. You've been my whole life, the wrong way—we've got to make up for that. What I thought was hate—it's been with me, you've been with me, night and day since I was a kid in knee-pants. I've thought more of you and about you and around you. . . . I've more right to you than Butch has!"

"I couldn't hurt him, Ty," said Bonnie tonelessly. "He's the grandest person in the world."

"You don't love him," said Ty with scorn.

Her eyes fell. "I'm—I can't think clearly now. It's happened so suddenly. He loves me."

"You've been my whole life, Bonnie." He tried to take her in his arms again, seeking her mouth.

"No, Ty. I want some . . . time. Oh, it does sound corny! But you can't expect . . . I've got to get used to so much."

"I'll never let go of you."

"No, Ty. Not now. You've got to promise me you won't say anything . . . about this to anyone. I don't want Butch to know yet. Maybe I'm wrong. Maybe . . . You've got to promise."

"Don't think of any one but me, Bonnie."

She shivered. "The only thing that's really emerged these last three days has been to see mother avenged. Oh, you simply can't say real things without sounding—dramatic! But I do want that . . . badly. She was the sweetest, most harmless darling in the world. Whoever killed her is a monster. He can't be human." Her mouth hardened. "If I knew who it was I'd kill him myself, just the way I'd put a mad dog out of the way."

"Let me hold you, darling—"

She went on fiercely: "Anybody—*anybody* who was in any way involved. . . . I'd hate him just as much as I'd hate the one who poisoned her." She took his hand. "So you see, Ty, why all this . . . why we have to wait."

He did not reply.

"Don't you want to find your father's murderer?"

"Do you have to ask me that?" he said in a low voice.

"Then let's search together. It's true—I see it now—we've always had at least one thing in common. . . . Ty, look at me." He looked at her. "I'm not refusing you, darling," she whispered, close to him. "When all this happened . . . I admit it, the only one I could think of was you. Ty, they—they died and left us alone!" Her chin began to quiver.

Ty sighed, and kissed it, and led her to the bed and sat her down.

"All right, partner; we're partners. A little private war on a little private crime." He said cheerfully: "Let's have it."

"Oh, Ty!"

"What's all the excitement about?"

Bonnie gazed up at him through tears, smiling back. And then the smile chilled to a bleak determination, and she withdrew an envelope from her bosom.

"For some time," Bonnie said, sniffling away the last tear, "mother'd been receiving certain letters. I thought it was the usual crank mail and didn't pay any attention to them. Now . . . I don't know."

"Threatening letters?" said Ty swiftly. "Let's see that."

"Wait. Do you know anybody who sends cards in the mail? Do cards mean anything to you? Did Jack ever get any?"

"No. Cards? You mean playing-cards?"

"Yes, from the Horseshoe Club."

"Alessandro again, eh?" muttered Ty.

"I've been searching for those other envelopes, the ones that came before the—accident. But they're gone. When I got back from the funeral I began going through a heap of letters and telegrams of condolence and found—this. That's what made me remember the others."

Ty seized the envelope. It was addressed in a washed-out blue ink, and the writing—block-letters crudely penned—was scratchy.

"But it's addressed to Blythe Stuart," said Ty, puzzled. "And from the postmark it was mailed in Hollywood last night, the nineteenth. That's two days *after* her death! It doesn't make sense."

"That's why," said Bonnie tensely, "I think it *is* important. Maybe when we add up all the things that don't make sense, we'll have something that does."

Ty took out what lay in the envelope and stared at it.

"And this is all there was?"

"I told you it was mad."

The only thing in the envelope was a playing-card with a golden horseshoe engraved on its blue back.

The card was the nine of clubs.

10
FREEDOM OF THE PRESS

Whether it was because of the story in the paper or because banishing indecision meant seeing Paula Paris again, Mr. Ellery Queen concluded a three-day struggle with himself by driving on Thursday morning to the white house in the hills.

And there, in one of the waiting-rooms intently conning Paula's *Seeing Stars* column in the previous Sunday's night-edition of the Monday morning paper, sat Inspector Glücke. When he saw Ellery he quickly stuffed the paper into his pocket.

"Are you one of Miss Paris's doting public, too?" asked Ellery, trying to conceal his own copy of the same edition.

"Hullo, Queen." Then the Inspector growled: "What's the use of beating around the bush? I see you've spotted that column. Darned funny, I call it."

"Not at all! Some mistake, no doubt."

"Sure, that's why you're here, no doubt. This dame's got some tall explaining to do. Give me the runaround since Monday, will she? I'll break her damned neck!"

"Please," said Ellery frigidly. "Miss Paris is a lady. Don't speak of her as if she were one of your policewomen."

"So she's hooked you, too," snarled Glücke. "Listen, Queen, this isn't the first time I've locked horns with her. Whenever she comes up with something important and I ask her—in a nice way, mind you—to come down to HQ for a chin, I get the same old baloney about her not being able to leave this house, this crowd phobia of hers—"

"I'll thank you," snapped Ellery, "to stop insulting her."

"I've subpoenaed her from Dan to Beersheba time after time and she always wriggles out, blast her. Doctor's affidavits—God knows what! I'll show her up for a phony some day, mark my words. Crowd phobia!"

"Meanwhile," said Ellery nastily, "the mountain again approaches Mohammed. By the way, what's doing?"

"No trace of that pilot yet. But it's only a question of time. My own hunch is he cached a plane somewhere near that plateau, maybe on the plateau itself. Then when he grounded Ty's plane he simply walked over to his own ship and flew off. You don't leave much of a trail in thin air."

"Hmm. I see Dr. Polk has confirmed my guess as to the cause of death officially."

"Autopsy showed an almost equal amount of morphine, a little over five grains, in each body. That means, Doc says, that a hell of a lot of morphine was dropped into those thermos bottles. Also some stuff Bronson calls sodium allurate, a new barbiturate compound—puts you rockababy."

"No wonder there was no struggle," muttered Ellery.

"Polk says the morphine and sodium allurate would put 'em to sleep in less than five minutes. While they were sleeping that terrific dose of morphine began to get in its licks, and they must have died in less than a half-hour."

"I suppose Jack went first, and Blythe thought he was merely dozing. The soporific performed an important function. You see that? While the first victim, whichever it was, was apparently asleep although really dying or dead the second one, unsuspicious because of that sleeping appearance of the other, would drink from the other thermos bottle. The allurate was a precaution—just in case they didn't both drink at the same time. Damned clever."

"Clever or not, it did the trick. Death by respiratory paralysis Polk calls it. The hell of it is we can't trace the stuff. Sodium allurate's now available in any drug store, and you know what a cinch it is to lay your hands on morphine."

"Anything new?"

"Well," said Glücke bashfully, "I'm not saying—much. I tried tracing the sender of that hamper, but no dice; we found the place it came from, but the order was mailed in and they threw away the letter. Phony name, of course. The plane's sterile; the only fingerprints are Jack's and Blythe's and Ty's—this guy must have worn gloves throughout. On the other hand . . . "

"Yes? You're eating my heart out."

"Well, we sort of got a line on Jack's lady-friends. I swear he was a man, that billy-goat! Got a couple of interesting leads." The Inspector chuckled. "From the way the gals in this town are running for cover you'd think—"

"I'm not in the mood for love," said Ellery somberly. "How about this man Park? Not a word about him in the news."

"Oh, he's dead."

"What!"

"Committed suicide. It'll be in tonight's papers. We found his duds intact in the cheap flophouse in Hollywood where he bedded down, with a note saying he was dying anyway, he was no good to his wife and crippled boy back East, who are on relief, he hadn't earned enough to keep his own body and soul together for years, and so he was throwing himself to the tuna."

"Oh," said Ellery. "Then you didn't find his body?"

"Listen, my large-brained friend," grinned Glücke. "If you think that suicide note is a phony, forget it. We verified the handwriting. For another thing, we've definitely established the old guy couldn't fly a plane."

Ellery shrugged. "By the way, do something for me after you get through boiling Miss Paris in oil."

"What?" demanded the Inspector suspiciously.

"Put a night-and-day tail on Bonnie."

"Bonnie Stuart? What the hell for?"

"Blamed if I know. It must be my Psyche sniffing." Then he added quite without humor: "Don't neglect that, Glücke. It may be of the essence, as our French friends say."

Just then one of Paula Paris's secretaries said with an impish smile: "Will you come in now, Inspector?"

When Inspector Glücke emerged from Paula's drawing-room he looked positively murderous.

"You like that dame in there, don't you?" he panted.

"What's the matter?" asked Ellery, alarmed.

"If you do, get her to talk. Sock her, kiss her, do anything—but find out where she picked up that story!"

"So she won't talk, eh?" murmured Ellery.

"No, and if she doesn't I'll drag her out of this house by that pretty gray streak in her hair and lock her up, crowd phobia or no crowd phobia! I'll book her on a charge of—of criminal conspiracy! Hold her as a material witness!"

"Here, calm down. You wouldn't try to coerce the press in this era of constitutional sensitivity, would you? Remember the lamentable case of that newspaperman Hoover."

"I'm warning you!" yelled Glücke, and he stamped out.

"All right, Mr. Queen," said the secretary.

Ellery entered the holy of holies soberly. He found Paula finishing an apple and looking lovely, serene, and reproachful.

"You, too?" She laughed and indicated a chair. "Don't look so tragic, Mr. Queen. Sit down and tell me why you've neglected me so shamefully."

"You do look beautiful," sighed Ellery. "Too beautiful to spend the next year in jail. I wonder—"

"What?"

"Which part of Glücke's advice to take—whether to sock you or kiss you. Which would you prefer?"

"Imagine that monster playing Cupid," murmured Paula. "Disgusting! Why haven't you at least phoned me?"

"Paula," said Ellery earnestly. "You know I'm your friend. What's behind this story?" He tapped the Monday newspaper.

"I asked a question first," she said, showing the dimple.

Ellery stared hungrily. She looked ravishing in a silver lamé hostess-gown with a trailing wrap-around skirt over Turkish trousers. "Aren't you afraid I'll take Glücke's advice?"

"My dear Mr. Queen," she said coolly, "you overestimate your capacity—and his—for inspiring fear."

"I," said Ellery, still staring, "am. Damned if I'm not!"

He advanced. But the lady did not retreat. She just looked at him. "I see," she said in a pitying way, "that Hollywood's been doing nasty things to you."

Mr. Queen stopped dead, coloring. Then he said sharply: "We've strayed from the point. I want to know—"

"How it is that my column ran a story in the night-edition of the Monday paper, appearing Sunday evening, to the effect that Jack and Blythe were kidnapped on their wedding trip?"

"Don't evade the question!"

"How masterful," murmured Paula, looking down demurely.

"Damn it," cried Ellery, "don't be coy with me! You must have written that item, judging by the relative times involved, *before* the actual kidnapping!" Paula said nothing. "How did you know they were *going* to be kidnapped?"

Paula sighed. "You know, Mr. Queen, you're a fascinating creature, but what makes you think you've the right to speak to me in that tone of voice?"

"Oh, my God. Paula, can't you see the spot you're in? Where'd you get that information?"

"I'll give you the same answer," replied Paula coldly, "that I gave Inspector Glücke. And that is—none of your business."

"You've *got* to tell me. I won't tell Glücke. But I must know."

"I think," said Paula, rising, "that will be all, Mr. Queen."

"Oh, no, it won't! You're going to tell me if I have to—"

"I'm not responsible for the care and feeding of your detective instincts."

"Blast my detective instincts. It's you I'm worried about."

"Really, Mr. Queen," cooed Paula.

Ellery scowled. "I—I didn't mean to say that."

"Oh, but you did." Paula smiled at him; there was that damned dimple again! "Are you *truly* worried about me?"

"I didn't mean it that way. I meant—"

She burst into laughter suddenly and collapsed in her chair. "Oh, this is so funny!" she gasped. "The great detective. The giant intellect. The human bloodhound!"

"What's so funny about what?" asked Ellery stiffly.

"You thinking I had something to do with those murders!" She dabbed at her eyes with a Batique handkerchief.

Ellery blushed. "That's—absurd! I never said anything like that!"

"But that's what you meant. I don't think so much of your finesse, Mr. Sherlock Holmes. Trying to put it on a personal basis! I ought to be furious with you. . . . I *am* furious with you!" And Ellery, bewildered, saw that she was indeed furious with him.

"But I assure you—"

"It's *contemptible*. You overlords, you Mussolinis, you strutting men! You were going to take the poor, psychically ill little newspaper-woman and give her a delightful free ride, weren't you? Make love to her, sweep her off her silly feet, talk dizzy pretty nonsense—dash gallantly into a romantic attack, hoping all the time you'd find out something damning about her!"

"I should like to point out, in self-defense," said Ellery with dignity, "that my 'romantic attack,' as you put it so romantically, was launched long before either Jack Royle or Blythe Stuart was murdered."

Paula half-turned her shapely back, applying the handkerchief to her eyes, and Ellery saw her shoulders twitch convulsively. Damn him for a clumsy fool! He had made her cry.

He was about to go to her and act terribly sympathetic and powerful, when to his astonishment and chagrin she faced him and he saw that she was laughing.

"I *am* a fool," he said shortly, pierced to the soul. And he stalked to the door. Laughing at *him*.

She flew past him to set her back against it. "Oh, darling, you are," she choked. "No. Don't go yet."

"I don't see," he said, not mollified, but not going, "why I should stay."

"Because I want you to."

"Oh, I *see*." Not frightfully clever, that remark. What had happened to his celebrated wits? It was bewildering.

"I'll tell you what," said Paula, facing him with large, soft eyes. "I'll give you something I didn't give that lout Glücke. Now will you stay?"

"Well . . . "

"There! We're friends again." She took him by the hand and led him back to the sofa. Ellery felt suddenly pleased with himself. Not badly handled, eh? Proved something, didn't it? She liked him. And her hand was so warm and small. She did have tiny hands for a woman of her size. Not that she was so big! Well . . . she wasn't small. But not fat. Certainly not! He didn't like small women. He had always maintained a man cheated himself when he took to his bosom a small woman; man was entitled to a "generous measure of devotion." Oho, not bad, that! He looked Paula over covertly. Yes, yes, generous was the word. The richness of the cornucopia and the aristocracy of a court sword. Beautiful patrician. Quite the grand lady. Queenly, you might say.

"Queenly," he chuckled, pressing her hand ardently.

"What?" But she did not withdraw her hand.

"Oh, nothing," said Ellery modestly. "A little pun I just thought of. Queenly . . . ha ha! I mean—what were you going to tell me?"

"You do talk in riddles," sighed Paula, pulling him down with her. "I think that's why I like you. It's so much fun just trying to keep up."

Ellery wondered what would happen if he let his arm—oh, casually, of course—slip around her shoulders. They did look so strong, and yet womanly; were they soft? Would she flee to the arms of her phobia? Science—yes, the pure spirit of science—made it mandatory to try the experiment.

"What," he mumbled, trying the experiment, "happened?"

For one delicious instant she endured the reverent pressure of his arm. Her shoulders *were* strong and yet soft; just right, just right. Mr. Queen, in a heat of scientific ardor, squeezed. She jerked away from him like a blooded mare; then she sat still, coloring.

"I'll tell you just this," said Paula to her handkerchief, in a voice barely audible. "I—" And she stopped and got up and went to the nearby table and took a cigaret from a box.

Ellery was left with his arm in empty air, feeling rather foolish.

"Yes?" he said abruptly.

She sat down in the Cape Cod rocker, busy with the cigaret. "About an hour before the plane was stolen, I received a telephone call. I was told Jack and Blythe were about to be kidnapped."

"Where was the call from?"

"I can't tell you that."

"Don't you know?" She did not reply. "Who called?" Ellery jumped up. "Paula, did you know Jack and Blythe *were going to be murdered*?"

Her eyes flashed then. "Ellery Queen, how dare you ask me such a filthy question!"

"You bring it on yourself," he said bitterly. "Paula, it's—very queer."

She was wordless for a long time. Ellery mooned down at her sleek hair with its fascinating band of gray. Teach him a lesson, he thought. The one thing he didn't know anything about was women. And this one was exceptionally clever and elusive; you just couldn't grasp her. He turned and for the second time made for the door.

"Stop!" Paula cried. "Wait. I'll—I'll tell you what I can."

"I'm waiting," he growled.

"Oh, I shouldn't, but you're so . . . Please don't be angry with me."

Her splendid eyes shed such soft, luminous warmth that Ellery felt himself beginning to melt. He said hastily: "Well?"

"I do know who called." She spoke in a very low tone, her lashes resting on her cheeks. "I recognized the voice."

"Then this man didn't give you his name?"

"Don't be clever; I didn't *say* it was a man. As a matter of fact, this—person did give a name. The right name, because the voice checked."

Ellery frowned. "Then there was no secret about this caller's identity? He—or she—made no effort to conceal it?"

"Not the slightest."

"Who was it?"

"That's the one thing I won't tell you." She cried out at his sudden movement. "Oh, can't you see I mustn't? It's against every rule of newspaper ethics. And if I betrayed an informant once, I'd lose the confidence of the thousands of people who sell me information."

"But this is murder, Paula."

"I haven't committed any crime," she said stubbornly. "I would have notified the police, except that as a precaution I had the call traced, found it came from the airport, and by the time I got my information the plane had left and the police already knew what had happened."

"The airport." Ellery sucked his lower lip.

"And besides, how was I to know it would wind up in murder? Mr. Queen . . . Ellery, don't look at me that way!"

"You're asking me to take a great deal on faith. Even now it's your duty as a citizen to tell Glücke about that call, to tell him who it was that called you."

"Then I'm afraid," she half-whispered, "you'll have to take it that way."

"All right." And for the third time Ellery went to the door.

"Wait! I—Would you like a real tip?"

"More?" said Ellery sarcastically.

"It's only for your cars. I haven't printed it yet."

"Well, what is it?"

"More than a week ago—that's the thirteenth, last Wednesday—Jack and Blythe took a quiet little trip by plane."

"I didn't know about that," muttered Ellery. "Where did they go?"

"To the Chocolate Mountain estate of Blythe's father."

"I don't see anything remarkable in that. Jack and Blythe had made up by that time. Quite natural for two people intending to be married to visit the bride-to-be's father."

"Don't say I didn't warn you."

Ellery scowled. "You possess an omniscience, Paula, that disturbs me. Who poisoned Jack and Blythe?"

"*Quien sabe*?"

"What's more to the point, *why* were they poisoned?"

"Oh," she murmured, "so that's bothering you, eh?"

"You haven't answered my question."

"Darling," she sighed, "I'm just a lonely woman shut up in a big house, and all I know is what I read in the papers. Nevertheless, I'm beginning to think . . . I could guess."

"Guess!" He wrinkled his nose scornfully.

"And I'm also beginning to think . . . you can, too." They regarded each other in sober silence. Then Paula rose and smiled and gave him her hand. "Goodbye, Ellery. Come and see me some time. Heavens, I'm starting to talk like Mae West!"

But when he had gone, definitely this time, Paula stood still, staring at the panels of the door, her hands to her flushed face. Finally she went into her bedroom, shut the door, and sat down at her vanity and stared some more, this time at her reflection.

Mae West. . . . Well, why not? she thought defiantly. It merely took courage and a—and a certain natural equipment. And he did seem . . .

She shivered all at once, all over her body. The shiver came from a sensitive spot in the area of her shoulder where Mr. Queen, in a spirit of scientific research, had squeezed it.

11

IT'S IN THE CARDS

Mr. Queen, even as he drove away from Paula's house admiring his own charms in thought, felt a premonitory chill. He had the feeling that he had not heard quite everything.

The infallibility of his intuition was demonstrated the instant he stepped into Jacques Butcher's office. The Boy Wonder was reading Paula's column in a grim silence, while Sam Vix tried to look unhappy and Lew Bascom conducted a monologue shrewdly designed to distract the Boy Wonder's mind.

"I'm like the Phoenix," Lew was chattering. "It's won'erful how I rise outa my own ashes. We'll go ahead with the original plans for the picture, see, only we'll have Bonnie and Ty double for Blythe and Jack, an'—"

"Can it, Lew," warned Sam Vix.

"Here's the mastermind," said Lew. "Looka here, Queen. Don't you think—"

Without taking his eyes from the newsprint, Butch said curtly: "It's impossible. For one thing, Bonnie and Ty wouldn't do it, and I wouldn't blame them. For another, the Hays office would crack down.

Too much notoriety already. Hollywood's always sensitive about murders."

"What's the matter, Butch?" demanded Ellery.

Butch looked up then, and Ellery was startled at the expression on his face. "Nothing much," he said with an ugly laugh. "Just another little scoop of Paula Paris's."

"Oh, you mean that Monday column?"

"Who said anything about Monday? This is today's paper."

"Today?" Ellery looked blank.

"Today. Paula says here that Ty and Bonnie are on their way to honeymoonland."

"What!"

"Aw, don't believe what that halfwit writes," said Lew. "Here, Butch, have a drink."

"But I just saw Paula," cried Ellery, "and she didn't say anything about that!"

"Maybe," said Vix dryly, "she thinks you can read."

Butch shrugged. "I guess I had to wake up some time. I think I've known all along that Bonnie and I . . . She's crazy about Ty; if I hadn't been so blind I'd have realized all that bickering covered up something deep." He smiled and poured himself a water-glass full of gin. "*Prosit!*"

"It's a dirty trick," mumbled Lew. "She can't do that to my pal."

"Do they know you know?" asked Ellery abruptly.

"I guess not. What difference does it make?"

"Where are they now?"

"I just had a call from Bonnie, gay as a lark—I mean, considering. They're going to the Horseshoe Club to play cops and robbers with Alessandro. Good luck to 'em."

Ellery departed in haste. He found Bonnie's scarlet roadster parked outside the Horseshoe Club; the interior was depressingly deserted, with charwomen scrubbing up the marks of the expensive shoes of Hollywood's élite and one bartender listlessly wiping glasses.

Bonnie and Ty were leaning side by side over the horseshoe-shaped desk in Alessandro's office, and Alessandro sat quietly before them, drumming a tune with his fingers.

"This seems to be my bad day," he remarked dryly when he saw Ellery. "It's all right, Joe; these folks don't pack rods. Well, shoot. What's on your mind?"

"Hello, Mr. Queen," cried Bonnie. She looked lovely and fresh in a tailored gabardine suit and a crimson jellyroll of a hat tipped on her honey hair; her cheeks were pink with excitement. "We were just asking Mr. Alessandro about those IOU's."

So they didn't know yet, Ellery thought. He grinned: "Coincidence. That's why I'm here, too."

"You *and* Inspector Glücke," chuckled the little fat gambler. "The flattie! Only he was here Monday."

"I don't care about that," barked Ty. "You admit my dad owed you a hundred and ten thousand dollars?"

"Sure I admit it. It's true."

"Then how is it those IOU's were found on his body?"

"Because," said Alessandro gently, "he paid up."

"Oh, he did, did he? When?"

"On Thursday the fourteenth—just a week ago."

"And with what?"

"With good stiff American dough. Thousand-buck bills."

"You're a liar."

The man called Joe growled. But Alessandro smiled. "I've stood a lot from you people," he said amiably, "you and your folks, get me? I ought to give Joe here the office to slug you for that crack, Royle. Only your old man just got his, and maybe you're a little excited."

"You and your gorillas don't scare me."

"So you think maybe I had something to do with those murders, hey?" Alessandro snarled. "I warn you, Royle, lay off. I run a clean joint and I got a reputation in this town. Lay off, if you know what's good for you!"

Bonnie sucked in her breath. But then her eyes snapped and she snatched an envelope from her purse and tossed it on the desk. "Maybe you can explain this!"

Ellery goggled as he saw Alessandro take a blue-backed playing-card out of the envelope and stare at it. One of those cryptic messages!

He groaned inwardly. They had utterly slipped his mind. He was growing senile.

Alessandro shrugged. "It comes from the Club, all right. So what?"

"That," growled Ty, "is what we're trying to find out."

The gambler shook his head. "No dice. Anybody could get hold of our cards. Hundreds play here every week, and we give dozens of packs away as souvenirs."

"I imagine," said Ellery hurriedly, "Alessandro is right. We're not learning anything here. Coming, you two?"

He herded them out before they could protest, and the instant they were in Bonnie's roadster he snapped: "Bonnie, let me see that envelope."

Bonnie gave it to him. He studied it intently, then put it into his pocket.

"Here, I want that," said Bonnie. "It's important. It's a clue."

"You're a better man than I am for spotting it as such," said Ellery. "I'll keep it, if you don't mind—as I happen to have kept the others. Oh, I'm an idiot!"

Bonnie almost ran over a Russian wolfhound. "You!" she cried. "Then it was you—"

"Yes, yes," said Ellery impatiently. "I fancy I'm better qualified for all my forgetfulness. Magna Studios, Bonnie."

Ty, who was scarcely listening, muttered: "He's lying. It couldn't be anything but a lie."

"What?"

"Alessandro. We've only got his word that those IOU's were paid. Suppose dad refused to pay, or what's more likely pointed out how impossible it was for him to pay? It would have been pie for Alessandro to get one of his plug-uglies to play the pilot and after poisoning dad and Blythe put the torn IOU's into dad's pocket."

"But why, Ty?" frowned Bonnie.

"Because he'd know he'd never get his money anyway. Because knowing that, he'd want revenge. And planting the IOU's on dad would make it seem to the police as if the money *was* paid, in that way eliminating in their minds any possible motive on Alessandro's part."

"A little subtle," said Ellery, "but conceivable."

"But even if that's so," said Bonnie, "why mother? Don't you see, Ty, that's the thing that confuses everything? Why was mother poisoned, too?"

"I don't know," said Ty doggedly. "All I know is dad couldn't possibly have laid his hands on a hundred and ten grand. He had no money, and nowhere to get any."

"By the way," remarked Ellery casually, "did you people know that in today's column Paula Paris hints you two have made up rather thoroughly?"

Bonnie went slowly pale, and Ty blinked several times. Bonnie pulled up to a curb and said: "What?"

"She says you're well on your way to love and kisses."

Bonnie looked for a moment as if she was going to have a crying spell again. But then her chin came up and she turned on Ty furiously. "And you *promised* me!"

"But, Bonnie—" began Ty, still blinking.

"You—*fiend!*"

"Bonnie! You certainly don't think—"

"Don't speak to me, you publicity hound," said Bonnie with a sick, heavy, hot loathing.

That was the start of an extraordinary day, and every one was thoroughly miserable; and when they got to the Boy Wonder's office Bonnie went to him and deliberately kissed his mouth and then took up the phone and asked Madge to get Paula Paris on the wire.

Butch looked bewilderedly from Bonnie to Ty; both their faces were red with anger.

"Miss Paris? This is Bonnie Stuart speaking. I've just heard that, with your usual cleverness, you've found out that Ty Royle and I are going to be married, or something as foul and lying as that."

"I'm afraid I don't understand," murmured Paula.

"If you don't want to be sued for libel you'll please print a retraction of that story at once!"

"But, Bonnie, I had it on excellent authority—"

"No doubt. Well, I detest him as much as I detest you for listening to him!"

"But I don't understand. Ty Royle—"

"You heard me, Miss Paris." Bonnie slammed the phone down and glared at Ty.

"Well, well," chuckled Lew. "This is like old times, for gossakes. Now about that picture—"

"Then it isn't true?" asked Butcher slowly.

"Of course not! And as far as this contemptible—person is concerned . . . "

Ty turned on his heel and walked out. Ellery hurried after him. "You didn't give that story to Paula?"

"What do you think I am?"

"Hmm. Very pretty scene." Ellery glanced at him sidewise. "I shouldn't be surprised if she did it herself."

"What!" exploded Ty. He stopped short. "Well, by God, maybe you're right. She's been stringing me along. I see it all now—the whole thing, leading me on just so she could turn around and slap me down the way she's always done. What a rotten trick!"

"That's women for you," sighed Ellery.

"I thought at first it was that damned Frenchwoman. She's the only other one who could possibly have overheard."

"Oh, then you did get cuddly?"

"Well. . . . But it's over now—finished! I'm through with that scheming little double-crosser for good!"

"Nobly resolved," said Ellery heartily. "Man's much better off alone. Where are you going now?"

"Hell, I don't know." They were standing before a row of pretty little stone bungalows. "That's funny. Here's dad's old dressing-room. Force of habit, eh?" Ty muttered: "If you don't mind, Queen, I think I'll sort of go in alone."

"Not a bit of it," said Ellery, taking his arm. "We've both been made fools of, so we ought to pool our misery."

And he went into John Royle's studio bungalow with Ty.

And found the key to the code.

* * *

He found it by accident, merely because he was in the dead man's room and it occurred to him that no one had disturbed it since the elder Royle's death. There was even a soiled towel, with the stains of make-up on it, lying on the make-up table beside a new-looking portable typewriter.

So Ellery poked about while Ty lay down on the couch and stared stonily at the oyster-white ceiling; and almost the first thing Ellery found in the table drawer was a creased and crumpled sheet of ordinary yellow paper, 8½ by 11 inches in size, one side blank and the other well-filled with typewritten words.

And Ellery took one look at the capitalized, underscored heading: MEANING OF THE CARDS, and let out a whoop that brought Ty to his feet.

"What is it? What's the matter?"

"I've found it!" yelled Ellery. "Of all the colossal breaks. The cards! All typed out. Thanks, kind Fates. Yes, here's the whole thing. . . . Wait a minute. Is it possible—"

Ty frowned over the sheet. Ellery whipped the cover off the portable typewriter, rummaged until he found a sheet of blank stationery, pushed it under the carriage, and began rapidly to type, referring to the crumpled yellow paper from time to time. And as he typed, the gladness went out of his face, and it became dark with thought.

He got up, replaced the cover of the typewriter, put the papers carefully into his pocket, picked up the machine, and said in a flat voice: "Come along, Ty."

They found Bonnie and the Boy Wonder in each other's arms, Bonnie's face still stormy and Butch looking wildly happy. Lew sat grinning at them both, like a benevolent satyr.

"We come bearing news," said Ellery. "Unhand her, Butch. This requires confabulation."

"Whassa matter?" asked Lew suspiciously.

"Plenty. I don't know whether you know it or not, Butch, but Ty and Bonnie do. Blythe for some time before last Sunday had been receiving anonymous messages."

"I didn't know that," said Butch slowly.

"What kind?" frowned Lew. "Threats?"

"Plain envelopes addressed in block letters by obviously a post-office pen, mailed in Hollywood, and containing nothing but playing-cards." He took out his wallet and tossed over a small bundle of envelopes bound by an elastic. Butch and Lew examined them incredulously.

"Horseshoe Club," muttered Lew.

"But what do they mean?" demanded Butch. "Bonnie, why didn't you tell me?"

"I didn't think they were important."

"I'm more to blame. I've been carrying these things around in my pocket and didn't once think of them after Sunday. But just now," said Ellery, "I found the key to those cards."

He laid down on Butcher's desk the yellow sheet. Lew and Butch and Bonnie read it with blank faces.

"I don't understand," murmured Bonnie. "It looks like some kind of fortune-telling."

"It told a remarkably grim fortune," drawled Ellery. "This—you might call it a codex—tells what each card sent through the mail means." He picked up the envelopes. "The first envelope Blythe received was mailed on the eleventh of this month and delivered on the twelfth. That was nine days ago, or five days before the murders. And what was in the envelope? Two playing-cards—the knave and seven of spades."

Automatically they craned at the yellow sheet. The meaning assigned to both the knave and seven of spades was: "An Enemy."

"Two enemies, then," said Ellery. "Just as if some one had written: 'Watch yourself. We're both after you.' "

"Two—enemies?" said Bonnie damply. There was horror in her eyes as she glanced, as if against her will, at Ty's pale face. "Two!"

"The second envelope arrived on Friday the fifteenth. And it contained two cards also—the ten of spades and the two of clubs. And what do they mean?"

" 'Great Trouble,' " muttered Ty. "That's the spade ten. And 'In Two Days or Two Weeks' on the deuce of clubs."

"Two days," cried Bonnie. "Friday the fifteenth—and mother was murdered on Sunday the seventeenth!"

"And on Sunday the seventeenth, at the field," continued Ellery, "I saw Clotilde deliver the third envelope. I picked it up after your mother, Bonnie, threw it away. It was this—the eight of spades, torn in half. If you'll refer to that note at the bottom of the sheet, you'll see that the meaning is intended to become reversed when a card is torn in half. Consequently the message becomes—only a few minutes before the plane is hijacked and the murder occurs: 'Threatened Danger Will NOT Be Warded Off!' "

"This," said Butcher pallidly, "is the most childish nonsense I've ever heard of. It's completely incredible."

"Yet here it is." Ellery shrugged. "And just now Bonnie gave me the last message—the nine of clubs enclosed, meaning: 'Last Warning.' That seems the most incredible nonsense of all, Butch, since this 'warning' was *sent to Blythe two days after her death*."

The Boy Wonder looked angry. "It was bad enough before, but this . . . Damn it, how can you credit such stuff? But if we must . . . it does look as if whoever mailed this last letter didn't know Blythe was dead, doesn't it? And since all the letters were obviously the work of the same person, I can't see the relevance of any of it."

"It's ridiculous," jeered Lew. "Plain nut stuff." Nevertheless he asked: "Say, where'd you find this sheet?"

"In Jack Royle's dressing-room." Ellery took the cover off the portable typewriter. "And what's more, if you'll examine this sample of typewriting I just made on this machine and compare it with the typing on the yellow sheet, you'll find that the small h's and r's, for instance, have identically broken serifs. Identically broken," he repeated with a sudden thoughtful note; and he seized a paperweight sunglass on Butcher's desk and examined the keys in question. Freshly filed! But he put the glass down and merely said: "There's no doubt about it. This code-sheet was typed on Jack Royle's typewriter. It was *your dad's, Ty?*"

Ty said: "Yes. Yes, of course," and turned away.

MEANING OF THE CARDS

	DIAMONDS	HEARTS	CLUBS	SPADES
KING	Man with Fair Hair	Man with Red Hair	Man with Dark Hair	Strange Man
QUEEN	Woman with Fair Hair	Woman with Red Hair	Woman with Dark Hair	Strange Woman
JACK	A Messenger	A Preacher	A Lawbreaker	An Enemy
TEN	Large Sum of Money	A Surprise	Gambling	Great Trouble
NINE	Lovers' Quarrel	Disappointment	Last Warning	Grief
EIGHT	A Jewel	Thoughts of Marriage	An Accident	Threatened Danger Will Be Warded Off
SEVEN	A Journey	Jealousy	Prison	An Enemy
SIX	Beware of Speculation	Beware of Scandal	Beware of Overwork	Beware of Malicious Gossip
FIVE	A Telegram	Unexpected Meeting	A Change	Unpleasant Meeting
FOUR	A Diamond Ring	Broken Engagement	A Secret	Have Nothing to Do With a Certain Person About Whom You Are Doubtful
THREE	Quarrel over Money	Obstacles in Way of Love	Obstacles in Way of Success	Obstacles in Way of Reconciliation
TWO	Trouble Caused by Deception	An Introduction	In Two Days or Two Weeks	Tears
ACE	Telephone Call	Invitation	Wealth	Death

(The Meaning Becomes Reversed When a Card Appears Torn in Half)

"Jack?" repeated Butch in a dazed voice.

Lew snarled: "Aw, go on. What would Jack want to play games for?" but the snarl was somehow unconvincing. He glanced uneasily at Bonnie.

Bonnie said huskily: "On Jack Royle's typewriter. . . . You're sure of that?"

"Absolutely. Those broken keys are as good as fingerprints."

"Ty Royle, did you hear that?" asked Bonnie of his back, her eyes flashing. "Did you?"

"What do you want?" muttered Ty, without turning.

"What do I want?" screamed Bonnie. "I want you to turn around and look me in the face! Your father typed that sheet—your father sent those notes with the cards in them to mother—*your father killed my mother!*"

He turned then, defensively, his face sullen. "You're hysterical or you'd know that's a stupid, silly accusation."

"Is it?" cried Bonnie. "I *knew* there was something funny about his repentance, about proposing marriage to mother after so many years of hating her. Now I know he was lying all the time, playing a game— yes, Lew, but a horrible one!—covering himself up against the time when he expected to—to murder her. The engagement, the wedding, it was all a trap! He hired somebody to pretend to kidnap them and then poisoned my mother with his own foul hands!"

"And himself, too, I suppose?" said Ty savagely.

"Yes, because when he realized what an awful thing he'd done he had the first decent impulse of his life and put an end to it!"

"I'm not going to fight with you, Bonnie," said Ty in a low voice.

"Enemies . . . *two* enemies! Well, why not? You *and* your father! The neat little love scene yesterday . . . oh, you think you're clever, too. You *know* he killed my mother and you're trying to cover him up. For all I know you may have helped him plan it—you murderer!"

Ty made two fists and then opened them. He rubbed the back of one hand for a moment as if it itched, or pained, him. Then without a word he walked out of the office.

Bonnie flew, weeping, into Butcher's arms.

But later, when she got home and Clotilde let her in, and she crept up to her room and without undressing lay down on her bed, Bonnie wondered at herself in a dark corner of her aching head. Was it really true? Could it really be? Had he been acting yesterday when he said he loved her? Suspicions were horrible. She could have sworn . . . And yet there it was. The facts were all against him. Who could have told Paula Paris about their reconciliation? Only Ty. And after she had begged him not to! And then, finding that sheet. . . . You couldn't wipe out years and years of hatred just by uttering three one-syllable words.

Oh, Ty, you monster!

Bonnie remained in her room, shut against the world, sleepless, sick, and empty. The night passed, and it was a long night peopled with so many shadows that at three o'clock in the morning, railing at her nerves and yet twitchy with morbid thoughts, she got up and switched on all the lights. She did not close her eyes the whole night.

At eight she admitted Clotilde, who was frantic.

"Oh, Bonnie, you shall make yourself ill! See, I have brought *p'tit déjeuner. Galettes et marmelade*—"

"No, thanks, 'Tilde," said Bonnie wearily. "More letters?"

She dipped into the heap of envelopes on the tray. "Dear Bonnie Stuart: My heart goes out to you in your grief, and I want to tell you how much I feel for you. . . ." Words. Why couldn't people let her alone? And yet that was ungrateful. They *were* dears, and they had loved Blythe so. . . .

Her heart stopped.

There was an envelope—it looked so horribly familiar. . . . She tore an end off with shaking fingers. But no, it couldn't be. This one was addressed in typewriting, sloppily. But the envelope, the Hollywood postmark . . .

A blue playing-card dropped out. The seven of spades.

Nothing more.

Clotilde stared at her open-mouthed. "*Mais chérie, il semble que tu*—"

Bonnie breathed: "Go away, 'Tilde."

The seven of spades. *Again* . . . "An Enemy" . . .

Bonnie dropped the card and envelope as if they were foul, slimy things. And for the first time in her life, as she crouched in her tumbled bed with Clotilde gaping at her, she felt weak with pure fright.

An enemy. Ty . . . Ty was her only enemy.

Before Ellery left the Magna lot he went on impulse, still toting Jack Royle's typewriter, to the studio street where the stars' stone bungalows were and quietly let himself into Blythe Stuart's dressing-room.

And there, as he had half-expected, he found a carbon copy on yellow paper of the "Meaning of the Cards." In a drawer, hidden away.

So Blythe *had* known what the cards meant! Ellery had been positive her too casual dismissal of the letters had covered a frightened knowledge.

He slipped out and made for the nearest public telephone.

"Paula? Ellery Queen."

"How nice! And so soon, too." Her voice was happy.

"I suppose," said Ellery abruptly, "it's useless for me to ask where you learned about Ty and Bonnie."

"Quite useless, Sir Snoop."

"I imagine it was that Clotilde—it couldn't have been any one else. There's loyal service for you!"

"You won't pump me, my dear Mr. Queen," she said; but from something defensive in her tone Ellery knew he had guessed the truth.

"Or why you didn't tell me this morning when I saw you. However, this is all beside the point. Paula, would you say Jack Royle killed Blythe Stuart—that his change of heart, the engagement, the wedding, were all part of a careful, murderous scheme to take his revenge on her?"

"That," said Paula crisply, "is the silliest theory of the crime I've heard yet. Why, Jack couldn't possibly . . . Is it yours?"

"Bonnie Stuart's."

"Oh." She sighed. "The poor child gave me Hail Columbia over the phone a few moments ago. I suppose running that yarn *was* a rotten trick, so soon after the funeral. But that's the trouble with newspaper work. You can't be nice, and efficient, too."

"Look, Paula. Will you do me one enormous favor? Print that retraction of the reconciliation story Bonnie demanded. Right away."

"Why?" Her voice was instantly curious.

"Because I ask you to."

"Ouch! You are possessive, aren't you?"

"Forget personalities or your job. This is—vital. Do you know the derivation of that word? Paula, you must. Swing back into the old line—their furious feud from childhood, how they detest each other, how the death of their parents has driven them farther apart. Feed them raw meat. Keep them fighting."

Paula said slowly: "Just why do you want to keep those poor mixed-up kids apart?"

"Because," said Ellery, "they're in love."

"How logical you are! Or are you a misogamist with a mission in the world? Keep them apart *because* they're in love? Why?"

"Because," replied Ellery grimly, "it happens to be very, very dangerous for them to *be* in love."

"Oh." Then Paula said with a catch in her voice. "Aren't we all?" and hung up.

PART THREE

12

INTERNATIONAL MAILERS, INC.

Ellery, Sam Vix, and Lew Bascom were having breakfast Friday morning in the Magna commissary when Alan Clark strolled in, sat down beside them on a stool, and said to the aged waitress behind the counter: "Coffee, beautiful."

"Oh, Alan."

"Here I am. What's on your mind?"

"I've been wondering," said Ellery. "Just what is my status now in the studio?"

"Status?" The agent stared. "What d'ye mean? You're on the payroll, aren't you?"

"His conscience is havin' an attack of the shakes," grinned Lew. "I never saw such a guy for virtue. Like the little studio steno I was out with last night. I says to her—"

"I know," protested Ellery, "but I was hired to work on the Royle-Stuart picture, and there is no Royle-Stuart picture any more."

"Isn't that too bad?" said Clark, shaking his head over the coffee. "My heart bleeds for you."

"But what am I supposed to do, Alan? After all, I'm drawing fifteen hundred a week!"

The three men shook their heads in unison. "He's drawing fifteen hundred a week," said Sam Vix pityingly. "Now that's what I call a stinking shame."

"Look, Queen," sighed the agent. "Was it your fault Jack Royle and Blythe got themselves purged?"

"I don't see what that has to do with it."

"Say, whose side are you on, anyway—labor or capital?" demanded Lew. "We writers got some rights!"

"Your contract wasn't drawn up, if I may say so," said Clark modestly, "by a cluck. You've got little Alan in there batting for you all the time, remember that. You contracted to work on a Royle-Stuart picture, and there's nothing in that immortal document about murders."

"That's just the point; the picture will never be made. It's been withdrawn from schedule. Butch announced its withdrawal only this morning."

"What of it? Your contract calls for an eight-week guarantee. So, picture or no picture, you stay here till you collect eight weeks' salary. Or, to put it crudely, till you've wrapped your bankbook around twelve thousand bucks."

"It's criminal," muttered Ellery.

"Nah, it's life," said Clark, rising. "Now forget it. Being ashamed to draw a salary! Who ever heard of such a thing?"

"But how can I take it? I can't just sit around here—"

"He can't just sit around here," exploded Lew. "Listen, drizzlepuss, I'm sittin' around here for a lot less than fifteen hundred bucks a week!"

"Me, too," sighed the publicity man.

"Work it out in detecting," suggested Clark. "You're a detective, aren't you?"

"I could use some o' that dough," Lew grumbled into his raw egg-and-tomato juice. "Say, Queen, how's about letting me have a couple o' C's till next Friday?"

"This is where I came in," said the agent hurriedly. "Got to bawl out a producer; he's knifing one of my best clients in the back."

"Just till next Friday," said Lew as Clark went away.

"If you let this pirate put the bee on you," growled Sam Vix, "you're a bigger sap than you pretend to be. Next Friday! What's the matter with this Friday? You get paid today, you fat bastard."

"Who asked you to butt in?" said Lew hotly. "You know I'm savin' up for my old age. I'm gonna start a chicken farm."

"You mean the kind that clucks 'Daddy'?" jeered Vix. "You save for your old age! You're not going to have an old age. Unless your stomach's lined with chromium."

"Anyway, I saw him first!"

"That," said the publicity man with a grin, "was one tough break— for him. Well, so long. I work for my lousy pittance."

"By the way, Sam," said Ellery absently. "I've been meaning to ask you. Where were you last Sunday?"

"Me?" The one-eyed man looked astonished. "Over at Reed Island, making arrangements for the wedding reception."

"I know, but when I phoned the Island after the plane was snatched Sunday, I was told you weren't there."

Vix scowled down at him. "What the hell you doing—taking Clark's advice seriously?"

"No offense," smiled Ellery. "I just thought I'd ask you before Glücke got around to it."

"Take a tip from me and lay off that kind of chatter. It isn't healthy." And Vix stalked off, the black patch over his eye quivering with indignation.

"What's the matter with *him*?" murmured Ellery, offering his coffee-cup to the waitress to be replenished.

Lew chuckled. "Some guys are born hatin' spinach and other guys work up a terrific peeve if you split an infinitive. Sam's weakness is he don't think it's funny to be suspected of a murder. And he thinks it's twice as not funny in the case of a double feature."

"Can't a man ask an innocent question?"

"Yeah," said Lew dryly. "Pretty soon you'll be askin' me an innocent question, too. Like: 'Was that really you standin' beside me when this masked guy hijacked Ty's plane?'"

"Well, you can't always believe your eyes," said Ellery with a grin.

"Sure not. I mighta been my twin brother."

"Have you a twin brother?" asked Ellery, startled.

"You know why I like you?" sighed Lew. "Because you're such a pushover for a gag. Of course I ain't got no twin brother!"

"I might have known that the Author of us all wouldn't repeat a mistake of *that* magnitude," said Ellery sadly. "Oh, Ty! Come over here and join us in some breakfast."

Ty Royle strode over, freshly shaven but looking as if he had spent a hectic night. "Had mine, thanks. Queen, I'd like to talk to you."

"Yes?"

Ty squatted on the stool Sam Vix had vacated, put his elbow on the counter, and ran his fingers through his hair.

"All right, all right," grumbled Lew, getting up. "I know a stage wait when I hear one."

"Don't go, Lew," said Ty wearily. "You may be able to help, too."

Ellery and Lew exchanged glances. "Sure, kid," said Lew, seating himself. "What's on your mind?"

"Bonnie."

"Oh," said Ellery.

"What's she pulled on you now?" asked Lew sympathetically.

"It's that business of yesterday afternoon." Ty fiddled with Vix's coffee-cup. "Her saying that dad was behind the—well, the whole thing. I've been up all night thinking it over. I was sore as a boil at first. But I found out something about myself last night."

"Yes?" said Ellery with a frown.

"Something's happened to me. Since Wednesday. I don't feel the way I used to about her. In fact, I feel . . . just the opposite." He banged the cup. "Oh, what the hell's the use of fighting myself any longer? I'm in love with her!"

"You feelin' good?" growled Lew.

"It's no use, Lew. I'm hooked for fair this time."

"With all the fluffs you've played!"

Ty smiled wryly. "That's almost exactly what I said to dad when I found out he'd decided he loved Blythe."

"Yes," murmured Ellery, "history has a fascinating way of repeating itself." He sent Lew a warning look, and Lew nodded.

"Listen kid, it's your imagination and this climate," said Lew in a fatherly tone. "Jack's death sort of knocked you out of kilter, and you know what the warm sun does to young animals. Listen to your Uncle Looey. This love stuff don't get you anything but trouble. Take me, for instance. You don't see me going woozy-eyed over any one dame, do you? Hell, if I had your pan I'd make Casanova look like Cousin Hiram heavin' his first pass at the college widow!"

Ty shook his head. "No go, Lew. I don't want any woman but Bonnie. That stuff's out for good."

"Well," shrugged Lew, "it's your funeral. Don't say I didn't warn you."

"Look, Lew." Ty seemed embarrassed. "You're about as close to Bonnie as . . . I mean, I was thinking you might try to talk to her."

Ellery shook his head violently over Ty's shoulder.

"Who, me?" said Lew in a shocked voice. "What d'ye wanta make me, accessory to a crime? I wouldn't have it on my conscience. I'm no John Alden. Do your own courtin'."

"How about you, Queen? Bonnie's convinced that dad—well, you heard her yesterday. Somebody's got to show her how wrong she is. She obviously won't listen to me."

"Why don't you let matters ride for a while?" said Ellery lightly. "Give her time to cool off. She'll probably realize by herself, in time, that it's all a mistake."

"Sure, what's the rush? Give the kid a chance to get her bearings. Besides," said Lew, "there's Butch."

Ty was silent. Then he said: "Butch . . . Maybe you're right. It *is* less than a week."

The cashier at the commissary desk called out: "Mr. Queen, there's a call for you on this phone."

Ellery excused himself and went to the desk.

"Hello—Mr. Queen? This is Bonnie Stuart."

"Oh," said Ellery. "Yes?" He glanced at Ty, who was listening glumly as Lew waved his arms in earnest exhortation.

"I've something to show you," said Bonnie strangely. "It . . . came this morning."

"Oh, I see." Then Ellery said in a loud tone: "How about lunch?"

"But can't you come over now?"

"Sorry, I've something important to do. Shall we say the Derby on Vine at one o'clock?"

"I'll be there," said Bonnie curtly, and hung up.

Ellery strolled back to the counter. Ty interrupted Lew in the middle of a sentence. "Just the same, there's one thing we ought to do right away."

"What's that?" asked Ellery.

"I've been thinking about those anonymous letters. I think Inspector Glücke ought to be told about them."

"That nut stuff," scoffed Lew. "No one but a screwloose would mail cards to a dame when she was dead."

Ellery lit a cigaret. "Coincidence! I've been giving the matter considerable thought, too. And I believe I've worked out a practical theory."

"You're a better man than I am, then," said Ty gloomily.

"You see, there are really only two plausible inferences to be drawn from the strange fact Lew's just mentioned—I mean, this business of mailing a letter to a dead woman. Oh, of course there's always the possibility that the sender didn't know Blythe was dead, but you'll agree we can dismiss that as a huge improbability; Sam Vix and the gentlemen of the press associations have taken care of that."

"Maybe this palooka can't read," said Lew.

"Is he deaf, too? Illiteracy is scarcely the answer in these days of news broadcasting via the radio. Besides, the envelopes were addressed by some one who could write. No, no, that can't be the answer."

"Don't you know a gag when you hear one?" said Lew disgustedly.

"The two inferences seem to me to be all-inclusive. The first is the normal, obvious inference you've already voiced, Lew: that is, that the sender is a crank; that the envelopes, the cards, the whole childish business indicate the workings of a deranged mentality. It's conceivable that such a mentality would see nothing unreasonable about continuing to send the cards even after the object of his interest has died."

"Well, that's my guess," said Lew.

"And yet I get the feeling," said Ty thoughtfully, "that while the sender of those cards may be slightly off, he isn't just a nut."

"A feeling," murmured Ellery, "I share. And if he *is* sane, the alternate inference arises."

"What's that?" demanded Lew.

Ellery rose and picked up his check. "I was going to devote the morning," he said with a smile, "to a line of investigation which would prove or disprove it. Would you care to join me, gentlemen?"

While Lew and Ty waited, mystified, Ellery borrowed the Los Angeles Classified Directory at the commissary desk and spent ten minutes poring over it.

"No luck," he said, frowning. "I'll try Information." He closeted himself in one of the telephone booths, emerging a few minutes later looking pleased.

"Simpler than I expected. We've got one shot in the dark—thank heaven there aren't dozens."

"Dozens of what?" asked Ty, puzzled.

"Shots in the dark," said Lew. "See how simple it is?"

Ellery directed Ty to drive his sport roadster down Melrose to Vine, and up Vine to Sunset, and west on Sunset to Wilcox. On Wilcox, between Selma Avenue and Hollywood Boulevard, Ellery jumped out and hurried up the steps of the new post-office, vanishing within.

Ty and Lew looked at each other.

"You got me," said Lew. "Maybe it's a new kind of treasure hunt."

Ellery was gone fifteen minutes. "The postmaster," he announced cheerfully, "says nix. I didn't have much hope."

"Then your idea is out?" asked Ty.

"Not at all. Visiting the Hollywood postmaster was a precaution. Drive around to Hollywood Boulevard, Ty. I think our destination's just past Vine Street—between Vine and Argyle Avenue."

Miraculously, they found a parking space near Hollywood's busiest intersection.

"Now what?" said Lew.

"Now we'll see. It's this building. Come on."

Ellery preceded them into the office building across the street from the bank and theatre. He consulted the directory in the lobby, nodded, and made for the elevator, Ty and Lew meekly following.

"Third," said Ellery.

They got out at the third floor. Ellery looked cautiously about, then drew a leather case out of his pocket. He took a glittering object from the case and returned the case to his pocket.

"The idea is," he said, "that I'm somebody in the L.A. police department and that you two are somebody's assistants. If we don't put up an imposing front, we'll never get the information I'm after."

"But how are you going to get away with whatever you're trying to get away with?" asked Ty with a faint smile.

"Remember the Ohippi case? I had something to do with solving it, and this"—he opened his hand—"is a token of your *pueblo's* gratitude, up to and including Glücke, poor devil. Honorary Deputy Commissioner's badge. Look tough, you two, and keep your mouths shut."

He walked down the corridor to a door with a pebbled glass front on which was daubed in unimposing black letters:

INTERNATIONAL MAILERS, INC.
T. H. LUCEY
Los Angeles Division

The office proved to be a box-like chamber with one streaky window, a scratched filing cabinet, a telephone, a littered desk, and a dusty chair. In the chair sat a depressed-looking man of forty-odd with thinning hair carefully plastered to his skull. He was sucking a lollipop morosely as he read a dog-eared copy of *True Murder Stories*.

"You Lucey?" growled Ellery, fists in his pockets.

The stick of the lollipop tilted belligerently as Mr. Lucey swung about. His fishy eyes examined the three faces.

"Yeah. So what?"

Ellery withdrew his right hand from his pocket, opened his fist, permitted the mote-choked sun to touch the gold badge in his palm for a moment, and returned the badge to his pocket.

"Headquarters," he said gruffly. "Few questions we want to ask you."

"Dicks, huh." The man took the lollipop out of his mouth. "Go peddle your eggs somewheres else. I ain't done nothin'."

"Climb down, buddy. What kind of business do you run?"

"Say, whadda ya think this is, Russia?" Mr. Lucey slammed the magazine down and rose, a vision of American indignation. "We run a legitimate racket, Mister, and you got no right to question me about it! Say," he added suspiciously, "you from the Fed'ral gov'ment?"

Ellery, who had not anticipated this sturdy resistance, felt helpless. But when he heard Lew Bascom snicker his back stiffened. "You going to talk now or do we have to take you downtown?"

Mr. Lucey frowned judiciously. Then he stuck the lollipop back into his mouth. "Aw right," he grumbled. "Though I don't see why you gotta bother me. I'm only the agent here for the company. Why don't you get in touch with the gen'ral manager? Our main office is in—"

"Don't give a hoot. I asked you what kind of business you run here?"

"We take orders from folks to mail letters, packages, greeting cards—any kind o' mailable matter—at specified dates from specified places." He jerked his thumb toward a profusely curlicued bronze plaque on the wall. "There's our motto: 'Any Time, Any Where.'"

"In other words I could leave a dozen letters with you and you would mail one from Pasadena tomorrow, the next one next week from Washington, D.C., and so on, according to my instructions?"

"That's the ticket. We got branch offices everywhere. But what's this Ogpu business? Congress pass another law?"

Ellery tossed an envelope on the man's desk. "Did you mail this envelope?"

The man looked at it, brows drawn in. Ellery watched him, trying hard to preserve the indifferent expression of the professional detective. He heard Lew and Ty breathing stertorously behind him.

"Sure thing," said Mr. Lucey at last. "Mailed it—let's see; Tuesday, I think it was. Tuesday late. So what?"

Ellery preened himself. His companions looked awed.

"So what?" said Ellery sternly. "Take a look at that name and address, Lucey!"

Mr. Lucey's lollipop stick tilted again as he bridled; but he looked, and the stick dipped like the mast of a flag being struck, and his mouth opened, and the lollipop fell out.

"B-Blythe Stuart!" he stuttered. His demeanor altered instantly to one of cringing apology. "Say, Officer, I didn't reco'nize—I didn't know—"

"Then you mailed the others, too, didn't you?"

"Yes, sir. Yes, sir, we did." Mr. Lucey betrayed liquid signs of an inner warmth. "Why, even now, even just now when you showed it to me, I read the name, but it sort of didn't register . . . I mean I spotted it because it looked familiar. The name—"

"Don't you read the names and addresses on mailable matter when you contract to take a job?"

"We don't contract. I mean—no, sir, I don't. I mean why should I? Get stuff to mail, and we mail 'em. Look, Officer, did you ever have to do the same thing day in, day out for years? Look, I don't know nothin' about these murders. I'm innocent. I got a wife and three kids. People just give us mail, see? Salesmen. People tryin' to put the dog on with their customers—as if they had branches in different cities, stuff like that—"

"And husbands supposed to be in one city but actually being in another," said Ellery. "Sure, I know. Well, keep your shirt on, Mr. Lucey; nobody's accused you of being mixed up in this thing. We just want your co-operation."

"Co-operation? That's me, that's me, Officer."

"Tell me about this transaction. You must have records."

The man swabbed his damp face. "Yes, sir," he said humbly. "Just a minute while I look it up."

The three men exchanged glances as Lucey stooped over his filing cabinet. Then they stared expectantly at the man.

"Who put this particular order through, Mr. Lucey?" asked Ellery casually. "What was the name of this customer?"

"I think," said Lucey, red-faced as he struggled with the file, "I think . . . it was . . . somebody named Smith."

"Oh," said Ellery; and he heard Ty curse under his breath. "What did this fellow Smith look like?"

"Dunno," said Lucey, panting. "He didn't come here in person, as I remember; sent the batch of letters in a package, with a note inside and a five-dollar bill. Here it is."

He straightened up, triumphant, waving a large manila envelope bearing a handwritten legend: "Egbert L. Smith."

Ellery seized the envelope, took one swift look at its contents, closed it, and tucked it under his arm.

"But it's still in our 'Open' file," protested Lucey. "There's still one letter in there to be mailed."

"Blythe Stuart won't need it any more. Did you have any further correspondence with this man Smith?"

"No, sir."

"Did he ever call up, or show up in person?"

"No, sir."

"Well, Lucey, you've been a great help. Keep your mouth shut about this. Understand?"

"Yes, *sir*," said Mr. Lucey eagerly.

"And if this Smith ever should write, or call up, you can get me at this number." Ellery scribbled his name and telephone number on the man's magazine. "Come on, boys."

The last thing he saw as he closed the door was Mr. Lucey stooping, dazed, to pick up his fallen lollipop.

13

MR. QUEEN, LOGICIAN

They dodged guiltily around the corner and hurried down Vine Street. When they were safely hidden in a private booth at the Brown Derby they all looked relieved.

Lew was fat with laughter. "I'd like to see Glücke's face when he hears about this," he choked, wiping his eyes dry. "That deadpan won't talk—much. He'll tell his wife and his cuties and his pals. Say, I'll bet he's on the phone right now!"

"I'll have to make up to Glücke some way," said Ellery contritely. "He doesn't even know these letters exist."

"For God's sake, Queen," said Ty, "what's in that envelope?"

Ellery took from the manila envelope a letter, *sans* envelope; a type-written schedule on a letterhead of International Mailers, Inc.; and a single envelope, sealed, addressed to Blythe Stuart in the scratchy, pale blue-inked block letters of the previous messages. Attached to this envelope by a steel clip was a slip of memorandum paper, bearing a typed date.

"Mr. Egbert L. Smith's letter," said Ellery, scanning it slowly. Then he passed it over to Ty.

Ty read it eagerly, Lew squinting over his shoulder. The letter had been typewritten on a sheet of white "second" paper of the flimsiest, cheapest grade. It was dated the twenty-seventh of the previous month.

International Mailers, Inc.
Hollywood Blvd. & Vine St.
Hollywood, Calif.

GENTLEMEN:

I have seen your ad in today's paper saying you run a mailing service and wish to avail myself of this service.

I have certain letters which must be mailed to a customer of mine on certain dates, but I find I have to leave town for an indefinite period and may not be in a position to keep up my correspondence, so I am enclosing the letters in the package with a five-dollar bill, not knowing what your rates are and not having time to make inquiries. I am sure the five dollars will more than take care of stamps and your charge.

You will find the envelopes bound by an elastic. I wish them mailed in Hollywood *in the order in which they are stacked*, the top one first, the one under the top one second, and so on. This is very important. Here is a schedule of dates for mailing:
(1) Monday 11th (next month)
(2) Thursday 14th   (")
(3) Saturday 16th   (")—*special delivery*
(4) Tuesday 19th   (")
(5) Thursday 28th   (")
Thanking you in advance, I am,

Very truly yours,
EGBERT L. SMITH

P.S.—Please note letter No. 3 is to be mailed special delivery. This is to insure its arriving on Sunday the 17th, when there is no regular mail.

E. L. S.

"Damned Borgia didn't even *sign* his phony name," muttered Ty.

"An irritating but wise precaution," said Ellery dryly. "No handwriting, no clue. And no address. Note, too, the carefully innocuous phraseology. Neither illiterate nor erudite. With a distinct businessman flavor, as if Mr. Egbert L. Smith were exactly what he was pretending to be."

"Say, this letter was typed on Jack Royle's machine!" exclaimed Lew. "If what you said yesterday was true, Queen. Look at the broken serifs on those h's and r's. I think we ought to turn this over to Glücke pronto."

Ellery nodded, picking up the sheet of the company stationery. "This is just Lucey's schedule, copied verbatim from the list in Smith's letter. Of course, the name is fictitious. And I imagine the paper will be found to be sterile of fingerprints."

A waiter came to hover over them, and Ty said absently: "Brandy."

Lew said: "Greetings, Gene."

"Double drinks, Mr. Bascom?"

"Bring the bottle, for gossakes. Can't you see I got a sucker? The fifteen-year Monnet."

The waiter grinned and padded away.

"Let's see," murmured Ellery, "what the last letter in Mr. Smith's kitbag had to say. The one that hadn't yet been mailed."

He ripped off one end of the sealed envelope and squeezed. A blue-backed playing-card dropped out.

The card was the ace of spades.

It was unnecessary to refer to the code sheet Ellery had found in John Royle's dressing-room.

All the world and his wife and children knew the cartomantic significance of the ace of spades.

"Death," said Ty nervously. "That's . . . But it came—I mean it was scheduled to come— She was killed *before* it came."

"Exactly the point," said Ellery, fingering the card.

"You and your points," snorted Lew. "How about tipping your mitt for a change?"

Ellery sat gazing at the card, and the envelope, and the memorandum slip attached to the envelope.

"One thing is sure," said Ty, his face screwed up. "It's the baldest kind of frame-up. Somebody had it in for Blythe and framed dad for the crime. Dad's feud with Blythe furnished an ideal background for a frame-up, gave him a motive. And anybody could have got to that typewriter of dad's."

"Eh?" said Ellery absently.

"It's true the date on this 'Smith's' note—twenty-seventh of last month—ought to give us a clue to where the note was typed; I mean as between the dressing-room on the lot and our house. But, damn it, dad was always lugging the machine from one place to the other. I can't remember in which place it was before the twenty-seventh."

"Why did he have a typewriter, Ty?"

"To answer fan mail. He despised secretaries and liked to correspond personally with the writers of the more interesting letters he received. Hobby of his. He wouldn't let the studio handle it at all. As a matter of fact, I do the same thing."

"You say any one could have used his machine?"

"The whole population of Hollywood," groaned Ty. "You know what our house was like, Lew, when dad was alive—a club for every hooch-hound in town."

"Am I supposed to take that personally?" chuckled Lew.

"And dad's dressing-room was a hangout for everybody on the lot. He was framed, all right—by some one who got hold of the typewriter either in the house or on the lot." He scowled. "Somebody? It could have been anybody!"

"But what I can't understand," said Lew, "is why this palooka Smith planned for two letters to be mailed to Blythe *after* she died. That in itself would screw up a frame against Jack, because Jack was knocked off, too; and dead men send no mail. And if Jack was meant to be framed, why was he murdered? It don't make sense."

"That," said Ty between his teeth, "is what I'd like to know."

"I believe," murmured Ellery, "we'll get along better if we take this problem scientifically. That alternate inference I mentioned this morning, by the way, was arrived at by mere common sense. On the assumption that the writer of those addresses was sane, not a crank, it was evident that the only sane reason ascribable to the fact that a letter was mailed to Blythe *after* Blythe's death was . . . that *the writer had no control over the source of mailing.*"

"I see," said Ty slowly. "That's what made you think of a mailing service."

"Precisely. I stopped in at the post-office on the off-chance that the writer may have arranged to have the letters mailed directly by the postmaster. But of course that was a far-fetched possibility. The only other one was an organization which made a business of mailing letters for people."

"But if Smith murdered Blythe and dad, why didn't he try to get the last two letters back from that outfit around the corner before they were mailed? Lucey said himself there's been no such attempt."

"And lay himself wide open to future identification?" jeered Lew. "Act your age, younker."

The waiter arrived bearing a bottle of brandy, a siphon, and three glasses. Lew rubbed his hands and seized the bottle.

"Of course," said Ellery, "that's perfectly true."

"As a matter of fact, why those last two letters at all?"

Ellery leaned back, clutching the glass Lew had filled. "An important question, with an important answer. Have you noticed the date, you two, on which our friend Smith intended this last letter to be mailed—the envelope bearing the unfriendly ace of spades?"

Lew looked over his glass. Ty merely looked. The date typed on the memorandum slip clipped to the envelope containing the ace of spades was "Thursday the 28th."

"I don't see the point," said Ty, frowning.

"Simple enough. What were the two cards mailed in one envelope to Blythe on Thursday the fourteenth—the envelope that arrived on Friday the fifteenth, two days before the murder?"

"I don't recall."

"The ten of spades and the deuce of clubs, meaning together: 'Great trouble in two days or two weeks.' The fact that the murders did actually occur two days after the receipt of that message was a mere coincidence. For what do we find now?" He tapped the card and envelope before him. "The ace of spades in this unmailed envelope, meaning 'Death,' is clearly marked for mailing on Thursday the twenty-eighth, or receipt by Blythe on Friday the twenty-ninth. So the murder of Blythe was obviously planned to occur not earlier than the twenty-ninth; or in other words she was scheduled to die, not two days, but two *weeks* after the Friday-the-fifteenth warning of 'Great Trouble.'"

"A week from today," growled Ty. "If he hadn't changed his plans, Blythe would still be alive. And dad, too."

"Exactly the point. For what was the murderer's original plan? To murder Blythe—*Blythe alone*. Corroboration? The fact that the playing-cards were sent only to Blythe, that the ace of spades was meant to go, as you can see by the address on the envelope, only to Blythe. Also the plan included a frame-up of Jack for the murder of Blythe when it should occur—witness the use of Jack's typewriter in the typing of the code-sheet, the planting of the code-sheet in his dressing-room."

"Well?"

"But what actually happened? Blythe was murdered, all right—but NOT alone. Jack was murdered, too. What made the murderer change his plans? What made him murder not only Blythe, as originally planned, but Jack as well—the very man scheduled to take the rap for that murder?"

They were both silent, frowning back at him.

"That, as I see it, is the most significant question arising out of the whole chain of events. Answer that question and I believe you'll be well on the road to an answer to everything."

"Yeah, answer it," muttered Lew into his brandy. "I still say it's baloney."

"But what I don't understand," protested Ty, "is why the date was advanced. Why did Smith hurry up his crime? It seems to me he could have waited until the ace of spades was delivered and then murdered the two of them. But he didn't. He abandoned his own time-schedule, the whole elaborate machinery of the letters which he had set up. Why?"

"Opportunity," said Ellery succinctly. "It's more difficult, you know, to contrive the killing of two people than of one. And the honeymoon jaunt in your plane gave Smith an opportunity to kill *both* Blythe and Jack which he simply couldn't pass up."

"As the situation stands, then, the frame-up against dad is a flop and the murderer knows it."

"But there's nothing he can do about that except make an effort to get back the letters and the code list, and particularly his own telltale note in the files of the mailing company. As Lew suggested, he probably figured the relative risks involved and chose not to make the attempt."

"At least we've got enough to convince Bonnie of the absurdity of her suspicions against dad. What you've just said proves dad was another victim, that's all. Queen, would you—"

"Would I what?" Ellery emerged from a cavernous reverie.

"Would you tell that to Bonnie? Clear dad for me?"

Ellery rubbed his jaw. "And you, I take it?"

"Well . . . yes."

"Now don't worry about anything, Ty," said Ellery with a sudden briskness. "Forget this mess. Go out and get some exercise. Or go on a bat for a couple of weeks. Why not take a vacation?"

"Leave Hollywood now?" Ty looked grim. "Not a chance."

"Don't be idiotic. You're only in the way here."

"Queen's right," said Lew. "The picture's out, and I know Butch'll give you a vacation. After all, he's engaged to the girl." He giggled.

Ty smiled and got to his feet. "Coming?"

"I think I'll sit here and cogitate for a while." Ellery surreptitiously glanced at his wrist-watch. "Think it over, Ty. Here, never mind the check! I'll take care of it."

Lew clutched the bottle to his bosom, reaching with his free hand for his hat. "My pal."

Ty waved wearily and plodded off, followed a little erratically by Lew.

And Mr. Queen sat and cogitated with an unusually perturbed expression in his usually expressionless eyes.

14

MR. QUEEN, MISOGAMIST

At ten minutes before one o'clock Bonnie scudded into the Brown Derby, looked about in panic, and made for Ellery's booth with a queer little rush. She sat down and pushed herself into a corner, breathing hard.

"Here, what's the matter?" said Ellery. "You look scared to death."

"Oh, I am. I'm being followed!" She peeped over the partition at the door, her eyes wide.

"Clumsy," mumbled Ellery.

"What?"

"I mean, it's probably your imagination. Who would want to follow you?"

"I don't know. Unless . . . " She stopped inexplicably, her brows almost meeting. Then she shook her head.

"You're looking especially lovely today."

"Yet I'm *positive*. . . . A big black car. A closed car."

"You should wear bright colors all the time, Bonnie. They do remarkable things to your complexion."

Bonnie smiled vaguely, removed her hat and gloves, and passed her hands over her face like a cat. "Never mind my complexion. It isn't that. I just won't wear mourning. It's—it's ridiculous. I've never believed in mourning. Black things are like a . . . *poster*. I keep fighting with Clotilde about it. She's simply horrified."

"Yes," said Ellery encouragingly. She was carefully made up, very carefully indeed, to conceal her pallor and certain tiny fine lines around her eyes; her eyes were large and dark with lack of rest.

"I don't have to go around advertising to the world that I've lost my mother," said Bonnie in a low voice. "That funeral . . . it was a mistake. I hated it. I hate myself for having consented to it."

"She had to be buried, Bonnie. And you know Hollywood."

"Yes, but—" Bonnie smiled and said in a sudden gay tone: "Let's not talk about it. May I have a drink?"

"So early in the day?"

She shrugged. "A daiquiri, please." She began to explore her handbag.

Ellery ordered a daiquiri, and a brandy-and-soda, and watched her. She was breathing hard again, under cover of her activity. She took out her compact and examined her face in the mirror, not looking at him, not looking at what lay plainly revealed in her open bag, picking at nonexistent stragglers of honey-hued hairs, pursing her lips, applying a dab of powder to her nose. And suddenly, without looking at it, she took an envelope out of her bag and pushed it across the table to him.

"Here," she said in a muffled voice. "Look at this."

His hand closed over it as the waiter brought their drinks. When the waiter went away Ellery opened his hand. In it lay an envelope. Bonnie studied him anxiously.

"Our friend's renounced the post-office pen, I see," said Ellery. "Typewritten address this time."

"But don't you *see?*" whispered Bonnie. "It's addressed to *me!*"

"I see quite clearly. When did it arrive?"

"In this morning's mail."

"Hollywood-posted last night, élite type, obvious characteristics three broken letters—b and d and t this time. Our friend had to use a different typewriter, since Jack's portable has been in my possession since yesterday afternoon. All of which tends to show that the letter probably wasn't written until last night."

"Look . . . at what's in it," said Bonnie.

Ellery withdrew the inclosure. It was the seven of spades.

"The mysterious 'enemy' again," he said lightly. "History seems on its way to being a bore. . . . Oh." He thrust the envelope and card into his pocket and rose suddenly. "Hello, Butch."

The Boy Wonder was standing there, looking down at Bonnie with a queer expression.

"Hello, Bonnie," he said.

"Hello," said Bonnie faintly.

He stooped, and she turned her cheek. He straightened up without kissing her, his sharp eyes veiled. "Having lunch here," he said casually. "Happened to spot you two. What's up?"

"Bonnie," said Ellery, "I think your estimable fiancé is jealous."

"Yes," said the Boy Wonder, smiling, "I think so, too." He looked ill. There were deep circles about his eyes, and his cheeks were sunken with fatigue. "I tried to get you this morning, but Clotilde said you'd gone out."

"Yes," said Bonnie. "I—did."

"You're looking better, Bonnie."

"Thank you."

"Will I see you tonight?"

"Why . . . Why don't you sit down with us?" said Bonnie, moving an inch on her seat.

"Yes, why don't you?" echoed Ellery heartily.

Those sharp eyes swept over him for an instant, stopping only long enough to touch on the pocket in which Ellery had thrust the envelope. "Thanks, no," smiled Butcher. "I've got to be getting back to the studio. Well, so long."

"So long," said Bonnie in a low voice.

He stood there for a moment more, as if hesitating over a desire to kiss her; then suddenly he smiled and nodded and walked away. They saw the droop of his shoulders as the doorman held open the door for him.

Ellery sat down and sipped at his brandy-and-soda. Bonnie jiggled her long-stemmed glass.

"Nice chap, Butch," said Ellery.

"Yes. Isn't he." Then Bonnie set down her glass with a little bang and cried: "Don't you see? Now that the cards have started coming to *me* . . ."

"Now Bonnie—"

"You don't think," she said in a shaky little voice, "you don't think . . . I'm . . . to be next?"

"Next?"

"Mother got the warnings, and she— Now I'm getting them." She tried to smile. "I'm scared silly."

Ellery sighed. "Then you've changed your mind about Jack Royle's having sent those previous letters?"

"No!"

"But, Bonnie, surely you're not afraid of a dead man?"

"No dead man mailed this letter last night," said Bonnie fiercely. "Oh, Jack Royle sent those other letters to mother. But this one to me . . ." Bonnie shivered. "I have only one enemy, Mr. Queen."

"You mean Ty?" murmured Ellery.

"I mean Ty. He's taking up where his father left off!"

Ellery was silent. He was powerfully tempted to demonstrate to Bonnie how unfounded her suspicions were; he would have given a good deal to dispel that look in her eyes. But he steeled himself. "You'll have to be careful, Bonnie."

"Then you *do* think—"

"Never mind what I think. But remember this. The most dangerous thing you can do is give yourself to Ty Royle."

Bonnie closed her eyes as she gulped down the dregs of her cocktail. When she opened them they were full of fear. "What shall I do?" she whispered.

Inwardly, Ellery cursed. But he merely said: "Watch your step. Care—care. Take care. Don't talk to Ty. Don't have anything to do with him. Avoid him as you would a leper."

"A leper." Bonnie shuddered. "That's what he is."

"Don't listen to his love-making," continued Ellery, not looking at her. "He's liable to tell you anything. Don't believe him. Remember, Bonnie."

"How could I forget?" Tears sprang into her eyes. She shook her head angrily and groped for her handkerchief.

"That car," muttered Ellery. "The one that's been following you. Don't worry about that. The men in it are protecting you. Don't try to get away from them, Bonnie."

But Bonnie scarcely heard him. "What good is my life?" she said dully. "I'm left alone in the world with a crazy beast after me, and—and—"

Ellery bit his lip, saying nothing, watching her pinch her nostrils with the handkerchief. He felt very like a beast himself.

After a while he ordered two more drinks, and when they came he urged one upon her. "Now stop it, Bonnie. You're attracting attention."

She dabbed at her reddened eyes very quickly then, and blew her little nose, and got busy with her powder-puff; and then she took up the second cocktail and began to sip it.

"I'm a fool," she sniffled. "It seems all I do is weep, like some silly heroine in a movie."

"Fine, fine. That's more like it. By the way, Bonnie, did you know that your mother and Jack Royle paid a visit to your grandfather Tolland Stuart a week ago Wednesday?"

"You mean just before their engagement was announced? Mother didn't tell me."

"That's odd."

"Isn't it." She frowned. "How do you know?"

"Paula Paris told me."

"That woman! How did *she* know?"

"Oh, she's really not so bad," said Ellery lamely. "It's just her job, Bonnie. You ought to be able to see that."

For the first time Bonnie examined him with the naked concentration of a woman seeking beneath the surface the signs of male weakness. "Oh, I see," she said slowly. "You're in love with her."

"I?" protested Ellery. "Absurd!"

Bonnie clothed the nakedness of her glance and murmured: "Sorry. I suppose it's immaterial where she found out. I do seem to recall now that mother was away all that day. I wonder why on earth she went to see grandfather. And with . . . that man."

"What's so surprising about that? After all, she'd decided to be married, and he *was* her father."

Bonnie sighed. "I suppose so, but it seems queer."

"In what way?"

"Mother hadn't visited or spoken to grandfather—oh, more than two or three times in the past dozen years. I myself hadn't been in that awful house in the Chocolate Mountains before last Sunday in at least eight years—I was wearing hair-ribbons and pinafores, so you can imagine how long ago that was. Why, if I'd passed grandfather on the street before Sunday I wouldn't have recognized him. He never came to see us, you see."

"I've meant to question you about that. Just what was the reason for the coldness between your mother and your grandfather?"

"It wasn't coldness exactly. It was . . . well, it's just that grandfather's naturally a selfish person, all wrapped up in himself. Mother used to tell me that even as a little girl she never got much affection from him. You see, my grandmother died in childbirth, when mother was born—she was an only child—and grandfather sort of . . . let go after that. I mean—"

"Cracked up?"

"He had a nervous breakdown, mother said. He was never quite the same after. He took grannie's death very hard, sort of blamed mother for it. If she hadn't been born—"

"It's not an uncommon masculine reaction."

"I don't want you to think he was brutal to mother, or anything like that," said Bonnie quickly. "He always had a sense of obligation towards her financially. He had her brought up very well, with governesses and nurses and heaps of clothes and European trips and finishing schools and all that. But when she grew up and went on the stage and got along very well by herself—why, I suppose he thought his duties as a father ended right there. And he's never paid the slightest attention to me."

"Then why did your mother visit him last Wednesday?"

"I'm sure I don't know," frowned Bonnie, "unless it was to tell him about her and Jack Royle getting married. Although certainly grandfather wouldn't care *what* she did; he took no interest in her first marriage, so why should he take any in her second?"

"Could it have been because your mother needed money? You said the other day she was always stony."

Bonnie's lip curled. "From him? Mother always said she'd beg before she'd ask him for a cent."

Ellery sat rubbing his upper lip with the tip of his finger. Bonnie finished her cocktail.

"Bonnie," said Ellery suddenly, "let's do something."

"What?"

"Let's get ourselves a plane and fly down to the Chocolate Mountains."

"After the horrible way he acted Sunday?" Bonnie sniffed. "No, indeed. Not even going to his own daughter's funeral! That's carrying eccentricity a bit *too* far, at least for me."

"I have a feeling," said Ellery, rising, "that it's important to find out why your mother and John Royle visited him nine days ago."

"But—"

Ellery looked down at her. "It may help, Bonnie, to clear away the fog."

Bonnie was silent. Then she tossed her head and got up. "In that case," she said firmly, "I'm with you."

15

MR. QUEEN, SNOOP

In the light of blessed day the Law of Dreadful Night reversed itself and Tolland Stuart's eyrie from the sun-shot air lay revealed in all its sprawling, weatherbeaten grandeur—a more fearsome scab upon the knife-edged mountain landscape than it had ever been invisible under darkness.

"It's a simply hideous place," shivered Bonnie, peering down as the hired airplane circled the landing-field.

"It's not exactly another Shangri-La," said Ellery dryly, "even though it does resemble the forbidden city at the roof of the world. Has your worthy grandfather ever visited Tibet? It might explain the geographical inspiration."

The gloomy pile crouched lifeless beneath them. And yet there was an illusion of life in the silent stones and turrets, lying still in the center of a web of power lines and telephone cables descending airily the slopes of the mountain.

"Is it my imagination," said Bonnie, "or does that thing down there look like a spider?"

"It's your imagination," replied Ellery quickly. When they trundled to a stop on the tiny field, he said to the pilot: "Wait for us. We shan't be long," and took Bonnie's arm in a casual but precautionary way. He helped her to the ground and hurried her towards the rift in the woods. As they passed the hangar he noted that its doors stood open and its interior was empty.

Bonnie noticed, too. "Do you suppose grandfather's flown off somewhere? I'd always understood he rarely left the estate."

"More likely it's Dr. Junius. I imagine the good leech has to do the shopping for cabbages and such. Picture yourself running a household up here!"

"And flying down to the grocer's for a bottle of olives," giggled Bonnie nervously.

The tree-canopied path was deserted. And when they emerged into the clearing where the house stood they saw that the front doors were shut.

Ellery knocked; there was no answer. He knocked again. Finally, he tried the knob. It turned.

"The obvious," he chuckled, "has a way of eluding me. Enter, Bonnie. The house, at least, won't bite you."

Bonnie looked doubtful; but she squared her boyish shoulders and preceded him bravely into the dim interior.

"Grandfather?" she called.

The syllables tumbled back, smothered and mocking.

"Mr. Stuart!" roared Ellery. The echo had a sneer in it. "Damn. That old man's exasperating. Do you mind if I shake some life into him?"

"Mind?" Bonnie looked angry. "I'd like to do some shaking myself!"

"Well," said Ellery cheerfully, "we'll have to find him first," and he led the way.

The living-room was empty. The kitchen, although there were bread-crumbs on the porcelain-topped table and the odor of freshly brewed tea, was also empty; so Ellery took Bonnie with him to the staircase, looking grim.

"He's up there sulking again, I'll bet a million. Mr. Stuart!"

No answer.

"Let me go first," said Bonnie firmly, and she ran up the stairs.

They found the old man lying in bed, the table by his side loaded with pill-boxes, medicine bottles, atomizers, and iron-stained spoons. His toothless jaws were doggedly munching on a cold meat sandwich, and he was gulping iced tea as he glared at them quite without surprise.

"Grandfather!" cried Bonnie. "Didn't you hear us?"

He glowered at her from under his hairy gray brows munching without a sign he had heard her.

"Grandfather!" Bonnie looked scared. "Can't you hear me? Are you *deaf?*"

He stopped munching long enough to growl: "Go away," and then he took another swallow of tea and another bite of the white bread.

Bonnie looked relieved and furious. "How can you treat me this way? Aren't you human? What's the *matter* with you?"

The hair on his cheeks and chin stopped wiggling as his jaws suddenly clamped together. Then they wiggled again as he said curtly: "What d'ye want?"

Bonnie sat down. "I want," she said in a low voice, "a little of the affection you never gave my mother."

Studying that aged, bitter physiognomy, Ellery was astonished to see a soft expression creep into the veined and rheumy eyes. Then the expression vanished. The old man said gruffly: "Too late now. I'm an old man. Blythe should have thought of that years ago. She never was a daughter to me." The lisp grew more pronounced as his voice rose. "I don't want anybody! Go away and let me alone. If that fool Junius wouldn't hop in and out like a jack rabbit, blast him, maybe I'd get some privacy!"

Bonnie made two tight little fists of her gloves. "You don't scare me one bit with your bellowing," she said evenly. "You know the fault was yours, not mother's. You never gave her the love she had a right to expect from you."

The old man banged down his glass and hurled the remains of the sandwich from him. "You say that to me?" he howled. "What do *you* know about it? Did she ever bring you to me? Did she ever—"

"Did you ever show her you wanted her to?"

The bony arms wavered, then fell to the coverlet with a curious weakness. "I'm not going to argue with a snip of a girl. You're after my money. I know what you want. My money. That's all children and grandchildren ever want!"

"Grandfather," gasped Bonnie, rising. "How can you say such a thing?"

"Get out, get out," he said. "That fool Junius! Going off to Los Angeles and letting this house become a Wayside Inn. Lord knows what germs you've brought in here, you and this fellow. I'm a sick old man. I'm—"

"Goodbye," said Bonnie. And she made for the door blindly.

"Wait," said Ellery. She waited, her lips trembling. Ellery faced the old man grimly. "Your life is your own to lead as you see fit, Mr. Stuart, but a capital crime has been committed and you can't shut yourself away from *that*. You're going to answer some questions."

"Who are you?" demanded the old man sourly.

"Never mind who I am. A week ago Wednesday—that's nine days ago—your daughter and John Royle paid you a visit. Why?"

It seemed to him that for an instant the old man showed astonishment; but only for an instant. "So you found that out, too, did you? You must be from the police, like that idiot Glücke who was up here early in the week. Police!"

"I asked you, Mr. Stuart—"

"You want to know why they came here, hey? All right, I'll tell you," said the old man unexpectedly, hitching himself up in bed. "Because they wanted money, that's why! That's all anybody ever wants."

"Mother asked you for money?" said Bonnie. "I don't believe it!"

"Call me a liar, do you?" said the old man venomously. "I say she asked me for money. Not for herself, I admit. But she asked me. For the good-for-nothing Royle!"

Bonnie looked at Ellery, and Ellery looked at Bonnie. So that was it. Blythe had come to her father against all her instincts—not for herself, but for the man she loved. Bonnie looked away, staring out the window at the cold sky.

"I see," said Ellery slowly. "And you gave it to her?"

"I must have been out of my mind that day," grumbled the old man. "I gave Royle a check for a hundred and ten thousand dollars and I told Blythe not to bother me again. Good-for-nothing! Something about gambling debts. She wanted to marry a gambler. Well, that was her hard luck."

"Oh, grandfather," sobbed Bonnie, "you're an old fraud." She took a step toward him.

"Don't come near me!" said the old man hastily. "You're not sterile. Full of germs!"

"You did love her. You wanted her to be happy."

"I wanted her to let me alone."

"You just pretend to be hard—"

"It was the only way I could get rid of her. Why can't people let me alone? Blythe said it would be her money some day, anyway, and all she asked was part of it before . . . " His hairy lips quivered. "Get out and don't come back."

And Bonnie hardened. "You know," she whispered, "I believe you did give it to her just to get rid of her. Don't worry, grandfather. I'll get out and I'll never come back. I'll never speak to you again as long as you live."

The old man waved his arms again, his sallow face livid. "I won't die for a long time!" he yelled. "Don't worry about *that!* Get out, the two of you!"

"Not yet," said Ellery. He glanced at Bonnie. "Bonnie, would you mind going back to the plane? I'll join you in a few minutes. I'd like to talk to your grandfather alone."

"I can't get away from here fast enough." Bonnie stumbled out. Ellery heard her running down the stairs as if some one were after her.

He did not speak until the front door slammed. Then he said to the glowering old man: "Now, Mr. Stuart, answer one question."

"I told you why Blythe and that gambler came up here," replied the old man in a sulky voice. "I've got nothing more to say."

"But my question has nothing to do with Blythe's visit."

"Eh? What d'ye mean?"

"I mean," said Ellery calmly, "what were you doing last Sunday night outside this house in an aviator's helmet?"

For a moment he thought the man would faint; the eyes rolled alarmingly, and the large bony nose twitched with a sort of nausea. "Eh?" said the old man feebly. "What did you say?"

And as he said it the faintness and alarm disappeared, and his gray beard came up belligerently. Game old cock, thought Ellery with a grudging admiration. For all his years he absorbed punishment very quickly.

"I saw you outside in the rain with a flying helmet on your head. At a time when Junius said you were up here behind a locked door."

"Yes," nodded the old man. "Yes, I was outside. Because I wanted to breathe God's clean air. I was outside because there were strangers in my house."

"In the rain?" Ellery smiled. "I thought you had certain fears about pneumonia and such."

"I'm a sick man," said the old man stolidly. "But I'd rather risk pneumonia than be mixed up with strangers."

"You almost said 'a murder,' didn't you? Why should you be so timid about being mixed up in this one, Mr. Stuart?"

"Any one."

"Your own daughter's? You don't feel—I almost made the mistake of calling it 'natural'—you don't feel a desire for vengeance?"

"I want only to be let alone."

"And the helmet on your head—that had nothing to do with . . . let us say . . . airplanes, Mr. Stuart?"

"There are a few helmets about. They're good protection against rain."

"Ah, amiable now. I wonder why? People who have something to conceal generally are anxious to talk amiably, Mr. Stuart. Just what are you concealing?"

For answer the old man reached over and snatched the shotgun from its position beside the testered bed. Without speaking, he placed the shotgun in his lap. He looked at Ellery steadily.

Ellery smiled, shrugged, and strolled out.

He made a deliberate clatter as he went down the stairs, and he set one foot loudly after another on the floor of the living-room as he went to the front door. The door he banged.

But he remained inside, listening. There was no sound from above. Frowning, he looked about. That door. . . . Tiptoeing, he crossed the living-room, opened the door carefully, glanced in, nodded, and slipped through, shutting the door behind him with the same caution.

He stood in a library, or study, vast and raftered and gloomy, like all the rooms in the house. This one, too, had a brooding atmosphere, as if it had stood too long untenanted. There was a thick layer of dust over everything, mute reflection on Dr. Junius's housekeeping talents.

Ellery went without hesitation to the huge flat-topped desk in the center of the room, a piece of solid carved oak with an ancient patina. But he was not interested in the antiquity of Tolland Stuart's desk; he was interested in its contents. A rapid glance about had convinced him there was no safe in the room; and the desk seemed the most likely repository for what he was seeking.

He found it in the second drawer he opened, sepultured in an unlocked green-painted steel box, although a lock with a key in it lay beside the box.

It was Tolland Stuart's will.

Ellery read it avidly, one ear cocked for sounds from the old man's room above.

The date on the will was nine and a half years old, and the paper was a sheet of heavy bond bearing the imprint of an old, solid banking house in Los Angeles. It was a holograph will, handwritten in ink by a crabbed fist—Ellery could visualize the old terrorist twisting his tongue in his withered cheek and refusing to allow any one at his bank to catch a glimpse of what he was writing. The will was signed with Tolland Stuart's signature, which had been witnessed by names meaningless to Ellery, obviously employees of the bank.

The will said:

"I, Tolland Stuart, being this day sixty years of age and of sound mind, make my last will and testament.

"The sum of one hundred thousand dollars in cash or negotiable bonds is hereby left to Dr. Henry F. Junius, of my employ, but only on the following conditions:

"(1) That until my death Dr. Junius shall have been continuously in my employ for not less than ten years from the date of this will, except for periods of illness or other such interruptions in his service to me which shall be reasonable beyond his control; at all other times he is to act as my physician and exclusive guardian of my health; and

"(2) That I, Tolland Stuart, shall have survived this ten-year period; that is to say, that my death shall have occurred after my 70th birthday.

"In the event of my death before the age of 70 from any cause whatsoever, or in the event that Dr. Junius shall have left my employ either voluntarily or by dismissal before the expiration of the ten-year period noted above, my bequest to him of $100,000.00 shall be considered cancelled; and my estate shall then go free and clear of any participating bequest to my legal heirs.

"I direct also that my just debts be paid, also the expenses of my funeral.

"The residue of my estate I leave to be divided as follows: One-half to go to my only child and daughter, Blythe, or in the event that she predeceases me, to her heirs. The other half to go to my granddaughter Bonita, Blythe's daughter, or in the event that Bonnie predeceases me, to Bonnie's heirs."

Except for an additional short paragraph in which the junior vice-president of the bank where the will had been drawn up and witnessed was named executor of the estate, there was nothing more.

Ellery replaced the document in its green box, shut the drawer, and stole out of the house.

As he stepped onto the landing-field he spied the stubby airplane which he had seen Sunday night in the nearby hangar. It was gliding down to a landing. It taxied to a stop beside the commercial plane which had flown Ellery and Bonnie up into the mountains. Dr. Junius jumped to the ground, looking like an elderly condor in the helmet which flapped about his ears.

He waved to Bonnie, who was waiting in the other plane, and hurried forward to greet Ellery.

"Paying us a visit, I see," he said companionably. "I would be out shopping! What's happening on the Hollywood front?"

"It's all quiet." Ellery paused. "We've just had the honor of an interview with your worthy benefactor."

"Since your skin is still whole," smiled the doctor, "it can't have been so terrifying." Then he said in quite a different tone: "Did you say 'benefactor'?"

"Why, yes," murmured Ellery. "Isn't he?"

"I don't know what you mean." The doctor's bright eyes retreated into their yellow sockets.

"Oh, come, Doctor."

"No. Really."

"Don't tell me you're unaware that the old crank has set aside a little something for your old age!"

Dr. Junius threw back his head and laughed. "Oh, that!" The laugh turned bitter. "Of course I'm aware of it. Why do you think I've buried myself up here?"

"I thought," said Ellery dryly, "there must be a sound reason."

"I assume he told you."

"Mmm."

"I'm not so sure," said Dr. Junius, shrugging, "that I got the better of the bargain. It's cheap at a hundred thousand, dirt cheap. Living with that old pirate and putting up with his tantrums and whims for ten years is worth closer to a million, even at a conservative estimate."

"How did he ever come to make such an odd arrangement with you, Doctor?"

"When we met he'd just been given a rather thorough going-over by a pair of quack 'specialists' who'd got hold of him and were milking him for thousands in fees. They told him he had cancer of the stomach, scared him into believing he had only a year or two at the most to live."

"You mean a deliberately false diagnosis?"

"I imagine so. I suppose they were afraid the sacred cow would stop giving milk sooner or later and thought they'd get much more out of him by concentrating their 'services' over a short period than by trying to pander to his hypochondria over a longer one. Anyway, some one recommended me to him, and I examined him and found he merely had ulcers. I told him so, and the quacks discreetly vanished."

"But I still don't see—"

"I told you you don't know Tolland Stuart," said the doctor grimly. "He was suspicious of them, but he couldn't get it out of his mind that perhaps there *was* a cancer in his stomach. My insistence that he hadn't, and that I could cure his ulcers very easily—he was in perfectly sound condition otherwise—gave him an idea. He remembered what the quacks had said about his having only a year or so to live. So, in view of my confidence, he engaged me to keep him alive for a minimum of ten years—he liked my honesty, he said, and if I kept him in reasonably good health five times longer than the other men had claimed he would live, I was entitled to a large fee."

"The Chinese system. You collect during the good health of your patient."

"Good health!" snorted Dr. Junius. "The man's as sound as a nut. It took me only a short time to heal the ulcers, and he hasn't had so much as a cold since."

"But all those medicines and pills by his bed—"

"Colored water and sugar-coated anodynes. It's a disgusting but essential therapy. I haven't used a legitimate drug from my little pharmacy in there in eight years. I've got to treat him for his imaginary ailments or he'd kick me out of the house."

"And then you wouldn't collect your hundred thousand when he dies."

The doctor threw up his hands. "When he dies! As far as I can tell, he'll live to be ninety. The chances are all in favor of his surviving me, and I'll get for my long years of martyrdom up here just two lines in an obituary column."

"But isn't he paying you a yearly retainer besides?"

"Oh, yes, quite handsome." The doctor shrugged. "But unfortunately I haven't any of it. I'd go crazy if I didn't sneak down into L.A. once in a while. When I do, it's only to lose money at roulette, or at the racetrack—I've dropped some in the stock market. . . ."

"Not Alessandro's?" said Ellery suddenly.

The doctor scowled at the jagged skyline. "Did you ever want something very badly?"

"Often."

"I recognized early in my career that I wouldn't make a go of medicine. Haven't the proper temperament. What I've always wanted more than anything else, and couldn't have for lack of money, was leisure."

"Leisure? To what purpose?"

"Writing! I've got a story to tell the world. Lots of stories!" He tapped his breast. "They're locked up in here, and they won't come free until my mind is relieved of financial worry and I've got time and a sense of security."

"But up here—"

"What about up here?" demanded Junius fiercely. "Security? Time? I'm a prisoner. I'm on my feet, from morning to night, catering to that old fool, cooking for him, wiping his nose, running his errands, cleaning his house. . . . No. Mr. Queen, I can't write up here. All I can do up here is run my feet off and hope he'll break his neck some day while he's out rabbit-hunting."

"At least," murmured Ellery, "you're frank."

The doctor looked frightened. He said hastily: "Goodbye," and plodded off towards the tree-masked house.

"Goodbye," said Ellery soberly, and he climbed into the waiting plane.

16

MR. QUEEN, RAT

Ellery was sitting at his kitchenette table Saturday morning clad in pajamas and robe and giving his divided attention simultaneously to a sooty slab of toast, the morning paper announcing the latest developments, which were nil, in the Royle-Stuart case, and a paperbacked book entitled *Fortune Telling by Cards*, when his telephone rang.

"Queen!" Ty's voice was eager. "What did she say?"

"What did who say?"

"Bonnie. Did you fix it up for me?"

"Oh, Bonnie." Ellery thought furiously. "Well, now, Ty, I've got bad news for you."

"What do you mean?"

"She won't believe a word of it. She's still convinced your father wrote those notes to her mother."

"But she can't!" howled Ty. "It's not reasonable. Didn't you tell her about that mailing company and the rest of it?"

"Oh, certainly," lied Ellery. "But you can't expect reasonableness from a woman, Ty; a man of your experience ought to know that. Why don't you give Bonnie up as a hopeless job?"

Ty was silent; Ellery could almost see him grinding his teeth together and sticking out his lean jaw. "I couldn't be mistaken," said Ty at last, in a sort of stubborn despair. "She gave herself to me too completely. She loves me. I know she does."

"Pshaw, the girl's an actress. Every woman has something of the mime in her, but when it's also her profession—"

"Since when do you know so much about women? I tell you she *wasn't* acting!"

"Look, Ty," said Ellery with simulated impatience, "I'm a sorely harassed man, and I'm not at my best at this hour of the morning. You asked me, and I told you."

"I've kissed too many girls in my time," muttered Ty, "not to recognize the real thing when it's dished out to me."

"Thus spake Casanova," sighed Ellery. "I still think you ought to take a vacation. Hop an Eastern plane. A whirl around Broadway's hot spots will get Bonnie out of your system."

"I don't want her out of my system! Damn it, if it's that bad I'll face the music in person. I should have done it in the first place."

"Wait," said Ellery, alarmed. "Don't go looking for trouble, Ty."

"I know if I talk to her, take her in my arms again—"

"Do you want a knife in your back when you do? She's been receiving letters again."

"More?" said Ty incredulously. "But I thought we bagged the whole batch in that mailing office!"

"She showed me one that came yesterday. Addressed to her."

"To *her?*"

"Yes, and with the seven of spades enclosed. 'An Enemy.'"

"But if it was mailed Thursday night—and we know it couldn't have come from the fellow Lucey's office—why, that *proves* dad couldn't have sent it!"

Ellery said desperately: "Oh, she knows your father couldn't have mailed this one. It's worse. She thinks *you* sent it."

"I?" Ty sounded dazed.

"Yes, she's convinced now the whole series of card messages has been inspired by the Royle family. The ones to Blythe by your father and now this one, apparently the first of a fresh series, by you."

"But that's ... why, that's mad! By me? Does she actually think *I* ... ?"

"I told you she was past reasoning with. You'll never rehabilitate this affair, Ty. Stop wasting your time."

"But she mustn't think I'm hounding her! I ought to be able to do something to convince her—"

"Don't you know that the only truly inert material in the universe is an idea rooted in a woman's skull? The winds do blow, but to no avail. I don't want to seem to be changing the subject, but do you own a typewriter?"

"What?" mumbled Ty.

"I said: Do you own a typewriter?"

"Why, yes. But—"

"Where is it?"

"In my dressing-room on the lot."

"Where are you going now?"

"To see Bonnie."

"Ty." Ellery winced at his own perfidy. "Don't. Take my advice. You may be ... in danger."

"Danger? What do you mean?"

"You understand English perfectly well."

"Look here," said Ty sharply, "are you trying to tell me that Bonnie would ... You're joking, or crazy."

"Will you do me one favor? Don't talk to Bonnie until I tell you it's safe to."

"But I don't understand, Queen!"

"You've got to promise."

"But—"

"I can't explain now. Have I your word?"

Ty was silent. Then he said wearily: "Oh, very well," and hung up.

Ellery did likewise, swabbing his moist brow. A close shave. Raw apprentice himself in the laboratory of love, he was just beginning to discover what powerful magnetic properties the grand passion possessed.

Damn that stubborn kid! At the same time, far and deep inside, Mr. Queen felt a great, consuming shame. Of all the black tricks he had ever played in the interests of ultimate truth, this was certainly the blackest!

Sighing, he plodded towards his kitchenette for a further perusal of the book on fortune-telling and a Star Chamber session with his own dark thoughts.

The doorbell rang.

Absently he turned about and went to the door and opened it.

And there stood Bonnie.

"Bonnie! Well, well. Come in."

Bonnie was radiant. She flew by, hurled herself on his sofa, and looked up at him with dancing eyes.

"What a lovely day! Isn't it? And that's the most fetching robe you're wearing, Mr. Queen. And I've just been followed by that same closed black car, and I don't care—whoever it is—and oh, the most wonderful thing's happened!"

Ellery closed the door slowly. What now?

Nevertheless, he managed to smile. "There's one pleasant feature of this case, anyway—it's thrown me into daily contact with one of the loveliest damsels of our time."

"One of the happiest," laughed Bonnie. "And are you trying to seduce me with that mustachioed old technique? Oh, I feel so chipper it's indecent!" She bounced up and down on the sofa like a gleeful little girl. "Aren't you going to ask me what it is?"

"What what is?"

"The wonderful thing that's happened?"

"Well," said Ellery, without elation, "what is it?"

She opened her bag. Ellery studied her. Her pixie features were ravaged to a degree that neither her present gaiety nor the art of make-up as taught by its most celebrated impresarios could conceal. There were gray hollows in her cheeks and her eyes were underscored by violet shadows. She looked like a sufferer from a serious ailment who has just been informed by her physician that she would live and get well.

She took an envelope out of her bag and offered it to him. He took it, frowning; why should the receipt of another warning note have this extraordinary effect on her spirits? Apprehension ruffled his spine as he removed the enclosed card. It was a four of spades.

He stared at it gloomily. So that was it. If he recalled the code sheet correctly . . .

"You needn't go looking for the yellow sheet," said Bonnie gaily. "I know all those meanings by heart. The four of spades means: 'Have Nothing More to Do with a Certain Person about Whom You Are Doubtful.' Isn't it scrumptious?"

Ellery sat down opposite her, scrutinizing the envelope.

"You don't look pleased," said Bonnie. "I can't imagine why."

"Perhaps," muttered Ellery, "it's because I don't understand in what way it's so scrumptious."

Bonnie's eyes widened. "But it says: 'Have Nothing More to Do with a Certain Person about Whom You Are Doubtful.' Don't you see," she said happily. "And I thought Ty sent that card yesterday!"

Bonnie, Bonnie. Ellery felt savage. First Ty, now Bonnie. Only the meanest man in the world would even attempt to wipe that blissful look from her drawn face, the first expression of pure happiness it had exhibited in the century-long week of doubts and torments and sorrow and death.

And yet, it had to be done. It was vitally important to wipe that look off her face. For an instant Ellery toyed with the notion to tell Bonnie the truth. That would stop her, if he gauged her character accurately. But then she wouldn't be able to keep it from Ty. And if Ty knew . . .

He steeled himself. "I don't see why you're so cheerful," he said, injecting a sneer into his voice.

Bonnie stared. "What do you mean?"

"You said you thought Ty sent that card yesterday. Apparently you don't think so any more. What's made you change your mind?"

"Why, this card—the one you're holding!"

"I fail," said Ellery coldly, "to follow your reasoning."

Her smile faded. "You mean you don't see—" She tossed her head. "You're teasing me. There's only one person in this world I could have been, and was, doubtful about. That was Ty."

"What of it?"

"No matter who sent this card, its meaning is plain—it warns me not to have anything more to do with Ty. Don't you see?" she cried, her cheeks pink again. "Don't you see that that clears Ty—that he couldn't have sent it? *Would he warn me against himself* if he were behind all this?" She paused triumphantly.

"He would under certain circumstances."

The smile flickered and went out for good. She lowered her gaze and began to pick aimlessly at the handle of her bag.

"I suppose," she said in a small voice, "you know what you're talking about. I'm—I'm not much at this sort of thing. It just seemed to me that . . ."

"He's been terribly clever," said Ellery in a flat tone. "He knows you suspect him, and therefore he's sent you the one message calculated to dispel your suspicions. As it did."

He rose, suddenly unable to endure the sight of her steady picking at the bag. At the same time he became conscious that she had raised her eyes again and was looking at him with a queer directness—a sad, sharp, questioning look that made him feel he had committed a great crime.

"You really believe that?" murmured Bonnie.

Ellery snapped: "Wait for me. I'll prove it." He went into his bedroom, shut the door, and quickly began to dress. Because it made things easier, he kept his mind blank.

Bonnie drove him to the Magna Studios, and when she had parked her roadster in the studio garage he said: "Where's Ty's dressing-room?"

"Oh," she said.

And without another word she led him to the little tree-shaded street of the stone bungalows and up the three steps to a door with Ty's name on it. The door was unlocked, and they went in.

A standard-sized typewriter stood on a table beside a chair. Bonnie was perfectly motionless at the door. Ellery went to the typewriter, took a sheet of clean paper from his pocket, and rapidly typed a few lines.

That he returned to Bonnie with the sheet, pulling out of his pocket the envelope which she had just received.

"Open and shut," he said tonelessly. "Here, Bonnie, compare these specimens. Notice the b's and d's and t's? Broken type." He did not mention that, like the h's and r's on John Royle's portable, the imperfect keys on Ty's machine had been freshly—and obviously—filed to make them so. "Also élite, which is unusual for a nonportable typewriter."

Bonnie moved then and looked, not at the paper specimens, but directly at the keys. She poked the b and examined the key, and the d, and the t. And then she said: "I see."

"Little doubt about it. This envelope and the one that came yesterday were both addressed on this machine."

"How did you know?" she asked, looking at him with that same queer, questioning gaze.

"It seemed likely."

"Then there ought to be a carbon copy of the yellow code sheet, too. It wouldn't be complete without that."

"Clever girl." Ellery rummaged through the table drawer. "And here it is, too! Looks like a third or fourth carbon." He offered it for her inspection, but she kept looking at him.

"What are you going to do?" Bonnie's voice was chill. "Expose Ty to Inspector Glücke?"

"No, no, that would be premature," said Ellery hastily. "No real evidence for a prosecutor." She said nothing. "Bonnie, don't say anything about this to any one. And keep away from Ty. Do you hear?"

"I hear," said Bonnie.

"As far away as you can." Bonnie opened the door. "Where are you going now?" Bonnie did not answer. "Be careful!" She looked at him, once, a long hard look that had in its depths a gleam of—that was strange—fright.

Her stride lengthened. Half a block away she was running.

Ellery watched her with grim eyes. When she vanished around a corner he closed the door and sank into the chair.

"I wonder," he thought miserably, "what the penalty is for murdering love."

17

"DANSE AMOUREUSE"

Mr. Queen sat in Ty's cool room and cogitated. He sat and cogitated for a considerable time. In many ways things were satisfactory; yes, quite satisfactory. In one important way, however, they were unquestionably not satisfactory. The most important way.

"Same old story," reflected Mr. Queen. "Find the nut and there's nothing to crack it with. Is it possible there's nothing to do but wait? Think, man, think!"

Mr. Queen thought. An hour passed; another. Mr. Queen kept on thinking. But it was no use.

He got to his feet, stretching to iron the kinks out of his muscles. It all gelled; the case lay smooth and shiny and whole before his critical appetite. The problem, which he found himself unable to solve, was how to wrap his fingers around it without causing it to disintegrate into a sticky, ruined, quivering mess.

Hoping fervently for an inspiration, Mr. Queen left the bungalow and the studio and took a taxi back to his hotel. In his apartment he called the desk clerk and instructed him to have his coupé brought around from the garage. While he was gathering the various letters in his collection and placing them under the lid of John Royle's portable typewriter, the telephone rang.

"Queen?" bellowed Inspector Glücke. "You come down to my office right away! Right away, d'ye hear?"

"Do I hear? I can't very well help myself, Glücke."

"I'm not saying anything now. You just get down here as fast as those smart legs of yours can carry you!"

"Mmm," said Ellery. "Shall I take a toothbrush and pajamas?"

"You ought to be in clink, damn you. Step on it!"

"As a matter of fact, I was on my way, Glücke—"

"You'd double-cross your own father," roared the Inspector. "I give you a half-hour. Not a minute more!" He hung up.

Ellery frowned, sighed, snapped down the lid of the typewriter, went downstairs, got into his coupé, and headed for downtown Los Angeles.

"Well?" said Mr. Queen, precisely a half-hour later.

Inspector Glücke sat behind his desk blowing out his hard cheeks and contriving to look both vexed and wounded at once. Also, he breathed hard and angrily.

"What's that you've got there?" he growled, pointing to the typewriter.

"I asked first," said Ellery coyly.

"Sit down and don't be so damned funny. Did you see Paula Paris's paper today?"

"No."

"Can't you read English, or aren't our newspapers classy enough for you? After all, you *are* a literary man."

"Ha, ha," said Ellery. "That, I take it, was meant to positively gore me. You see how much I love you, darling? I even split an infinitive with you! Come on, spill." Glücke hurled a newspaper at Ellery. Ellery caught it, raising his brows, and began to read a passage marked in red pencil in Paula Paris's column.

"What you got to say for yourself?"

"I say she's wonderful," said Ellery dreamily. "My lady Paula! A woman with brains. Glücke, tell me truthfully: Have you ever met a woman who combined intellect, beauty, and charm so perfectly?"

The Inspector smote his desk with the flat of his hand, making things jump and tremble. "You think you're damned cute—you and that pest of a newspaperwoman! Queen, I don't mind telling you I'm raving mad. Raving! When I read that piece I had a good mind to issue a warrant for your arrest. I mean it!"

"Looking for a goat, eh?" said Ellery sympathetically.

"Collecting all those letters! Holding out on me all week! Posing as a Headquarters dick!"

"You've worked fast," said Ellery with admiration. "All she says here, after all, is that Blythe Stuart was receiving anonymous letters and that they were mailed through the agency of a mailing service. Good work, Glücke."

"Don't salve me! There's only one mailing service in town, and I had this guy Lucey on the carpet just a while ago. He told me all about you—recognized you from his description. And you left your name and hotel phone number with him. The cheek of it! That proved his story. I suppose the other two were Ty Royle and Lew Bascom, from Lucey's description."

"Wonderful."

"I've been having the Stuart house searched—no letters—so I know you have 'em." The Inspector looked as if he were about to cry. "To think you'd pull a lousy trick like that on *me*." He jumped up and shouted: "Fork over!"

Ellery frowned. "Nevertheless, the inevitability of secrets finally coming to rest in Paula's column is beginning to give me the willies. Where the devil does she get her information?"

"I don't care," yelled Glücke. "I didn't even call her this morning on it—what the hell good would it do? Listen, Queen, are you going to give me those letters or do I have to slap you in the can?"

"Oh, the letters." Ellery kicked the typewriter between his legs. "You'll find them in here, with the cards and the machine the scoundrel used to type his code sheet, and his letter to International Mailers."

"Cards? Code sheet?" gaped Glücke. "Machine? Whose machine?"

"Jack Royle's."

The Inspector sank back, feeling his brow. "All right," he choked.

"Let's have the story. I'm just in charge of the Homicide Detail. Just give me a break, a handout." He bellowed: "Damn it, man, GIVE!"

Ellery gave, chuckling. He launched into a long exposition, beginning at the beginning—the very beginning, which was his acquisition of the first two cards from Blythe Stuart herself in Jack Royle's house—and concluding with the story of the new series of letters sent to Bonnie.

The Inspector sat glowering at the typewriter, the yellow sheets, the cards, the envelopes.

"And when I found that the two letters to Bonnie were typed on Ty's machine," shrugged Ellery, "that was the end of it. Honestly, Glücke, I was on my way to give you all this stuff when you phoned me."

The Inspector rose, grunting, and took a turn about the room. Then he summoned his secretary. "Take all this stuff down to Bronson and have him check it, along with the fingerprint detail." When the man left, he resumed his pacing.

Finally, he sat down. "To tell you the truth," he confessed, "it doesn't mean an awful lot to me. That letter signed Smith is a phony, of course; just a neat way of wiping out the trail to himself. The only thing I get out of the whole set-up is that the original plan was to bump Blythe off, and that something happened to make this Smith give Jack the works, too."

"The essential point," murmured Ellery.

"But why *was* Jack knocked off? Why were the warnings sent at all?" The Inspector waved his arms. "And what's the idea of starting on Bonnie Stuart now? Say!" His eyes narrowed. "So that's why you had me put a day-and-night tail on her!"

"If you'll recall, I asked you to have her watched before the first warning was sent to her."

"Then why—"

"Call it a hunch. The cards to Bonnie later confirmed it."

"So now she's elected," muttered Glücke. "No savvy."

"Have you seen her today?"

"I tried to locate her when I found out about the anonymous letters, but she's not home, and my men haven't reported. Matter of fact, Royle isn't around, either."

A chilly finger pressed on Ellery's spine. "You haven't been able to locate Ty?"

"Nope." The Inspector looked startled. "Say, you don't think *he's* behind these letters? That he's the one—!" He jumped up again. "Sure! You say yourself these last messages to Bonnie were typed on his machine!" He grabbed his phone. "Miller! Hop down to the Magna Studios on the double and bring back the typewriter in Ty Royle's dressing-room. Careful with it—prints." He hung up, rubbing his hands. "We'll have to go easy, of course. Proving he sent the cards doesn't prove he pulled the double murder. But just the same it's a start. Motive galore—"

"You mean he killed his father, too?"

Glücke looked uncomfortable. "Well, I said we'd go easy. There's a lot of questions to clear up. Keep this under your hat, Queen, while I start the ball rolling."

"Oh, I will," said Ellery dryly.

The Inspector grinned and hurried out. Ellery mused over a cigaret. When the Inspector came back he was beaming.

"We'll locate him in short order, of course. Then a day-and-night tail without his knowledge. I'm having his house fine-combed. Maybe we'll turn up something on the morphine and sodium allurate, too— check over his movements for a couple of weeks, drug purchases, and so on. It's a start; it's a start."

"Of course, you know Ty physically couldn't have been that masked pilot," Ellery pointed out.

"Sure not, but he could have hired some one as a blind. Swell blind, too, having himself held up with a gun and tied like a rooster. With the girl as witness, too."

Ellery sighed. "I hesitate to dampen your enthusiasm, Glücke, but you're all wrong."

"Hey? Wrong? How's that?" Glücke looked startled.

"Ty never wrote those letters—no, any more than Jack wrote the ones that came to Blythe."

The Inspector sucked his finger. "How come?" He looked disappointed.

"You might examine," drawled Ellery, "the faces of the h and r keys on this machine."

Glücke did so, frowning. The frown disappeared magically, to be replaced by a scowl. "Filed!"

"Exactly. And when you examine Ty's typewriter, you'll find that the b and d and t are similarly filed. There could be only one purpose in a deliberate mutilation of typewriter keys—identification of the machine from a sample of its writing. Well, who would want Jack Royle's machine to be easily identified as the machine which typed the code sheet behind the anonymous letters? Jack Royle? Hardly, if he was sending them. And the same goes for Ty and his machine."

"I know, I know," said Glücke irritably. "Framed, by God."

"So we can be sure of several things. First, that Jack Royle did *not* send those card messages to Blythe. Second, that Ty Royle did *not* send those card messages to Bonnie. And third—this follows a pattern of probability—from the fact that the same method of mutilation was used on both machines, filing of keys, a conclusion that *the same person* mutilated both, and consequently the same person sent both series of messages."

"But a frame of *two* men!"

"See what we have. Originally a plan to murder Blythe, and in doing so to frame Jack for the murder by the device of sending those otherwise infantile messages, leaving a trail to them through Jack's typewriter."

"But Jack was killed, too."

"Yes, but we also know the murderer had to change his original plans. Somehow that change necessitated the killing of Jack and the abandonment of the frame-up against him by virtue of the very fact that he had to be murdered."

"But the cards kept coming."

"Because the murderer had set up the machinery for having them mailed and didn't want to risk stopping it. Think now, Glücke. We have a change of plan. Jack's murder. Then the cards start coming to Bonnie. Had the original plans been followed through, it's reasonable to assume that Jack would continue to be framed. But with Jack dead, some one else must be framed for the threats against Bonnie. Who?

Well, we know now it's Ty being framed for those threats. It all adds up to one thing."

"Keep talking," said the Inspector intently.

"Some one is using the Royle-Stuart feud as a motive background for his crime. He's throwing you a ready-made motive. So the feud can't be the motive at all."

"The pilot!"

Ellery looked thoughtful. "Any trace of the pilot yet?"

"Damned shadow simply vanished. We're still plugging along on it. I've sort of become discouraged myself." He eyed Ellery. "Did you know I've cleared Alessandro?"

"Cleared?" Ellery elevated his brows.

"That hundred and ten grand Jack owed him was really paid. No doubt about it."

"Was there ever any?"

The Inspector looked suspicious. "You knew it!"

"As a matter of fact, I did. How did you find out?"

"Checked over bank accounts. Found that Jack had cashed a check for a hundred and ten thousand dollars in the bank on the morning of Thursday, the fourteenth."

"Not his bank, surely; they wouldn't honor a check of that size for him so quickly. Tolland Stuart's bank?"

"How'd you know that?" exploded Glücke.

"Guessed. I do know the check was signed by old man Stuart and was dated the thirteenth. I know because I asked the terrible-tempered old coot just yesterday."

"How come Stuart forked over all that dough to Jack? Jack didn't mean anything to him. Or did he?"

"I think not. It was Blythe's work. She took Jack with her that Wednesday to see her father, pleaded for the money for Jack's sake, not for her own. He says he gave it to her to get rid of both of them."

"Sounds screwy enough to be true. Even if it wasn't the reason, the signature's genuine; we know the old gent did make out a check for that amount."

"Anything else turn up?"

"Nope. Our leads on Jack's lady-friends petered out; every one of 'em had an alibi. And the poison—not a trace." Ellery drummed on the arm of his chair. Glücke scowled. "But this frame-up, now. If Ty's being framed, this last card was an awful dumb one to send the girl! What kind of cluck are we dealing with, anyway?"

"A cluck who puts morphine into people's cocktails and sends 'em dumb messages. Perplexing, isn't it?"

"Maybe," muttered the Inspector hopefully, "maybe there's a lead in this fortune-telling stuff after all. I do know Blythe was a little cracked on the subject, like most of the wacky dames out here."

"No self-respecting fortune-teller would tolerate the salmagundi of which that yellow code sheet is the recipe."

"Come again?"

"I've been delving into the occult art. The little I've read convinces me that those cards simply couldn't have been sent by a professional fortune-teller, or even by one who knew much about fortune-telling."

"You mean those meanings for each card were just made up?"

"Oh, the meanings are authentic enough, one by one. The only liberty the poisoner took that I could find was in the meaning of the nine of clubs, which in one system of divination means 'warning.' Our friend Egbert improved that; he made it 'last warning.' Otherwise, the meanings can be found in any work on the subject.

"The trouble is that the ones on the yellow sheet represent a haphazard mixture of meanings from a number of *different* systems—there are lots of them, you know. Some from the fifty-two card system, some from the thirty-two, one from the so-called 'tableau of twenty-one' system; and so on. Also, no account is taken of the different meanings for upright cards as against reversed; there's no mention of specific methods such as Incantation, Oracle, Old English, Romany, Witch, Gypsy; or of specific arrangement, such as Rows of Nine, Lover's Tableau, Lucky Horseshoe, Pyramid, Wheel of Fortune. Also, the tearing of a card in two to reverse its meaning—absolute innovation on the part of friend Egbert; can't find it mentioned anywhere. Also—"

"For God's sake, I've had enough hocus-pocus!" cried the Inspector, seizing his head.

"I trust," said Ellery, "I've made my point?"

"The whole damned thing," groaned Glücke, "adds up to one beautiful headache."

"*La vie*," said Ellery philosophically, and he strolled out.

He made straight for the Hollywood hills, like a faithful homing-pigeon. The very sight of the white frame house calmed his ruffled spirit and laid a blanket over his tossing thoughts.

Paula kept him cooling his heels for twenty minutes, succeeding admirably in undoing all the good work achieved by her house.

"You can't do that to me," he said in reproach, when her secretary sent him in. He devoured her with his eyes. She was gowned in something svelte and clinging; she looked delectable. Remarkable how every time he saw her he discovered something new to admire! Her left eyelid, now; there was a tiny mole on it. Simply adorable. Gave her eyes interest, character. He seized her hands.

"Can't do what to you?" Paula murmured.

"Keep me waiting. Paula, you look so tasty I could eat you."

"Cannibal." She laughed, squeezing his hands. "What can you expect if you don't tell a lady in advance you're coming?"

"What difference does that make?"

"Difference! Are you really as stupid as you sound? Don't you know that every woman looks forward to an excuse to change her dress?"

"Oh, that. You don't have to primp for me."

"I'm *not* primping for you! This is one of my oldest rags—"

"The ancient plaint. And you're using lipstick. I don't like lipstick."

"*Mr.* Queen! I'll bet you still wear long underwear."

"A woman's lips are infinitely more attractive in their natural state." He pulled her toward him.

"Well, it stays on," said Paula hurriedly, backing away. "Oh, you infuriate me! I always say to myself I'm going to be as cool and remote as a queen with you, and you always manage to make me feel like a silly little girl on her first date. Sit down, you beast, and tell me why you've come."

"To see you," said Ellery tenderly.

"Don't give me *that*. You never had a decent, honest, uncomplicated impulse in your life. What is it this time?"

"Uh . . . there *was* a little matter of an item in your column today. I mean, about those letters—"

"I knew it! You are a beast."

"You don't begin to fathom how true that is."

"You're not even polite. You might lie about it, just once. Make me think you've come for no other reason than to see me."

"But that is the reason. In fact," said Ellery, brightening, "the letter business was just an excuse. That's what it was, an excuse."

She sniffed. "*You* needing an excuse for anything!"

"Paula, did I ever tell you how beautiful you are? You're the woman I've dreamed about since the days when I mooned over movie actresses. The perfect supplement to my soul. I think—"

"You think?" she breathed.

Ellery ran his finger under his collar. "I think it's warm in here."

"Oh."

"Warm in here, all right. Where are your cigarets? Ah. My brand, too. You're a jewel." He nervously lit a cigaret.

"You were about to say?"

"I was about to say? Oh, yes. That item in your column about the letters to Blythe."

"Oh," she said again.

"Where'd you dig up that nugget?"

She sighed. "Nothing up my sleeve. One of my informants was told about your visit to International Mailers, Inc., by a friend of a friend of your friend Mr. Lucey. And so it got to me, as almost everything that happens in this town does. I put two and two together—"

"And got three."

"Oh, no, a cool and accurate four. The description was too, too perfect. A lean and hungry galoot with a rapacious glint in his eye. Besides, you left your name." She eyed him curiously. "What's it all about?"

He told her. She listened in a perfect quiet. When he had finished she reached for a cigaret. He held a match to it and she thanked him with a glance. Then she frowned into space.

"It's a frame-up, of course. But why did you ask me to keep peppering away in my column at the Ty-Bonnie feud?"

"Don't you know?"

"If Bonnie's in danger, it seems to me that Ty, being innocent . . ." She stopped. "Look here, Ellery Queen, you've got something up your sleeve!"

"No, no," said Ellery hastily.

"You just told me yourself you've done everything short of kidnapping to keep those two apart. Why?"

"A—whim. At any rate, if I must say so myself, I think I've done it very well."

"Oh, have you? Well, I don't know why you've done it, but I *don't* think you've done it well, Mister."

"Eh?"

"You've handled that part of it very badly."

Ellery regarded her with some annoyance. "I have, have I? Tell me, my omniscient Minerva, how you would have handled it?"

She gazed at him, her beautiful eyes mocking. "How true to type," she murmured. "Such magnificent sarcasm arising from such magnificent egoism. The great man himself condescending to listen to a mere layman. And a woman, at that. Oh, Ellery, sometimes I think you're either the smartest man in the world or the dumbest!"

Ellery's cheeks took on a strong reddish cast. "That's not fair," he said angrily. "I admit I've been a good deal of an ass in my conduct towards you, but as far as the Ty-Bonnie situation is concerned—"

"You've been even more of an ass, darling."

"Damn it all," cried Ellery, springing to his feet, "where? How? You're the most exasperating female I've ever known!"

"In the first place, Mr. Queen," smiled Paula, "don't shout at me."

"Sorry! But—"

"In the second place, you should have asked my advice, confided in me—"

"In you?" said Ellery bitterly. "When you could have cleared up that business of the mess at the airport so easily?"

"That was different. A question of professional ethics—"

"There's a woman's logic for you! That was different, she says. Let me tell you, Paula, it was precisely the same in principle. Besides, why should I confide in you? What reason have I to believe—" He stopped very suddenly.

"For that," said Paula with a glint in her eye, "you'll suffer. No. I think I'll give you the benefit of my wisdom after all. It may reduce the swelling above your ears. You bungled that Ty-Bonnie situation because you don't know women."

"What has that to do with it?"

"Well, Bonnie's very much the woman, and from what you've told me about the exact nature of your lies and her reaction to them . . . Mr. Queen, you are due to get the surprise of your life, I think very shortly."

"*I* think," said Mr. Queen nastily, "you're talking through your hat."

"Brr! don't we look mean! Smile, darling. Come, come. You look as if you wanted to eat me up, all right—but not from amorous motives."

"Paula," said Mr. Queen through his teeth, "I can stand just so much and no more. You need a lesson. Even the rat stands and fights at last."

"Such a humble metaphor!"

"Paula," thundered Mr. Queen, "I challenge you!"

"My, how formal," smiled Paula. "Touch a man's vanity and you send it screaming into the night. Challenge me to what?"

Mr. Queen seated himself again, smiling a wintry smile. "To tell me who killed Jack Royle and Blythe Stuart." Nevertheless, his eyes were curiously intent.

She raised her brows. "Don't you know—you, who know everything?"

"I asked *you*. Have you figured it out?"

"How tedious." She wrinkled her little nose. "Oh, I imagine I could guess if I wanted to."

"Guess." Ellery sneered. "Of course, it wouldn't stand to reason. I mean, that's the point. A woman doesn't reason. She guesses."

"And you, you great big powerful man, you've arrived at it by simply herculean efforts of the mind, haven't you?"

"Who is it?" said Ellery.

"You tell me first."

"Good Lord, Paula, you sound like Fanny Brice doing Baby Snooks!"

"Why should I trust you?" murmured Paula. "You'd only claim it was your guess, too. Only you wouldn't use the word 'guess.' You'd say 'ratiocination,' or something like that."

"But for Pete's sake," said Ellery irritably. "I *don't* do these things by guesswork. It's a science with me!"

"Nothing doing." Again mockery. "You write your name down—the name you've guessed—and I'll do the same, and we'll exchange papers."

"Very well," groaned Ellery. "You've disrupted my whole intellectual life. It's childish, but you've got to be taught that lesson I mentioned."

Paula laughed, and procured two sheets of stationery, and gave him a pencil, and turned her back and wrote something quickly on her paper. Ellery hesitated. Then, with heavy strokes, he wrote a name, too. His eyes were veiled as she turned around.

"Wait," said Ellery. "I have an improvement to suggest. Get two envelopes."

She looked perplexed, but obeyed.

"Put yours in that envelope, and I'll put mine in this."

"But why?"

"Do as I say."

She shrugged and sealed the envelope over her sheet. Ellery did likewise. Then he stowed her envelope away in his wallet and handed his envelope to her.

"Not to be opened," he said grimly, "until our friend's ears are pinned back."

She laughed again. "Then I'm afraid they'll never be opened."

"Why?"

"Because," said Paula, "the criminal will never be caught."

"Is that so?" said Ellery softly.

"Oh, I know it's so," murmured Paula.

They looked at each other for a long time in silence. The mockery in her eyes had deepened.

"And what makes you so sure?" asked Ellery at last.

"No proof. Not a shred of evidence you could take into court. Unless you've been holding out on me."

"If I snap the trap," said Ellery with bright eyes, "on friend Egbert, will you admit you were wrong?"

"That would prove me wrong, wouldn't it?" she murmured. "But you won't."

"Willing to stake something on that?"

"Certainly. If you'll assure me," she looked at him through her long lashes, "you've got no evidence at this moment."

"I haven't."

"Then I can't lose—unless the creature goes completely haywire and confesses for no reason at all."

"I have an idea," said Ellery, "this creature won't do any such thing. You'll bet, eh?"

"Anything you say."

"Anything?"

She lowered her lashes. "Well . . . that's a broad term. Anything within reason."

"Would it be reasonable," murmured Ellery, "to make the loser take the winner out to the Horseshoe Club?"

Once before he had seen that terrified glimmer in her eyes. It almost made him contrite. But not quite. And then it passed very quickly.

"No guts," jeered Ellery. "If that disgusting term may be applied to a lady's anatomy. Well, I knew you wouldn't."

"I didn't . . . say . . . I wouldn't."

"Then it's a bet!"

She began to laugh softly. "Anyway, there's not the slightest danger of your winning."

"Either a bet's a bet, or it isn't."

"And either a bet has two hazards, or it's no bet either. What are *you* giving up if you lose, as you will?"

"Probably my . . . "

Something new leaped into Paula's eyes, and it was not terror. "Your what?" she asked swiftly.

"Uh—"

"What were you going to say?"

"You know, Paula," said Ellery, avoiding her eager gaze, "I really have you to thank for my solution of this case."

"But you were about to say—"

"You were the one who supplied me with the vital clues." His tone dried out and became impersonal. "The two vital clues."

"Ellery Queen, I could shake you! Who cares about that?"

"Consequently," said Ellery in the same dry way, "I'll be grateful to you for those tips all my life."

"All your life?" said Paula tenderly. "*All* your life?"

And she went slowly up to him and stood so close that the sweet odor of her filled his nose, and his head began to swim, and he began to back away like a dog sniffing danger.

"All your life?" she whispered. "Oh, Ellery . . . "

One of the telephones on her desk rang.

"Damn!" cried Paula, stamping her foot; and she ran to the desk.

Mr. Queen wiped his damp cheeks with his handkerchief.

"Yes?" said Paula impatiently into the telephone. And then she said nothing at all. As she listened everything live went out of her face, leaving it as blank and set as a *papier-mâché* mask. She hung up in the same odd silence.

"Paula, what's the matter?"

She sank into the Cape Cod chair. "I knew your *modus operandi* was wrong, and I was sure Bonnie saw through your transparent masculine tactics. But I never thought—"

"Bonnie?" Ellery stiffened. "What's happened?"

"My dear Mr. Know-It-All, prepare for a shock." Paula smiled vaguely. "You've been trying to keep Bonnie and Ty at each other's throats. Why? You've got to tell me."

"So that a—certain person should see, believe, and be content." Ellery gnawed his lip. "Paula, for heaven's sake. Don't torment me. Who was that, and what did he say?"

"That was a friend of mine, a U.P. man. I'm afraid your certain person, unless afflicted by total paralysis, including eyes and ears, will in a matter of minutes learn the awful truth."

"What awful truth?" asked Ellery hoarsely.

"An hour ago Bonnie Stuart, hanging onto Ty Royle's neck as if she were afraid he'd fly away, gave an interview to the press—called 'em all in to her house in Glendale—in which she made a certain announcement to the world."

"Announcement?" Ellery said feebly. "What announcement?"

"To the effect that tomorrow, Sunday the twenty-fourth, she, Bonita Stuart, intended to become Mrs. Tyler Royle."

"My God!" howled Ellery, and he dived for the door.

18

THE SORCERER'S APPRENTICES

Ellery, scraping the fender of his coupé in his haste to park outside Bonnie's house in Glendale, caught sight of three men, patently detectives, speaking to a tall familiar figure who had just descended from a police car.

"Glücke! Is anything—has anything—"

"What brings you here?"

"I just heard the news. Is she still alive? There's been no attack on her?"

"Attack? Alive? Who are you talking about?"

"Bonnie Stuart."

"Of course not." The Inspector grunted. "Say, what's the matter with you? I just got the flash myself."

"Thank the Lord." Ellery swabbed his neck. "Glücke, you'll have to put a cordon around this house. As many men as you can scrape up."

"Cordon? But I've got three men—"

"Not enough. I want the place surrounded. I want it so well guarded that not even a mouse will get through. But it mustn't be obvious. The men are to stay out of sight. Get those flatfeet off this sidewalk!"

"Sure, but—"

"But nothing." Ellery raced for the gate.

Inspector Glücke ran back to the police car, rasped something, and pounded the pavement to the gate again. The police car shot away, and the three detectives strolled off.

Glücke caught up with Ellery, puffing. "What's this all about?"

"Something's wrong somewhere. Of all the idiotic stunts!"

The buxom, mousy Clotilde admitted them, her woman's black eyes sparkling with romantic excitement.

"Oh, but *Messieurs*, they cannot be—"

"Oh, but *Ma'm'selle*, they can, and they shall be," said Ellery rudely. "Ty! Bonnie!"

A muffled noise came from the nearest room, and he and the Inspector hurried towards its source. They burst into the drawing-room to find young Mr. Royle and his fiancée, considerably disheveled, disengaging themselves from each other's arms. Mr. Royle's mouth looked as if it were bleeding all round. But it was only Bonnie's liprouge.

"So here you are," said Ellery. "What the devil's the idea?"

"Oh, it's you," said Mr. Royle, in a grim tone, removing his lady's hands from about his neck.

"Hell of a mess," said Ellery, glaring at them. "Can't you two keep out of each other's hair for so much as two consecutive days? And if you can't, can't you at least keep your pretty mouths shut? Did you have to shout your goo-goo to the whole damned world?"

Mr. Royle rose purposefully from the sofa.

"Ty, your mouth," said Bonnie. "Oh, there's the Inspector. Inspector Glücke, I *demand*—"

"I think," said Ty in the same grim tone, "I know how to handle the situation."

"Oh, you do," said Ellery bitterly. "That's what comes of dealing with a couple of empty-headed kids who—"

A bomb exploded against his chin. It exploded, and little colored stars all gold and blue and scarlet, dancing like mad, filled the range of his vision, and the world swam languidly, and the next thing he knew it was a long long time after and he was lying on the floor blinking up at the chandelier and wondering when the war had broken out. The ceiling was insubstantial, too, heaving and rippling like a spread sail in a gale.

And he heard Ty blowing on his knuckles and saying in a hot, far-away voice: "There's your man, Inspector!"

"Don't be a jackass," said the Inspector's voice remotely. "Come on, Queen, get up. You'll dirty your nice pants."

"Where am I?" murmured Mr. Queen.

"He is, too!" shrieked Bonnie. "Sock him again, Ty. The sneaky devil!" Squinting for better visibility, Mr. Queen received a wavering impression of two slim ankles, a billowing skirt like a smaller sail, and a tiny stamping alligator. No, it was an alligator shoe. "I *knew* there was something wrong! When he took me to Ty's dressing-room . . . oh, it was so *pat!* That typewriter, and his smart 'deductions,' and Ty would *never* have sent me that warning against himself if he were the one, and then I saw with my own eyes how that b and d and t were *filed* down, so I knew Ty wouldn't do that if he really sent them, and everything." Bonnie paused for breath, but not for long. "You see? He was lying all the time! And so I went right to Ty, that's what I did, and—"

It went on and on, and Mr. Queen lay there surveying the ceiling. Why did it shift and sway so? He had it. It was an earthquake, a temblor. California was doing the Big Apple!

"Yes," growled Ty, "and we compared notes—should have done it a long time ago—and, Inspector, you'd be amazed at the things this fellow told us separately. Why, he actually tried to get each one of us to believe the other was a killer!"

"Yes, he told *me*—"

"The damned murderer told *me*—"

It went on and on and on. Somebody was making a fuss about something, Mr. Queen decided, but for the life of him he could not make out what it was. He groaned, trying to rise.

"Come on, come on," said Glücke in the most unfeeling way. "It was just a clout on the whiskers. Not that you don't deserve it, you lone wolf, you." And the detestable creature actually chuckled as he hauled Mr. Queen to a sitting position. "How you feeling? Terrible, I hope."

"My jaw is broken," mumbled Mr. Queen, waggling the organ in question. "Ooh, my head." He struggled to his feet.

"Try to tell Bonnie I sent those notes, hey?" snarled Ty, cocking his fist again.

"Why would he do that," cried Bonnie triumphantly, linking her arms about her hero's neck, "if he didn't send them himself? Answer that one!"

"Well, I had a reason," said Ellery shortly. "Where's a mirror?"

He wobbled to the mirror in the hall and examined his physiognomy. As he tenderly surveyed the damage, which was concentrated in a rapidly swelling heliotrope lump at the point of his chin, the doorbell rang and Clotilde hurried past him to admit two men. To Ellery's foggy gaze one was slow and grim and the other quick and excited. He rubbed his eyes and leaned against the wall, dizzy.

"Let 'em through," he muttered. "Glücke, didn't I tell you—"

Apparently the Inspector had the same notion, for he hurried out to talk to his men.

The slow one went slowly past Ellery, with no sign of recognition, into the drawing-room; and the quick one went quickly. Mr. Queen, satisfied that his jaw was still in one piece, tottered to the drawing-room doorway and closed his eyes.

The slow one stood just inside the room, looking at Bonnie. Looking. There was a sort of permanent flush under the top-most layer of his skin.

"It's Butch," said Bonnie faintly.

"Oh, say, Butch," began Ty in a defiant mutter. "We were going to tell you, call you, sort of—"

"The hell with that!" yelled the quick one. "I don't care a hoot about how you two bedbugs conduct your private lives, but I'll be damned if I see why you played such a dirty trick on your own studio!"

"Lay off, you," said Ty. "Butch, we really owe you—"

"Lay off?" Sam Vix glared out of his one eye. "He says lay off. Listen, me fine bucko, you haven't *got* a private life, see? You're a piece of property, like this house. You belong to Magna Studios, see? When Magna says jump—"

"Oh, go away, Sam," said Bonnie. She took one step towards the Boy Wonder, who stood exactly where he had stopped on entering the room and was still regarding her with that fixed and awful sadness of a man who sees the coffin-lid being screwed down over the face of his child, or mother, or sweetheart.

"Butch dear." Bonnie pinched her dress. "We were both so excited. ... You know, I think, how I've always felt towards you. I never really told you I loved you, did I, Butch? Oh, I know I've treated you shamefully, and you've been a perfect angel about everything. But something happened today. ... Ty is the only man I'll ever love, Butch, and I'm going to marry him just as quickly as I can."

Jacques Butcher took off his hat, looked around, put on his hat, and then sat down. He did not cross his legs, but sat stiffly, like a ventriloquist's dummy; and as he began to talk the only part of his face that moved was his lips.

"I'm sorry to have to intrude at such a time," he said, and stopped. Then he started again. "I wouldn't have come at all. Only Louis Selvin asked me to. Louis is—well, a little put out. Especially by you, Ty."

"Oh, Butch—" began Bonnie, but she stopped helplessly.

"By me?" said Ty.

Butcher cleared his throat. "Damn it all, I wouldn't—I've got to talk to you not as myself but as vice-president of Magna, Ty. I've just come from a long talk with Selvin. As president of Magna he feels it his duty to warn you—not to get married."

Ty blinked. "You don't mean to tell me he's going to hold me to that ridiculous marriage clause in my contract!"

"Marriage clause?" Bonnie stared. "Ty! What marriage clause?"

"Oh, Selvin stuck an anti-marriage clause into my contract the last time," said Ty disgustedly. "Prevents me from getting married."

"Sure, why not?" said Vix. "Great lover. You don't think the studio's going to build you up into a national fem-killer and let you spoil it by getting hitched!"

200

"I didn't know that, Ty," said Bonnie, distressed. "You didn't tell me."

"Forgot all about it. Anyway, it doesn't make any difference. Louis X. Selvin isn't going to tell me how to run my life!"

"Selvin asked me to point out," said Butcher in his cold, flat voice, "that you'll breach your contract if you marry Bonnie."

"The hell with Selvin! There are plenty of other studios in Hollywood."

"All Hollywood studios respect one another's star-contracts," said Butcher drearily. "If you breach a Magna contract you're through, Ty."

"Then I'm through!" Ty waved his arms angrily.

"But, Ty," cried Bonnie, "you *can't!* I won't let you throw away your career. We can wait. Maybe when you sign your next contract—"

"I don't want to wait. I've waited long enough. I'm marrying you tomorrow, and if Selvin doesn't like it he can go to hell."

"No, Ty!"

"No more arguments." Ty turned away with a stubborn, final gesture.

"All right, then," said Butcher in the same dreary way. "Louis anticipated that you might be stubborn. He could break you, Ty, but he admits you're too valuable a piece of property. So he's prepared to dicker."

"Oh, he is, is he?"

"But he warns you that his proposal is final. Take it or leave it."

"What proposal?" said Ty abruptly.

"If you insist on being married to Bonnie, he's willing to waive the anti-marriage clause. But only on the following conditions. First, you are to let Magna handle the details of your wedding. Second, after your wedding you and Bonnie are to co-star in a picture biography of Jack and Blythe, taking the rôles of your parents."

"Wait a minute, wait a minute," said Ty. "Does that wedding stunt mean a lot of this noisy publicity?"

"It means whatever Magna wants to do."

"And the picture—does that mean the murders, too?" asked Bonnie, looking ill at the very thought.

"The story," said Butcher, "is entirely up to me. You will have nothing to say about it."

"Oh, yes, we have," shouted Ty. "We say no—right now!"

Butcher rose. "I'm sorry. I'll tell Selvin."

"No—wait, Butch," cried Bonnie. She ran over to Ty and shook him. "Ty, please. You can't throw everything away like this. If—if you're stubborn I won't marry you!"

"Let 'em make monkeys out of us with one of those studio weddings?" growled Ty. "Make us put dad and Blythe on the screen in God knows what? Nothing doing."

"Ty, you've *got* to. I don't like it any more than you do; you know that. I'm fed up with—with all this. But we've got to look to the future, darling. Neither of us has anything. You can't throw up the only thing we've got. It won't be so bad. The wedding won't take long, and then we'll go away somewhere by ourselves—"

Ty glowered at the rug. He lifted his head and said sharply to Butcher: "If we go through with this, do we get a rest? A vacation? A honeymoon without brass bands?"

"Hell, no," said Vix quickly. "We can use that honeymoon swell. We can—"

"Please, Sam," said Butcher. Vix fell silent. "Yes, I can promise you that, Ty. Our wedding, your honeymoon. We realize that you're both upset, not yourselves, won't be able to do your best work immediately. So you may have as long for your honeymoon as you feel you need."

"And privacy!"

"And privacy."

Ty looked at Bonnie, and Bonnie looked pleadingly at Ty. Finally Ty said: "All right. It's a deal."

The Boy Wonder said: "Revised contracts will be in your hands in the morning. Sam here will handle all the details of the wedding." He turned on his heel and quietly went to the door. At the door he hesitated; then he turned around. "I'll convey my congratulations—tomorrow." And he walked out.

"Swell," said Sam Vix briskly. "Now look. You want to tie the knot tomorrow?"

"Yes," sighed Ty, sitting down. "Anything. Just get out of here."

"I've figured it all out on the way down. Here's the angle. We use the Jack-Blythe marriage as a model, see?"

"Oh," began Bonnie. Then she said: "Yes."

"Only we smear it on, see? Go the whole hog. You won't be married on the field. You'll—"

"You mean another airplane shindig?" growled Ty.

"Yeah, sure. Only we'll get old Doc Erminius to hitch you *in* your plane. Get it? Wedding *over* the field. In the air. Microphones for everybody in the plane. Broadcast through a radio telephone hook-up via the field station right to the thousands on the field as the plane circles it. Do it right, and with that Jack-Blythe background it'll be the biggest stunt this or any other town ever saw!"

"My God," yelled Ty, rising, "if you think—"

"Go on, Sam, get out of here," said Bonnie hurriedly, pushing him. "It'll be all right. I promise. Go on now."

Vix grinned and said: "Sure. Got plenty to do. Be seein' you," and he dashed out.

"Ty Royle, you listen to me," said Bonnie fiercely. "I *hate* it. But we're caught, and we're going to do it. I don't want to hear another word out of you. It's settled, do you hear? Whatever they want!"

Ellery detached himself from the support of the doorway and said dryly: "Now that all the masterminds have had their say, may I have mine?"

Inspector Glücke came in with him. He said, frowning: "I don't know. I'm not sure I like it. What do you think, Queen?"

"I don't give a damn what anybody thinks," said Ty, going over to a liquor cabinet. "Will you guys please clear out and leave Bonnie and me alone?"

"I think," said Ellery grimly, "that I'll find myself a nice deep hole, crawl into it, and pull it after me. I don't want to be around when the explosion comes."

"Explosion? What are you talking about?" said Ty, tossing off a quick one. "You and your riddles!"

"Oh, this is a lovely one. Don't you realize yet what you've done?"

cried Ellery. "Announcing your marriage was bad enough, but now this! Spare me these Hollywood heroes and heroines."

"But I don't understand," frowned Bonnie. "What have we done? We've only decided to get married. That's our right, and it's nobody's business, either!" Her lip trembled. "Oh, Ty," she wailed, "and it was going to be so beautiful, too."

"You'll find out very shortly whose business it is," snapped Ellery.

"What's this all about?" demanded Glücke.

"You're like the sorcerer's apprentice, you two, except that you're a pair. Sorcerer goes away and you start fiddling with things you don't understand—dangerous things. Result, grief. And plenty of it!"

"What grief?" growled Ty.

"You've done the worst thing you could have done. You've just agreed to do the one thing, in fact, that's absolutely fatal to both of you."

"Will you get to the point?"

"I'll get to the point. Oh, yes. I'll get to the point. Hasn't it occurred to either of you that you're the designs in a pattern?"

"Pattern?" said Bonnie, bewildered.

"A pattern formed by you and Ty and your mother and Ty's father. Hang it all, it's so obvious it simply shrieks." Ellery raced up and down the room, muttering. Then he waved his arms. "I'm not going to launch into a long analysis now. I'm just going to open your eyes to a fundamental fact. What happened to Blythe and Jack when *they* married? What happened to them, eh? Only an hour *after* they married?"

Intelligence leaped into Inspector Glücke's eyes; and Ty and Bonnie gaped.

"Ah, you see it now. They were both murdered, that's what happened. Then what? Bonnie gets warnings, winding up with one which tells her in so many words to have nothing more to do with Ty. What does that mean? It means lay off—no touch—hands off. And what do you idiots do? You promptly decide to be married—in such loud tones that the whole world will know not only the fact but the manner, too, in a matter of hours!"

"You mean—" began Bonnie, licking her lips. She whirled on Ty and buried her face in his coat. "Oh, *Ty.*"

"I mean," said Ellery tightly, "that the pattern is repeating itself. I mean that if you marry tomorrow the same thing will happen to you that happened to Jack and Blythe. I mean that you've just signed your death warrant—that's what I mean!"

PART FOUR

19

THE FOUR OF HEARTS

Ty recovered a little of his color, or perhaps it was the Scotch. At any rate, he said: "I don't believe it. You're trying to frighten us with a bogey-man."

"Doesn't want us to be *married?*" said Bonnie in a daze. "You mean mother . . . too? That that—"

"It's nonsense," scoffed Ty. "I'm through listening to you, anyway, Queen. All you've ever done to me is mix me up."

"You poor fool," said Ellery. "You don't know what I've done to you. You don't know what I've done *for* you. How can people be so blind?"

"That's me," said the Inspector. "Not just blind; stiff. Queen, talk some sense, will you? Give me facts, not a lot of curly little fancies."

"Facts, eh?" Ellery glowered. "Very well, I'll give you—"

The front doorbell rang. Bonnie called wearily: "Clotilde, see who it is." But Ellery and the Inspector jostled each other crowding through the doorway. They pushed the Frenchwoman out of their way. Ty and Bonnie stared after them as if the two men were insane.

Ellery jerked open the door. A stout lady, hatless but wearing a broadtail coat over a flowered house-dress, stood indignantly on the *Welcome* mat trying to shake off the grip of one of Glücke's detectives.

"You let go of me!" panted the lady. "Of all things! And all I wanted to do—"

"In or out?" asked the detective of his superior.

Glücke looked helplessly at Ellery, who said: "I daresay we may invite the lady in." He stared at the woman with unmoving eyes. "Yes, Madam?"

"Of course," sniffed Madam, "if a person can't be *neighborly* . . . "

Bonnie asked from behind them: "What is it? Who is it?"

"Oh, Miss *Stuart*," gushed the stout lady instantly, barging between Ellery and the Inspector and bobbing before Bonnie in a ponderous figure that was almost a curtsy. "You *do* look just the way you look in pictures. I've always remarked to my husband that you're one of the *loveliest*—"

"Yes, yes, thank you," said Bonnie hurriedly. "I'm a little busy just now—"

"What's on your mind, Madam?" demanded Inspector Glücke. For some reason of his own Ellery kept watching the stout lady's hands.

"Well, I *hope* you won't think I'm intruding, Miss Stuart, but the funniest thing just happened. I'm Mrs. Stroock—you know, the *big* yellow house around the corner? Well, a few minutes ago my doorbell rang and the second maid answered it after a delay and there was nobody there, but an envelope was lying on my mat outside the door, and it wasn't for me at all, but was addressed to *you*, Miss Stuart, and to Mr. Royle, and I thought to myself: 'Isn't that the queerest mistake?' Because after all your address is plain enough, and the names of our streets are so different—"

"Yes, yes, envelope," said Ellery impatiently, extending his hand. "May I have it, please?"

"I *beg* your pardon," said Mrs. Stroock with a glare. "This happens to be *Miss Stuart's* letter, not yours, *whoever* you are, and you aren't Mr. Royle, I know *that*. Anyway, Miss Stuart," she said, turning to Bonnie again, all smiles, "here it is, and I assure you I ran over here just as fast as I could, which isn't fast," she giggled, "because my doctor says I *am* running the least bit to flesh these days. How *do* you keep your figure? I've always said that you—"

"Thank you, Mrs. Stroock," said Bonnie. "May I?"

The stout lady regretfully took an envelope out of her coat pocket and permitted Bonnie to take it from her. "And may I congratulate you on your engagement to Mr. Royle? I just heard the announcement over the radio. I'm sure it's the nicest, sweetest thing for two young people—"

"Thank you," murmured Bonnie. She was staring with a sort of horror at the envelope.

"By the way," said Ellery, "did you or your maid see the person who rang your bell, Mrs. Stroock?"

"No, indeed. When Mercy went to the door there was nobody there."

"Hmm. Thank you again, Mrs. Stroock." Ellery shut the door politely in the stout lady's face. She sniffed again and marched down the steps, followed to the gate by the detective, who watched her until she turned the corner and then drifted away.

"Thank you," said Bonnie for the fourth time in a stricken voice to the closed door.

Ellery took the envelope from her fingers and, frowning, returned to the drawing-room. Inspector Glücke gently took Bonnie's arm.

Ty said: "What's the matter now?"

Ellery opened the too familiar envelope, addressed in pencilled block letters to "Miss Bonnie Stuart and Mr. Tyler Royle"—no stamp, no other writing except Bonnie's address—and out tumbled two playing-cards with the blue-backed design.

"The . . . four of hearts?" said Bonnie faintly.

Ty snatched both cards. "Four of hearts? And the ace of spades!" He went to Bonnie and pulled her close to him suddenly.

"I told you this morning, Glücke, we were dealing with a playful creature," remarked Ellery. He stared at the cards in Ty's fist. "Perhaps now you'll believe me."

"The ace of *spades*," said the Inspector, as if he could not credit the evidence of his own eyesight.

"What does it mean?" asked Bonnie piteously.

"It means," said Ellery, "that the interview you two gave the press today has already borne fruit. I suppose the extras have been on the streets for an hour, and you heard that awful woman mention the radio. Our friend Egbert was in such haste to get this message to you he refused to wait for the regular mails, which would have brought the cards Monday, or even a special delivery, which would have brought them some time tomorrow."

"But what's it *mean?*"

"As an intelligible message?" Ellery shrugged. "Together the cards say: 'Bonnie Stuart and Tyler Royle, break your engagement or prepare to die.'"

The Inspector made a sound deep in his throat and nervously looked about the room.

Bonnie was pale, too; paler than Ty. Her hand crept into his.

"Then it *is* true," she whispered. "There *is* a pattern. Ty, what are we going to do?"

"The reason," Mr. Queen remarked, "that Egbert delivered this message in such haste is that Monday—obviously—will be too late. Even tomorrow may be too late. I trust you get his implication?"

Ty sat down on the sofa, his shoulders sagging. He said wearily: "I get it, all right. It's true, and we're not to marry, and if we do it's curtains for us. So I guess we've got to satisfy everybody—Butch, the studio, Egbert L. Smith—and drop our marriage plans."

Bonnie moaned: "Oh, Ty. . . ."

"Why kid ourselves, honey?" Ty scowled. "If I was the only one concerned, I'd say the hell with Egbert. But I'm not; you're in it, too. I won't marry you and lay you wide open to an attack on your life."

"Oh, you *are* stupid!" cried Bonnie, stamping. "Don't you see that isn't so? *I* received threats even before we announced our plans. Those threats were mailed to *me*. The only time *you* were threatened was just now, *after* we'd announced our intention to be married!"

"Hurrah for the female intelligence," said Ellery. "I'm afraid Bonnie scores there, Ty. That's perfectly true. I refrained from mentioning it before, but I can't hold it back any longer. All my efforts to keep you two apart have been exerted in *your* behalf, Ty, not Bonnie's. It's your life that's involved in this association with Bonnie. Bonnie's life, with or without you, has been in danger from the day her mother died."

Ty looked confused. "And I socked you!"

"Marry Bonnie and you're on the spot. Don't marry Bonnie and you're not on the spot. But she is whether you marry her or not. It's a pretty thought."

"In again, out again." Ty grinned a twisted grin. "I've given up trying to make sense out of this thing. If what you say is true, we're going to be married. I'm not going to let her face this alone. Let that sneaking son try to kill me—let him try."

"No, Ty," said Bonnie miserably. "I can't have you doing that. I can't. Why should you endanger your life? I don't pretend to understand it, either, but how can I let you share a danger that's apparently directed at me alone?"

"You," said Ty, "are marrying me tomorrow, and no arguments."

"Oh, Ty," whispered Bonnie, creeping into his arms. "I'd hoped you'd say that. I *am* afraid."

Inspector Glücke was prowling about in a baffled sort of way. "If we only knew who it was," he muttered. "If we knew, we might be able to do something."

"Oh, but we do know," said Ellery. He looked up at their exclamations. "I forgot you didn't know. I do, of course, and I tell you we can do nothing—"

"'Of course,' he says!" shouted the Inspector. He pounced on Ellery and shook him. "Who is it?"

"Yes," said Ty in a funny voice. "Who is it, Queen?"

"Please, Glücke. Just knowing who it is doesn't solve this problem." He began to pace up and down, restlessly.

"Why not?"

"Because there's not an atom of evidence to bring into court. The case wouldn't get past a Grand Jury, if it ever got to a Grand Jury at all. It would be thrown out for lack of evidence, and you'd have missed your chance to pin the crimes on the one who committed them."

"But, good God, man," cried Ty, "we can't just sit around here waiting for the fellow to attack. We've got to do something to trim his claws!"

"Let me think," said Ellery irritably. "You're making too much noise, all of you."

He walked up and down, head bent. There was no sound at all except the sound of his march about the room.

"Look," interrupted the Inspector. "A cop has just as great a responsibility protecting life as investigating death. You say you know who's behind all this, Queen. All right. Let's go to this bird, tell him we know, warn him he'll be watched until the day he dies by a squad of detectives on twenty-four-hour duty. He'd be a bigger fool than any one could be if he didn't give up his plans then and there."

"I've thought of that, of course," said Ellery crossly. "But it has one nasty drawback. It means Egbert will never hang for the murder of Jack and Blythe; and if there's one little fellow I'd have no objection to seeing hanged, it's Egbert."

"If it means safety for Bonnie," said Ty, "let him go. Let him go! Glücke's right."

"Or why couldn't we," began Bonnie, and stopped. "*That's* it! Why couldn't Ty and I be married right this minute and then vanish? Go off somewhere without anybody's knowing where. *Anybody.* Then we'd be safe!"

"And go through the rest of a long life looking over your shoulder every time you heard a sound behind you?" asked Ellery. And then he stared at Bonnie. "Of course! That's it. Vanish! Exactly. Exactly. Force his hand. He'd have to . . . " His voice trailed off and he began to run madly, like an ant, his lips moving silently.

"Have to what?" demanded the Inspector.

"Try to murder them, of course. . . . Yes, he would. Let's see now. If we pulled the stunt—"

"Try to *murder us?*" repeated Bonnie, blinking.

Ellery stopped racing. "Yes," he said briskly. "That's exactly what we'll do. We'll jockey this bird into the position of *trying* to murder you. If the compulsion is strong enough—and I think we can make it strong enough—he *must* try to murder you . . . Bonnie." Ellery's eyes were shining. "Would you be willing to run the risk of an open attack on your life if by running that risk we stood a good chance of catching your mother's murderer red-handed?"

"You mean," said Bonnie slowly, "that if it were successful I'd be free? Ty and I—we'd both be *free?*"

"Free as the air."

"Oh, yes. Oh, yes, I'll do anything for that!"

"Not so fast," said Ty. "What's the plan?"

"To go through with the announced marriage, to utilize it as a trap for the murderer."

"And use Bonnie as a guinea-pig? Nuts."

"But I tell you Bonnie's life is in danger in any event," said Ellery impatiently. "Even if she's surrounded by armed guards day and night, do you want her to spend the rest of her life waiting for the ax to fall? I assure you, Ty, it's either Egbert or Bonnie. Take my word for that. The creature's gone too far to stop now. *His plans make it mandatory for Bonnie to die.*"

"It's a hell of a decision to make," muttered Ty.

"Ty, will you listen to me? I tell you it's the safest course in the long run. Don't you see that by setting a trap we force his hand? We make him attempt Bonnie's life when *we* want him to, under conditions *we* have established—yes, lure him unsuspecting right into a spot where we know what he'll do and be prepared for him. By taking the bold step we reduce the danger to a minimum. Don't you see?"

"How do you know," said Glücke intently, "he'll attack?"

"He's got to. He can't wait too long; I'm positive of that, never mind how. If part of our plan is to announce that immediately after the wedding tomorrow Bonnie and Ty are taking off for an unknown destination, to be gone an indefinite length of time, he *must* attack; I know he must. He can't let Bonnie, living, vanish; he'll have to try to kill her tomorrow or give up his whole plan."

"Why shouldn't he give up his whole plan?"

"Because," said Ellery grimly, "he's already killed two people in pursuance of his objective. Because we'll give him another opportunity he can't pass up. Because he's desperate, and cold-blooded, and his motive—to him—is overwhelming."

"Motive? What motive? I thought he was crazy."

"Yes, what motive?" asked Bonnie tensely. "Nobody could possibly have a reason for killing me."

"Obviously some one has, as this last message indicates. Let's not go down byroads now. The big point is: Are you game to try?"

Bonnie laid her head on Ty's shoulder. Ty twisted his head to look down at her. She smiled back at him faintly.

"All right, Queen," said Ty. "Let's go."

"Good! Then we've got to understand this clearly, all four of us. You, too, Glücke. You'll have an important job.

"We'll let Sam Vix's plans for the wedding stand; in fact, we use them. As it's turned out, that studio mix-up just now was a break for us; it happened naturally, and that's what we need most—natural events arousing no possible suspicion on the part of . . . let's continue to call him Egbert.

"All right. We can depend on Sam to ring the <u>welkin</u> tonight; there will be plenty of ballyhoo between now and tomorrow afternoon. We make it clear that you two are to be married in the plane; we make it even clearer—this is vital—that you two are leaving for an unannounced destination, for an indefinite stay. That no one, not even the studio, will know where you're going or when you're coming back. That you're sick and tired of it all, and want to be alone, to chuck Hollywood and all its sorrows for a while. If possible you must tell that to the press . . . convincingly."

"The way I feel," grinned Ty, "don't worry about that."

"Now what does Egbert do? He's got to murder Bonnie—yes, and after the wedding you, too, Ty—before you slip out of his grasp. How is he going to do it? Not by poisoning food or drink, as in the case of Jack and Blythe; he'll realize that, with the manner of their deaths so fresh in your minds, you just won't touch untested gifts of food or drink. So he'll have to plan a more direct assault; that's inevitable. The most direct is a gun."

"But—" began the Inspector, frowning.

"Let me finish. To shoot and get away safely, he can't attack on the field; even if he succeeded in taking two accurate potshots from the crowd, he'd never live to leave the field. So," snapped Ellery, "he'll have only one course to follow. In order to make sure of a successful double murder and a successful getaway, *he'll have to get into that plane with you.*"

"Oh ... I see," said Bonnie in a small voice. Then she set her smooth jaw.

"I get it, I get it," mumbled Glücke.

"Moreover, since we know he'll try to get into that plane, we also know how. He can get in, reasonably, only as *the pilot.*"

"The way he did it in the case of Jack and Blythe!" exclaimed the Inspector.

"Since we're reasonably certain he'll take the opportunity if he's given the opportunity, all we have to do is give it to him. So we engage a professional aviator. That's part of our announcement. We see to it that the pilot isn't openly under surveillance, we permit Egbert to decoy the pilot into a dark corner, to incapacitate him—I don't believe he'll be in serious danger, but we can take steps to keep it down to a minimum—and we permit Egbert to take the pilot's place in the plane."

"Why a pilot at all? I run my own ship. Won't that sound phony?" asked Ty.

"No, because you're taking a pilot in order to have him drop you off somewhere to make connections with a train or a boat—not even the pilot, we'll announce, will know where he's going until after the take-off. So, of course you'll need a pilot, ostensibly, to bring the plane back after he dumps you. That's all right. At any rate, friend Egbert will hop into the plane and take off, secure in the feeling that he's left no trail and will be able to commit his crime in mid-air."

"Wait a minute," said Glücke. "I like your scheme, but it means putting these two youngsters in a plane with a dangerous criminal, alone except for some fool of a minister who'll probably only make things worse."

"This minister won't."

"Erminius is an old woman."

"But it won't be Erminius. It will be some one who just looks like

214

Erminius," said Ellery calmly.

"Who?"

"Your obedient servant. Erminius has a beautiful set of black whiskers, which makes him a cinch to impersonate. Besides, Egbert won't be paying much attention to the preacher, I can promise you that. He'll be too intent on getting that plane off the ground unsuspected. Anyway, Ty and I will both be armed. At the first sign of trouble, we shoot."

"Shoot," repeated Bonnie, licking her lips and trying to look brave.

"We'll subdue him if we can, but we must give him the opportunity to show his hand. And *that* can be brought out in court."

"Hell," protested the Inspector, "you ought to know even catching the guy in an attempted homicide won't pin the murders of Jack and Blythe on him."

"I rather think it won't make any difference. I think that, once caught, our friend will collapse like a straw man and tell all. If the stunt works, sheer surprise at finding himself trapped at a moment when he thought his plans were about to be consummated will put him off guard. At any rate, it's our only chance to catch him at all."

There was a little uncomfortable interval, and then Glücke said: "It sounds screwy as the devil, but it might work, it might work. What do you say, you two?"

"I say, yes," said Bonnie quickly, as if she were afraid that if she hesitated she might not say yes at all. "What do *you* say, darling?"

And Ty kissed her and said, "I love you, Pug Nose." Then he said to Ellery in an altogether different tone of voice: "But if anything goes wrong, Queen, I swear I'll strangle you with my bare hands. If it's the last thing I do."

"It probably will be," muttered Ellery. "Because Egbert's plan will undoubtedly be to stage a second St. Valentine's Day massacre in that plane with his popgun and then bail out, leaving the plane to crash in the desert somewhere."

20

CASTLE IN THE AIR

Time, which had been floating by, suddenly took on weight and speed. Ellery kept looking at his wristwatch in despair as he went into the details of his plan, instructing Ty and Bonnie over and over in their rôles.

"Remember, Ty, you'll have to handle all the arrangements; Glücke and I can't possibly appear in this. In fact, we'll stay as far away from you as we can until tomorrow. Have you a gun?"

"No."

"Glücke, give him yours." The Inspector handed his automatic over to Ty, who examined it expertly and dropped it into his jacket pocket. "Now what's your story to the press?"

"Bonnie has received a warning to break our engagement, but we both agree it's the work of some crank and intend to be married at once. I show the cards."

"Right. Not a word about our real plans to any one. In a half-hour call Erminius and engage him to perform the ceremony. Bonnie."

Bonnie peeped out from the cradle of Ty's arms.

"You're all right?"

"I'm feeling fine," said Bonnie.

"Good girl! Now do a little of that acting Butch pays you for. You're happy—just the proper combination of happiness and grief. You're marrying Ty because you love him, and you also know that Blythe and Jack must be happy somewhere knowing what you're about to do. The feud is over, never to be resurrected. You've got all that?"

"Yes," said Bonnie in a shaky little voice.

"By George, I feel like a director!" Ellery grinned with a confidence he did not feel and stuck his hand out to Ty. "Good luck. By this time tomorrow night the nightmare will be over."

"Don't worry about us, Queen," said Ty, shaking hands soberly. "We'll come through. Only—get into that plane!"

Glücke said abruptly: "Stay here. Send for your duds, Ty. Don't leave this house. It's surrounded right now, but I'll send two men in here to watch from a hiding-place—just in case. Don't do anything foolish, like those heroes you play in the movies. At the first suspicion of trouble, yell like the devil."

"I'll take care of that part of it," said Bonnie with a grimace; then she tried to smile, and they shook hands all around, and Ellery and the Inspector slipped out by the back way.

The next twelve hours were mad on the surface and madder underneath. The necessity for boring from within was a bother; Ellery was constantly answering telephone calls in his hotel apartment and giving cautious instructions. He could only pray that Ty and Bonnie were carrying off their end successfully.

The first assayable results came booming in via radio late that night. Towards the end of an expensive Saturday-night program a studio announcer interrupted with the detailed news of the projected wedding. Apparently Sam Vix had sailed into his assignment with his customary energy. Within two hours four of the largest radio stations on the Pacific Coast had broadcast the announcement of the Sunday airplane wedding of Tyler Royle and Bonnie Stuart. A famous female studio commentator climbed panting on the air to give the palpitating public the intimate details of the plan, as transmitted directly from the mouths of the lovers themselves. The interview, reported this lady, had been too, too sweet. Somebody, she said sternly, had had the bad taste to "warn" Bonnie against marriage. This was, it seemed, a frank and brutal case of *lèse majesté*. Those two, poor, sorrowing children! panted the lady. She hoped every friend Ty and Bonnie had within driving distance of Griffith Park airport would be on hand Sunday to show Ty and Bonnie what the *world* thought of their coming union.

The newspapers erupted with the news late Saturday night, chasing a scarehead concerning the Japanese war in China off the front page.

And so on, interminably, far into the night.

Ellery and the Inspector met secretly at Police Headquarters at two o'clock in the morning to discuss developments. So far, so good. Dr. Erminius had been duly, and unsuspectingly, engaged to perform the unique ceremony. Dr. Erminius was delighted, it appeared, at this heaven-sent opportunity to join two fresh young souls in holy wedlock with God's pure ether as a background, although he fervently prayed to the Lord that there would be no repetition of the ghastly aftermath of the first Royle-Stuart wedding at which he had officiated.

The pilot had also been engaged; he had been selected without his knowledge more for his character than for his skill as an aviator. He was known to have a healthy respect for firearms.

In his office at Headquarters Glücke had several photographs of the eminent divine ready for Ellery, who came down with a make-up box stolen from one of the Magna dressing-rooms; and the two men spent several anxious hours making Ellery up and comparing him with Dr. Erminius's photographs. They agreed finally that a bundling, muffling overcoat with a beaver collar, such as Dr. Erminius affected in brisk weather, would help; and parted with plans to meet early in the morning.

Ellery returned to Hollywood, snatched three hours of uneasy sleep, and at eight Sunday morning met the Inspector and two detectives outside Dr. Erminius's expensive house in Inglewood. They went in; and when they came out they were minus the two detectives and richer by a fur-collared coat. The good man howled ungodly imprecations from within.

Several telephone calls, a final check-up. . . . Ellery crossed his fingers. "Nothing more for us to do," he sighed. "Well, so long, Glücke. See you in the Troc or in hell."

At noon Sunday the parking spaces about the Griffith Park airport were almost filled. At one o'clock there was a jam over which a hundred policemen sweated and cursed. At one-fifteen all cars were halted at the intersection of Los Feliz and Griffith Park boulevards and detoured; and at one-thirty it seemed as if every automobile-owner in the State of California had come to see Ty and Bonnie married.

Ty's red-and-gold plane stood in a cleared area considerably larger than the area in which it had stood a week before. But the jam threatened to burst the ropes on the field, and the police heaved against them, shouting. When Dr. Erminius's royal-blue limousine rolled onto the field under motorcycle escort and the good dominie descended, complete with shiny black whiskers and beaver-collared coat, muffled to the ears—the doctor had a bad cold, it appeared—a cheer shook the heavens. And when Ty and Bonnie arrived, pale but smiling, the din frightened a flock of pigeons into swooping for cover.

Cameras were leveled, reporters yelled themselves hoarse, and Ty and Bonnie and Dr. Erminius were photographed from every conceivable angle and in every position commensurate with the moral tone of the family newspaper.

Meanwhile, the pilot who had been engaged, very natty in his flying suit, received a puzzling message and wandered off to the empty hangar in which only a week before Ty and Bonnie had been held up. He went into the hangar and looked about.

"Who wants me?" he called.

Echo answered; but answer also materialized, and the man's jaw dropped as a bulky, shapeless figure in flying togs, wearing a face-concealing pair of goggles and a helmet, stepped from behind a tarpaulined airplane and leveled a revolver at the pilot's chest.

"Huh?" gasped the pilot, elevating his arms.

The revolver waved an imperious order. The pilot stumbled forward, fascinated. The butt described a short, gentle arc and the pilot crumpled to the floor, no longer interested in the proceedings.

And from a rent in the tarpaulin, behind which he had been suffocating for two hours, Inspector Glücke, automatic in hand, watched the pilot fall, watched the bundled figure stoop over the man and drag him into a corner. The Inspector did not so much as stir a finger; the tap had been gentle, and the interference just then would have been disastrous to the plan.

Because of his position, Glücke could see only the inert body. He did see a pair of hands begin to undress the pilot, divesting him of his outer clothing; it struck Glücke suddenly that the two flying-suits were of different cut; of course, little Egbert would have to put on his victim's suit and helmet and goggles.

It was all over in two minutes. Glücke saw the flying-suit of the attacker flung down on the unconscious pilot, then the helmet, the goggles; and the quick disappearance of the pilot's rig.

Then the attacker appeared again, dressed as the pilot, goggled and unrecognizable; he appeared stooping over the motionless figure. He began to bind and gag the pilot. Still the Inspector did not move.

The attacker pushed his bound victim under the very tarpaulin behind which Glücke crouched, pocketed the revolver, and with a certain grim jauntiness strode out of the hangar.

Glücke moved then, quickly. He clambered out of the covered ship, made a low warning sound, and three plainclothes men stepped out of steel lockers. Leaving the unconscious man in their hands, he ducked out of the hangar by a rear door and strolled around the building to merge briefly with the crowd. Then he sauntered casually up to the group of shouting, gesticulating people around the red-and-gold plane.

The "pilot" was busily engaged in picking up the tumbled luggage and depositing it, piece by piece, in the plane. No one paid any attention to him. Finally he climbed into the plane and a moment later the propeller turned over and began to spin with a roar.

He looked out the window and waved his arm impatiently.

The Reverend Dr. Erminius looked startled. But he caught the eye of Inspector Glücke, who nodded, and heaved a relieved sigh.

"All set," he said in Ty's ear.

"What?" yelled Ty above the roar of the motor.

Dr. Erminius gave him a significant look. Bonnie caught it, too, and closed her eyes for a second; and then she smiled, and waved, and Ty, looking rather grim, picked her slender figure up in his arms and carried her into the plane to the howling approval of the mob. The Reverend Dr. Erminius followed more sedately. The pilot came out of his cubicle, shut the door securely, went back to his cubicle; the police and field attendants cleared the runway; and finally the signal came, and the red-and-gold plane began slowly to taxi down the field, picking up speed . . . its tail lifting, its wings gripping the air. And then it left the solid ground and soared into the blue, and they were alone with their destiny.

Afterwards, in recollection, it all seemed to have happened quickly. But at the time there was an interminable interval, during which the thousands on the field below grew smaller and smaller as the plane circled the field, and finally became only animated dots, and the hangars and administration buildings looked like toys, and the runway, the crowd released, suddenly took on the appearance of a gray patch overrun with bees.

Bonnie kept looking out the window as Ty adjusted the speaking tube to her head, and put one on himself, and gave one to Dr. Erminius. Bonnie was trying to look gay, waving idiotically at the mobs below, steadfastly keeping her eyes averted from the cubicle in which the pilot sat quietly at the controls.

Ty's arm was tightly about her, and his right hand gripped the automatic in his pocket. And his eyes never left the back of the pilot's helmeted head.

As for the Reverend Dr. Erminius, that worthy beamed on the earth and on the sky, and fumbled with the Word of God, obviously preparing to preside over the coming union of two young, untried souls.

And the plane began imperceptibly to nose towards the northeast, where the desert lay, leveling off at eight thousand feet and throbbing steadily.

"I believe," announced Dr. Erminius solemnly, and at his words the bees being left behind stopped swarming and froze to the ground as the amplifiers on the field caught his voice, "that the time has come to join you children in the ineffable bliss of matrimony."

"Yes, Doctor," said Bonnie in a low voice. "I'm ready." And she turned around, and gulped, and the gulp was audible as a hollow thunder below. She rose to stand at Ty's knee and clutch his shoulder. Ty rose quickly then, placing her behind him. His right hand was still in his pocket.

"Oh, pilot," called Dr. Erminius over the mutter of the motor.

The pilot turned his goggled head in inquiry.

"You have automatic controls there, have you not?"

Ty answered in a flat voice: "Yes, Doctor. This is my plane, you know. The Sperry automatic pilot."

"Ah. Then if you will come back here, pilot, after locking the controls you may act as the witness to this ceremony. It will be more comfortable than crowding about your cockpit, or whatever it is called."

The pilot nodded and they saw him adjust something on the complex control-board in front of him. He spent a full minute there, his back to them; and none of them spoke.

Then he got out of his seat, and turned, and stooped, and came into the body of the plane with a swift lurch of his bulky body, looking like a hunchback with the protuberance of the unopened parachute between his shoulder-blades. The Reverend Dr. Erminius had his Book open and ready, and he was beaming on Ty and Bonnie. Ty's hand was still in his pocket, Bonnie was by his side and yet somehow a little behind him, sheltered by his body and the body of the beaming preacher.

And the preacher said: "Let us begin. Bless my soul, we're leaving the field! Weren't we supposed—"

The pilot's hand darted into his pocket and emerged with a snub-nosed automatic, and he brought his hand up very swiftly, his finger tightening on the trigger as the muzzle came up to aim directly at Bonnie's heart.

At the same moment there was a flash of fire from Ty's right pocket, and a flash of fire as if miraculously from the pages of the Good Book in the no longer beaming dominie's hands; and the pilot coughed and lurched forward, dropping the snub-nosed automatic from a gloved hand which suddenly spouted blood.

Bonnie screamed, once, and fell back; and Ty and Dr. Erminius pounced on the swaying figure.

The pilot lashed out, catching Ty with his good fist on the jaw and sending him staggering back against Bonnie. Dr. Erminius snarled and fell on the cursing man. The two tumbled to the floor of the plane, pummeling each other.

Ty lunged forward again.

But somehow, by exactly what means they never knew, the pilot managed to shake them off. One moment they were all struggling on the floor and the next he was on his feet, goggles and helmet torn away from his flushed face, screaming: "You'll never hang *me!*"

And before either of the men on the floor could get to his feet, the pilot darted to the door, wrenched it open, and flung himself out into the sky.

He bounced once on the metal wing.

His body hurtled toward the distant wrinkled face of the earth.

They watched that plummet dive with the paralysis of horror.

The tumbling figure waved frantic arms, growing smaller and smaller.

But no parachute blossomed, and the body became a shrinking mote that suddenly stopped shrinking and spread infinitesimally on the earth.

21

EXCURSION INTO TIME

The field was the surface of a bubbling pot when they landed. Police were using their night-sticks. Men with cameras and men with note-books were fighting openly to break through the cordon.

Ellery, one whisker askew, cooing over Bonnie, saw Inspector Glücke in a small army of detectives gesticulating near the hangar; and he grinned with the satisfaction of sheer survival.

"It's all right, Bonnie," he said. "It's all over now. You've got nothing more to worry about. That's right. Cry it out. It's all right."

"Just wait," growled Ty. "Wait till I get this damned thing standing still."

"I'm waiting," sobbed Bonnie. "Oh, Ty, I'm waiting!" And she shuddered over the palpable sight of a small leggy figure tumbling end over end through empty air, like a dead bug.

The Inspector hurried them into the hangar, out of sight of the frenzied crowd. He was red-faced and voluble, and he grinned all over as he pumped Ty's hand, and Ellery's hand, and Bonnie's hand, and listened to details, and shouted instructions, and swore it had all come in like a movie. Outside a police plane managed to find a space clear enough for a take-off; it headed northeast on the funereal mission of locating and gathering the splattered remains of the one who had sought escape and found death.

Ty seized Bonnie and began shoving through the crowd of detectives to the hangar door.

"Here, where are you going?" demanded Ellery, grabbing his arm.

"Taking Bonnie home. Can't you see the poor kid's ready to collapse? Here, you men, get us off this field!"

"You wouldn't run out on me now, Bonnie?" smiled Ellery, chucking her chin. "Come on, square your shoulders and get set for another sky-ride."

"Another?" yelled Ty. "What now, for the love of Mike? Haven't you had enough sky-riding for one day?"

"No," said Ellery, "I have not." He began to rip off his false whiskers, glancing inquiringly at the Inspector; and the Inspector nodded with a certain grimness, and before Ty could open his mouth to protest he and Bonnie were hurried onto the field and through lanes of police into a large transport plane drawn up on the line with its motor spitting.

"Hey, for God's sake!" shouted a reporter. "Glücke! Give us a break. Glücke!"

"Ty!"

"Bonnie!"

But the Inspector shook his head, and followed Ty and Bonnie into the plane; and there, huddled in a pale-faced group, were several familiar faces.

They were looking at Ty and Bonnie, and Ty and Bonnie were looking at them; and Glücke hauled Ellery in and said something in a low voice to the pilot.

And then they all stared at the rushing, congested field as the plane took off and headed southeast.

And soon they were settling down on the little landing-field near Tolland Stuart's mountain mansion; and as they landed another plane, which had been following from Los Angeles, settled down after them.

Ellery, his face his own, jumped to the ground almost before the plane stopped. He waved to its oncoming pursuer, and ran over to the hangar before which the emaciated figure of Dr. Junius was waiting. The doctor's mouth was open and his eyes were glary with confusion.

Police poured out of the second plane and scattered quickly into the woods.

"What's this?" stammered Dr. Junius, staring at the numerous figures getting out of the first plane. "Mr. Royle? Miss Stuart? What's happened?"

"All in good time, Doctor," said Ellery brusquely, taking his arm. He shouted to the others: "Up to the house!" and began to march the physician along.

"But . . . "

"Now, now, a little patience."

And when they reached the house, Ellery said: "Where's the old fire-eater? We can't leave him out of this."

"Mr. Stuart? In his room, sulking with a cold. He thinks he's catching the grippe. Wait, I'll tell him—" Dr. Junius broke away and ran up the living-room steps. Ellery watched him go, smiling.

"Upstairs," he said cheerfully to the others. "The old gentleman's indisposed for a change."

When they got upstairs they found Dr. Junius soothing the old man, who sat propped up in bed against two enormous pillows, wrapped in an Indian blanket almost to the hairline, his two bright eyes glaring out at them.

"I thought I told you," he began to complain, and then he spied Bonnie. "Oh, so you've come back, hey?" he snarled.

"Yes, indeed," said Ellery, "and with a considerable escort, as you see. I trust, Mr. Stuart, you won't be as inhospitable this time as you were the last. You see, I've got a little tale to tell, and it did seem a pity to keep it from you."

"Tale?" said the old man sourly.

"The tale of an escapade just now in the California clouds. We've captured the murderer of John Royle and your daughter Blythe."

Dr. Junius said incredulously: "*What?*"

226

And the old man opened his toothless mouth, and closed it again, and then reopened it as he stared from Ellery to Inspector Glücke. His mouth remained open.

"Yes," said Ellery, nodding over a cigaret, "the worst is over, gentlemen. A very bad hombre's come to the end of the line. I shouldn't have said 'captured.' He's dead, unless he learned somewhere to survive an eight-thousand-foot drop from a plane with a parachute that didn't open."

"Dead. Oh, I see; he's dead." Dr. Junius blinked. "Who was he? I can't imagine. . . . " His eyes, bulging out of their yellow-violet sockets, began timidly to reconnoitre the room.

"I think it would be wisest," said Ellery, blowing a cloud of smoke, "to clean this sad business up in an orderly manner."

"So I'll begin at the beginning. There were two elements in the double murder of John Royle and Blythe Stuart which pointed to our now departed friend as the only possible culprit: motive and opportunity.

"It was in a consideration of motive that this case has been most interesting. In one way, unique. Let's see what we had to work with.

"Neither Blythe nor Jack left an estate worth killing for, so murder for monetary gain was out. Since there were no romantic entanglements, such as jealous inamoratos of either victim—Blythe was stainless morally and all of Jack's lady-friends have been eliminated by Glücke because of alibis—then the only possible emotional motive would have had to arise out of the Royle-Stuart feud. But I have been able, as some of you know, to rule out the feud as the motive behind these crimes.

"If the feud is eliminated, then neither Jack Royle nor Ty Royle could have been criminally involved—the feud being their only possible motive.

"But if the feud is eliminated, we're faced with a puzzling situation. No one gained by the double murder, either materially or emotionally. In other words, a double murder was committed *apparently without motive*.

"Now this is palpably absurd. The only kind of crime which can even be conceived to lack motivation is the crime of impulse, the passion of a moment—and even this kind of crime, strictly speaking, has some deep-seated motive, even though the motive may manifest itself only in a sudden emotional eruption. But the murder of Jack and Blythe did not fall into even this classification. It was clearly a crime of great deliberation, of much planning in advance of the event—the warnings, the hamper, the frame-ups of Ty and Jack, the poison, and so on.

"Why, then, was Blythe Stuart, against whom the crime was originally and exclusively directed, marked for death? We agree there must have been a motive in so deeply premeditated a crime. But what?

"This raises," said Ellery slowly, "one of the most extraordinary questions in my experience. The question being: How is it possible for a murder-motive to exist and yet elude the most searching analysis? It's there; we know it's there; and yet we can't see it, we can't even glimpse its ghost; it lies in pure darkness, in the vacuum of the void.

"Well," said Ellery, "maybe we can't see the motive for the simplest reason imaginable. Maybe we can't see it because it doesn't exist . . . yet."

He paused, and Inspector Glücke said with an exasperation which flicked the hide from his words: "You just said there must be a motive, that Blythe Stuart was murdered because of that motive, that all we have to do is find that motive. And now you say we can't find the motive because it doesn't exist yet! But if it didn't exist when the murderer planned his crime, why the devil did he plan it? Do you know what you're talking about?"

"This fascinating discussion," drawled Ellery, "shows the limitations of language. Glücke, it's so simple it's absurd. It's merely a question of *time*—I used the word 'yet,' you'll recall."

"Time?" repeated Bonnie, bewildered.

"Time—you know, that invisible thing made visible by your wristwatch. The background of *The Magic Mountain* and Albert Einstein's mathematical researches. Time—what time is it? Have you the time? I'm having a great time."

He laughed. "Look. Whatever the great intellects may call time, mankind has divided it for practical purposes into three classifications:

the past, the present, and the future. All living is motivated by one, two, or all of these classifications. The businessman pays a sum of money to his bank because he took a loan *in the past*; certainly his current headaches are directly attributable to a past event. I am smoking this cigaret because I have the impulse to satisfy a craving for tobacco *in the present.* But isn't the future just as important in our lives? In many ways, more important? A man scrimps to provide against the rainy day—our way of nominating the future. A woman buys a steak at the butcher's in the morning because she knows her husband will be hungry in the evening. Magna plans a football picture in May because they know that in October people will be excited about football. Future, future, future; it dictates ninety percent of our actions."

He said sharply: "In the same way, it struck me that crime—murder—is dictated by time just as inexorably as any other human activity. A man might murder his wife because she was unfaithful to him yesterday. Or a man might murder his wife if he catches her in the act of being unfaithful to him—which means the present. But mightn't a man also murder his wife because he overhears her planning to be unfaithful to him tomorrow?"

And Ellery cried: "So not having found a past event to account for Blythe Stuart's murder; not having found a present event, one contemporaneous with the crime, to account for it—it struck me with force that Blythe Stuart might have been murdered *because of an event which was destined to happen in the future!*"

Inspector Glücke said queerly: "You mean . . . " He did not finish. But after that he kept his gaze riveted on one person in the room with a vague curiosity that was half suspicion.

"But what event," Ellery went on swiftly, "was destined to happen in the future which could have provided a strong motive for the murder of Blythe Stuart? Of all the factors which made up Blythe Stuart—the woman, the actress, the member of a social unit we call 'family'—one factor stood out. Some day . . . in the future . . . some day Blythe Stuart's father would die. And when Blythe Stuart's father died *she would inherit a large fortune.* She was not yet an heiress, but *she was destined to be.*"

The old man in the bed sank deeper into his swathings, fixing his eyes bitterly on Bonnie.

And Bonnie grew paler and said: "But that means . . . If mother died, *I* would inherit . . . "

"Queen, are you crazy?" cried Ty.

"Not at all; your hands are clean, Bonnie. For after your mother's death wasn't it apparent that you, too, were marked for death? Those threatening messages? The ace of spades?

"No," said Ellery, "you were the only one who would *directly* gain by your mother's death, from the standpoint of a future inheritance. But, equally as restrictive, there was only one person who would gain by the deaths of both your mother *and* you, the only one who stood in the direct line after you two women should have died.

"And that was how I knew that the sole living relation of Tolland Stuart, once you and your mother were dead, must be the driving force behind the entire plot. That was how I knew the murderer was Lew Bascom."

22

BEGINNING OF THE END

And there was an interval in time in which the only sound was the asthmatic breathing of the old man in the bed.

And then he muttered: "Lew? My cousin Lew Bascom?"

And Dr. Junius kept blinking, saying nothing.

But Ellery said: "Yes, Mr. Stuart, your cousin Lew Bascom, who conceived and was well on his way to executing a brilliant reversal of the usual procedure in murdering to-gain-a-fortune. A strange creature, Lew. Always broke, too erratic to settle down and put his undeniable talents to a humdrum and sustained economic use, Lew planned murder as the easy way. Of course it was the hard way, but you could never have convinced a man like Lew of that.

"Lew was no sentimentalist, and naturally he was cracked. All deliberate killers are out of plumb somewhere. But the rift in his psychological make-up did not prevent him from seeing that a man stood a much better chance of getting away with murder *if he concealed the motive*. Usually, in murders for gain through inheritance, the rich man is killed first, to insure the passing of the estate. Then the heir or heirs are eliminated, the estate passing legally from one to the other until

231

finally, with no one left but the last legal heir, it becomes his property. There are numerous cases on record of such crimes. But the trouble with them, as many murderers have discovered to their sorrow, is that the method leaves a plain motive trail.

"It was too plain for Lew. If your daughter Blythe were killed while her father Tolland Stuart remained alive, he saw that the real motive for her murder would be a hopeless enigma to the police. Originally, of course, he hoped the frame-up of Jack Royle would provide an instant motive to the police. But even when he had to kill Jack and destroy the force of his own frame-up, he still felt safe; Tolland Stuart was still alive. Then he planned to kill Bonnie, and again it would seem as if Bonnie's death had been a result of the Royle-Stuart feud; the whole childish business of the card-messages had only this purpose—to lay a trail which led back to the Royles. And all the while Tolland Stuart would live, not suspecting that it was *his death*, and not the deaths of his daughter and granddaughter, that was the ultimate goal of the murderer."

"Oh, grandfather!" said Bonnie, and she went to him and sat down on the bed. He sank back on the pillows, exhausted.

"He meant to kill me, then?" mumbled the old man.

"I think not, Mr. Stuart. I think—I know—he meant to let Nature take her course. You are an old man. . . . Well, we'll get to that in a moment.

"Now for element two—opportunity. How had Lew Bascom committed the murders at the airport? That took a bit of figuring."

"That's right, too," said Alan Clark suddenly, from his position between Sam Vix and silent, grim Jacques Butcher. "Lew was with you and me last Sunday, Ellery, when this fake pilot made off with the plane. So Lew couldn't possibly have been that pilot. I don't understand."

"True, Alan; he couldn't have been the kidnapper of the plane. I saw that, if I could clear the kidnapper of complicity in the murder, I could pin the actual poisoning by a stringent process of elimination on Lew.

"Well, who was the kidnapper? One thing I knew beyond question, as you've just pointed out; whoever the kidnapper was, he wasn't Lew."

"How did you know," asked Inspector Glücke, "that he mightn't have been Bascom's accomplice? That's the way I would figure it."

"No, he couldn't have been Lew's accomplice, either, Inspector. Paula Paris gave me the necessary information—the first of the two clues which I got through her."

"The Paris woman? You mean she's mixed up in this, too?"

"Lord, no! But Paula *was* tipped off to the kidnapping before it happened by some one who phoned her from the airport—she didn't tell you that, but she told it to me. Who could have known of the kidnapping and phoned Paula *before* it took place? Only the person who planned, or was involved in the plan, to do it. But this person, in tipping off Paula, *made no secret of his identity*—she admitted that to me, although she wouldn't for ethical reasons divulge the name."

"The interfering little snoop!" snarled Glücke. "I'll break her now. Suppressing evidence!"

"Oh, no, you won't," said Ellery. "Before we're finished you'll thank her, Glücke; if not for her this case would never have been solved.

"Now, if the kidnapper had been involved in the murders as Lew's accomplice, would he have revealed his identity to a newspaperwoman, especially before the crime occurred? Absurd. And if he had been the criminal himself—not Lew—would he have revealed himself to Paula, putting himself in her power? Utterly incredible. No, indeed; his telephone call to her, his willingness to let her know who he was, indicated that he had no idea murder was about to occur, eliminated him either as the poisoner or as the poisoner's accomplice; *or even, for that matter, as a kidnapper.*"

"This gets worse and worse," groaned Glücke. "Say that again?"

"I'll get around to it," grinned Ellery. "For the moment let me push along on the Lew tack. I was satisfied that the kidnapper wasn't involved in the murders in any way. That meant he didn't poison the thermos bottles.

"If the kidnapper didn't, who did? Well, who could have? The bottles were all right when the last round of cocktails was drunk before the plane—obvious from the fact that no one who drank, and many did, suffered any ill effects. Therefore the morphine-sodium allurate mixture must have been slipped into the bottle *after* the last round was poured.

"Exactly when? Well, it wasn't done in the plane, because we've eliminated Jack, Blythe, and the kidnapper as the possible murderers, and they were the only three who entered the plane between the last round of drinks and the take-off. Then the bottles were poisoned before the hamper was stowed away in the plane, but after the last round. But after the last round I myself sat on that hamper, and I got up only to hand it to the kidnapper when he was stowing the luggage away in the plane.

"So you see," murmured Ellery, "I arrived by sheer elimination to only one conceivable time and only one conceivable person. The bottles must have been poisoned *between the time the last round was poured and the time I sat down on the hamper*. Who suggested the last round? Lew Bascom. Who immediately after returned the bottles to the hamper? Lew Bascom. Therefore it must have been Lew Bascom who dropped the poison into the bottles, probably as he was screwing the caps back on after pouring the last round."

The Inspector grunted a little crossly.

"So both elements—motive and opportunity—pointed to Lew as the only possible criminal. But what proof did I have that would satisfy a court? Absolutely none. I had achieved the truth through a process of reasoning; there was no confirmatory evidence. Therefore Lew had to be caught red-handed, trapped into giving himself away. Which occurred today."

"But who the hell *was* the kidnapper?" asked Butch.

"I said, you'll recall, that he wasn't even that, really. Had the kidnapper seriously intended to spirit Jack and Blythe away by force, hold them for ransom, or whatever, would he have told a newspaperwoman first? Naturally not. So I saw that it wasn't intended to be a real kidnapping at all. The wraith we were chasing had staged a *fake* kidnapping!"

"Fake?" shouted Glücke. "The hell you say! After we've worn our eyes out looking for him?"

"Of course, Inspector. For who would stage a kidnapping and inform a famous newspaper columnist about it in advance? Only some one who was interested in a news story, publicity. And who could have been interested in a publicity splash centering about Jack Royle and Blythe Stuart?" Ellery grinned. "Come on, Sam; talk. You're caught with the goods."

Vix grew very pale. He gulped, his one eye rolling wildly, looking for an avenue of escape.

The Inspector gasped: "*You?* Why, you ornery, one-eyed baboon—"

"Peace," sighed Ellery. "Who can quell the instincts of the buzzard or the dyed-in-the-wool publicity man? It was the opportunity of a life-time, wasn't it, Sam?"

"Yeah," said Vix with difficulty.

"The marriage of two world-famous figures, the gigantic splash of that airport send-off ... why, if those two were thought to be kid-napped, the Magna picture Butch was going to make would get a million dollars' worth of publicity."

"A million dollars' worth of misery to me, as it turned out," groaned Vix. "It was to be a surprise; I didn't even tell Butch. I figured I'd let on to Jack and Blythe once we were safely away, and then we'd hide out somewhere for a few days. They wanted a little peace and quiet, anyway. . . . Oh, nuts. When I turned around and saw those two dead, my stomach turned over. I knew I was in the worst kind of jam. If I gave myself up and told the truth, nobody'd believe me, certainly not a one-cylinder flattie like Glücke. I could see myself tagged for a twin killing and going out by the aerial route, kicking. What could I do? I set the plane down on the first flat place I could find and took it on the lam."

"You," said Inspector Glücke venomously, "are going up on charges. I'll give you publicity!"

"Take it easy, Inspector," growled Jacques Butcher. "Why make the studio suffer? It was a dumb stunt, but Sam can't be considered in any way responsible for what happened; if there'd been no murder there wouldn't have been any harm done. He'll take his rap in the papers, anyway; and you've got your man."

"Not only have you got your man," said Ellery pleasantly, "but if you're a good doggie, Glücke, maybe I'll give you something else."

"Isn't this nightmare over yet?" Glücke threw up his hands.

"Well, what forced Lew to change his plans?" asked Ellery. "What forced him to kill not only Blythe, but Jack Royle? What happened between the inauguration of his playing-card threats against Blythe and the day of the murder?

"Only one important thing happened—Blythe buried the hatchet, gave up her long feud with Jack; in fact, announced her intention to marry him, and did so.

"But how could Blythe's marriage have forced Lew to kill not only Blythe but the man she married? Well, what was behind his whole scheme? To get for himself the entire Stuart estate. Who were his obstacles? Blythe and Bonnie. But when Blythe married Jack Royle, then Jack Royle became an obstacle, too! For by the terms of Tolland Stuart's will half the estate went to Blythe, if living, *or to Blythe's heirs if dead*; and her heirs in that case would be her daughter Bonnie and her husband Jack. Only if Jack Royle died, too, before the estate passed would Jack cease to be an heir; living, he would inherit, but if dead his own estate would collect nothing and Bonnie, Blythe's only heir, would consequently get everything.

"So Lew killed Jack, too. Now he must kill Bonnie. But what happened before he got the opportunity to kill Bonnie? History repeated itself: Bonnie announced her intention to marry Ty. Therefore Ty became an obstacle in the way of Lew, for if Bonnie married Ty and Lew killed only Bonnie, Ty would get the entire estate, since according to the will if Bonnie predeceased her grandfather her portion would go to *her* heirs . . . or Ty, her surviving husband.

"Therefore Lew tried to prevent the marriage because if he could scare Bonnie into not marrying Ty he would have to kill only Bonnie; whereas if she did marry Ty he would have to kill both of them; and one murder was preferable to two for obvious reasons."

"That's all very well," muttered Glücke, "but what I can't understand is how Bascom expected to be able to control Mr. Stuart's will.

How could he be sure Mr. Stuart, when he saw his daughter murdered, wouldn't write a new will which would make it impossible for Lew ever to collect a cent, murders or not?"

"Ah," said Ellery. "A good point, Glücke. In discussing that, and Mr. Bascom's good fortune, I'm forced to refer again to my invaluable friend, Paula Paris. A pearl, that woman! The very first time I met her she painted an interesting word-picture of Tolland Stuart. She told me of his hypochondria, of his pamphlets inveighing against the evils of stimulants, even unto coffee and tea; of his drinking cold water with a teaspoon, obviously because he was afraid of what cold water would do, drunk normally, to his stomach—chill it, I suppose; of his diatribes against white bread."

"But I don't see what that—"

"That's quite true," said Dr. Junius unexpectedly, clearing his throat. "But I, too, fail to see the relevance—"

"I imagine, Doctor," said Ellery, "that you're due for a nasty shock. Your faith in humanity is about to be destroyed. Can you imagine Tolland Stuart being inconsistent in a matter like that?"

Dr. Junius's face looked like a yellow paste. "Well, now, of course—"

"That disconcerts you, naturally. You're amazed to learn that Tolland Stuart *could* be inconsistent in his hypochondriasis?"

"No, really, it happens. I mean I don't know what you're referring to—"

"Well, Doctor," said Ellery in a hard voice, "let me enlighten you. Friday afternoon Miss Stuart and I, as you will recall, came up here to visit her grandfather. You were away—shopping, I believe? Too bad. Because when we came upon Mr. Tolland Stuart lying in this room— yes, in this very bed—what was he doing? The man who had a horror of white bread was eating a cold meat sandwich made of white bread. The man who sipped cold water from a teaspoon because he was afraid of chilling his stomach, the man who avoided stimulants as he would the plague, that man was *gulping* down quite callously large quantities of *iced tea!*"

The old man in the bed whimpered, and Dr. Junius shrank within himself like a withering weed. As for the others, they stared in perplexity from Ellery to the old man. Only Inspector Glücke looked aware; and he gave a signal to one of his men. The detective went to the bed and motioned Bonnie away. Ty jumped forward to grasp Bonnie's arm and draw her from the bed.

And the man in the bed dropped the Indian blanket with the swiftness of desperate purpose and reached for the shotgun which stood close to his hand. But Ellery was swifter.

"No," he said, handing the gun to the Inspector, "not yet, sir."

"But I don't understand," cried Bonnie, her glance wavering between the old man and Ellery. "It doesn't make sense. You talk as if . . . as if this man weren't my grandfather."

"He isn't," said Ellery. "I have every reason to believe that he's a man supposed to have committed suicide—an old and desperate and dying man known to the Hollywood colony of extras as Arthur William Park, the actor."

If Inspector Glücke had seen the revelation coming, at least he had not seen it in its entirety, for he gaped at the cowering old man in the bed, who covered his face with his wrinkled hands.

"Because of that sandwich and iced drink," continued Ellery, "I saw that it was possible Tolland Stuart was being impersonated. I began to put little bits together; bits that had puzzled me, or passed me by, but that coalesced into a significant whole once my suspicions were aroused.

"For one thing, an imposture was not difficult; in this case it was of the essence of simplicity. The improbability of most impostures lies in the fact that doubles are rare, and that even expert make-up will not stand the test of constant inspection by people who knew the one impersonated well.

"But—" and Ellery shrugged "—who knew Tolland Stuart well? Not even his daughter, who had visited him only two or three times in the last ten years. But granting that Blythe might have seen through an imposture, Blythe was dead. Bonnie? Hardly; she had not seen her grandfather since her pinafore days. Only Dr. Junius of the survivors. Dr. Junius saw Tolland Stuart every day and had seen him every day for ten years. . . . No, no, Doctor; I assure you that's futile. The house is surrounded, and there's a detective just outside the door."

Dr. Junius stopped in his slow sidle toward the door, and he wet his lips.

"Then there was the incident last Sunday, when we flew up here after the discovery of the bodies in Ty's plane on that plateau. I thought I heard the motors of a plane during the thunder-and-lightning storm. I went out and, while I couldn't see the plane, I did see this man, now in bed, crouching outside the house with a *flyer's helmet* on his head. At the time it merely puzzled me; but when I suspected an imposture I saw that the explanation was simple: this man had just been landed on the Stuart estate by an airplane, whose motors I had heard. Undoubtedly piloted by Lew Bascom, who had departed from the plateau that Sunday before we did in an Army plane. Lew flew a plane, as I knew because he offered to pilot the wedding plane when the original Royle-Stuart wedding stunt was being discussed; moreover, he even offered the use of his own plane. So Lew must have returned to the airport with the Army pilot, picked up Park at his rooms, landed Park on this estate, and returned quietly to Los Angeles. You *are* Park, aren't you?"

The old man in the bed uncovered his face. Dr. Junius started to cry out, but closed his mouth without uttering the cry.

"You aren't Tolland Stuart."

The old man said nothing, did nothing. His face was altered; the sharp lines were even sharper than before, but no longer irascible, no longer lines of evil; he merely looked worn out, like an old stone, and weary to death.

"There's a way of proving it, you know," said Ellery with a sort of pity. "In the desk in the study downstairs there's Tolland Stuart's will, and that will is signed with Tolland Stuart's signature. Shall we ask you, Mr. Park, to write the name Tolland Stuart for comparison purposes?"

Dr. Junius said: "Don't!" in a despairing burst, but the old man shook his head. "It's no use, Junius. We're caught." He lay back on the pillows, closing his eyes.

"And there were other indications," said Ellery. "The way Dr. Junius

239

acted last Sunday. He put up a colossal bluff. He knew there was no Tolland Stuart upstairs. He was expecting Park; our sudden appearance must have made him frantic. When we finally came up here and found Park, who must have blundered about after sneaking into a house he's never been in before, found Stuart's room, and hastily got into Stuart's night-clothes, Junius was so surprised he fled. He hadn't heard those airplane engines. Oh, it was all cleverly done; Mr. Park is an excellent actor, and he was told everything he must know to play his part perfectly. After Sunday, of course, he was given further instruction."

"Then the doctor here was Bascom's confederate?" asked the Inspector, open-mouthed.

"Of course. As was Mr. Park, although he's the least culpable, I suspect, of the three.

"Now, convinced that Tolland Stuart was being impersonated, I could find only one plausible reason for it. Lew's plans depended on Stuart's remaining alive until after the murder of Blythe and Bonnie; if Tolland Stuart was being impersonated, then it could only mean that Tolland Stuart was dead. When had he died? Well, I knew Stuart had been alive four days before the murder of Jack—"

"How did you know that?"

"Because on that day, when Blythe and Jack visited here, she saw him, for one thing; she might have spotted an impersonation. But more important, he gave her a check for a hundred and ten thousand dollars, which she turned over to Jack. Would Stuart's bank have honored Stuart's signature if it had not been genuine? So I knew that four days before the murders Stuart had still been in the land of the living.

"Apparently, then, Stuart had died between that day and the following Sunday. Probably Saturday night, the night before the crime, because we know Lew got hold of Park Sunday, hurried him up here under the most difficult and dangerous conditions—something he would not have done Sunday had he been able to do it before Sunday. So I imagine Dr. Junius telephoned Lew Saturday night to say Tolland Stuart had suddenly died, and Lew thought of Park, and instructed the doctor to bury his benefactor in a very deep hole, and immediately got busy on the Park angle. Park left a suicide note to efface his trail and vanished—to turn up here the next day as Bonnie's grandfather."

"This is—extraordinary," said Jacques Butcher, staring from Junius to Park. "But why? What did Park and Junius hope to get out of it?"

"Park? I believe I can guess. Park, as I knew from Lew himself long ago, is dying of cancer. He's penniless, has a wife and crippled son back East dependent on him. He knew he couldn't last long, and for his family a man will do almost anything—a certain type of man—if there's enough money in it to insure his family's security.

"Dr. Junius? I have the advantage of you there; I've read Tolland Stuart's will. In it he engaged to pay the doctor a hundred thousand dollars if the doctor kept him alive until the age of seventy. From the wording of the will and its date—it was made out at the age of sixty and was dated nine and a half years ago—it was obvious that Stuart had died at the age of *sixty-nine and a half*. Dr. Junius had spent almost ten years of his life in a living hell to earn that hundred thousand. He wasn't going to let a mere matter of a couple of murders stand in the way of his getting it. Nevertheless, he wouldn't have risked his neck unless he felt reasonably certain Stuart wouldn't live to reach the age of seventy. Consequently, I was convinced that, far from being a healthy man, Stuart was really a very sick man; and that Junius was putting on an act when he claimed his patient was just a hypochondriac. I was convinced that Stuart, who I knew had died suddenly, had died probably of his illness—not accidentally or through violence, since violence was the last thing Lew wanted in the case of the old man."

"There's something," whispered Dr. Junius, "of the devil in you."

"I imagine the shoe fits you rather better," replied Ellery. "And, of course, it must have been you who supplied Lew Bascom with the morphine and the sodium allurate in the proper dose—no difficult feat for a physician."

"I went into it with Bascom," said Dr. Junius in the same whisper, "because I knew Stuart wouldn't survive. When he engaged me nine and a half years ago he had a badly ulcerated condition of the stomach. I treated him faithfully, but he developed a cancer, as so often occurs. I felt . . . cheated; I knew he probably wouldn't live to reach seventy.

When Bascom approached me, I fell in with his scheme. Bascom knew, too, that the old man was dying. In a sense our—interests lay in the same direction: I wanted Stuart to live to seventy, and Bascom wanted him to live until after Blythe and Bonnie Stuart were . . . " He stopped and wet his lips. "Bascom had got the cooperation of Park, here, in advance, just in case the old man died prematurely, as he did. Park had plenty of time to study his physical rôle."

"You animal," said Bonnie.

Dr. Junius said nothing more; he turned his face to the wall. And the old man in the bed seemed asleep.

"And since Park had a cancer, too," said Ellery, "and couldn't live very long, it was just dandy all around, wasn't it? When he died, there'd be nobody to suspect he wasn't Stuart; and even an autopsy would merely have revealed that he died of cancer, which was perfectly all right. And by that time, too, he'd have grown real hair, instead of the false hair and spirit gum he's got on his face now. Oh, an ingenious plan." He paused, and then he said: "It makes me feel a little sick. Do you sleep well at night, Dr. Junius?"

And after a moment Glücke asked doggedly: "But Bascom didn't know exactly when Stuart would die. You still haven't answered the question of how he could control the old man before he died, how he could be sure the old man wouldn't make out a new will."

"That was simple. The old will, the present will, existed; all Lew had to do was see—probably through Junius—that the old man didn't get his hands on his own will. Then, even if he did make out a new will, they could always destroy it, leaving the old will in force.

"When Stuart died prematurely, it was even simpler. There would be no question of a new will at all. Park, playing Stuart's rôle, couldn't make out a new one, even if he wanted to. The old will would remain, as it has remained, the will in force.

"Incidentally, I was sure Lew would fall for our trap today. With Park dying of cancer, his survival for even a short time doubtful, Lew couldn't permit Bonnie and Ty to vanish for an indefinite period. If Park died while they were off on their honeymoon at an unknown place, Lew's whole scheme was nullified. His scheme was based on Bonnie's dying before her grandfather, to conceal the true motive. If he killed Bonnie—and Ty, as he would have to—after the death of Park-acting-as-Stuart, his motive would be clearly indicated. So I knew he would take any risk to kill Bonnie and Ty before they went away and while Park was still alive."

Ellery sighed and lit a fresh cigarette, and no one said anything until Inspector Glücke, with a sudden narrowing of his eyes, said: "Park. You there—Park!"

But the old man in the bed did not answer, or move, or give any sign that he had heard.

Ellery and Glücke sprang forward as one man. Then they straightened up without having touched him. For in his slack hand there lay a tiny vial, and he was dead.

And Dr. Junius turned from the wall and collapsed in a chair, whimpering like a child.

23

END OF THE BEGINNING

When Ellery turned the key in his apartment door Sunday night, and let himself in, and shut the door, and flung aside his hat and coat, and sank into his deepest chair, it was with a spent feeling. His bones ached, and so did his head. It was a relief just to sit there in the quiet living-room thinking of nothing at all.

He always felt this way at the conclusion of a case—tired, sluggish, his vital energies sapped.

Inspector Glücke had been gruff with praises again; and there had been invitations, and thanks, and a warm kiss on the lips from Bonnie, and a silent handshake from Ty. But he had fled to be alone.

He closed his eyes.

To be alone?

That wasn't quite true. Damn, analyzing again! But this time his mind dwelt on a more pleasant subject than murder. Just what *was* his feeling for Paula Paris? Was he sorry for her because she was psychologically frustrated, because she shut herself up in those sequestered rooms of hers and denied the world the excitement of her company? Pity? No, not pity, really. To be truthful about it, he rather enjoyed the feeling when he went to see her that they were alone, that the world was shut out. Why was that?

He groaned, his head beginning to throb where it had only ached dully before. He was mooning like an adolescent boy. Tormenting himself this way! Why think? What was the good of thinking? The really happy people didn't have a thought in their heads. That's why they were happy.

He rose with a sigh and stripped off his jacket; and as he did so his wallet fell out. He stooped to pick it up and suddenly recalled what was in it. That envelope. Queer how he had forgotten it in the excitement of the last twenty-four hours!

He took the envelope out of the wallet, fingering its creamy vellum face with appreciation. Good quality. Quality, that was it. She represented a special, unique assortment of human values, the tender and shy and lovable ones, the ones that appealed mutely to the best in a man.

He smiled as he tore the envelope open. Had she really guessed who had murdered Jack Royle and Blythe Stuart?

In her free, clear script was written: "Dear Stupid: It's inconceivable to you that a mere woman could do by intuition what it's taken you Siegfriedian writhings of the intellect to achieve. Of course it's Lew Bascom. Paula."

Damn her clever eyes! he thought angrily. She needn't have been so brash about it. He seized the telephone.

"Paula. This is Ellery. I've just read your note—"

"Mr. Queen," murmured Paula. "Back from the wars. I suppose I should offer you the congratulations owing to the victor?"

"Oh, that. We were lucky it all went off so well. But Paula, about this note—"

"It's hardly necessary for me to open your envelope now."

"But I've opened yours, and I must say you made an excellent stab in the dark. But how—"

"You might also," said Paula's organ voice, "congratulate *me* for having made it."

"Well, of course. Congratulations. But that's not the point. Guessing! That's the point. Where does it get you? Nowhere."

"Aren't you being incoherent?" Paula laughed. "It gets you the answer. Nor is it entirely a matter of guesswork, O Omniscience. There was reason behind it."

"Reason? Oh, come now."

"It's true. I didn't understand why Lew did it—his motives and things; the murder of Jack didn't fit in . . . you'll have to explain those things to me—"

"But you just said," growled Ellery, "you had a *reason*."

"A feminine sort of reason." Paula paused. "But do we have to discuss it over the phone?"

"Tell me!"

"Yes, sir. You see, I did know the kind of person Lew was, and it struck me that Lew's character exactly matched the character of the crime."

"What? What's that?"

"Well, Lew was an idea man, wasn't he? He conceived brilliantly, executed poorly—that was characteristic not only of him but of his work, too."

"What of it?"

"But the whole crime, if you stop to think of it, as I did, was exactly like that—brilliantly conceived and poorly executed!"

"You mean to say," spluttered Ellery, "that *that* sort of dishwater is what you call reasoning?"

"Oh, but it's so true. Have you stopped," said Paula sweetly, "to think it out? The playing-card scheme was very, very clever—a true Lew Bascom idea; but it was also fantastic and devious, and wasn't it carried out shoddily? Lew all over. Then the frame-up of Jack, followed by the frame-up of Ty . . . two frame-ups that didn't jibe at all. And that clumsy device of filing those typewriter keys! Poor execution."

"Lord," groaned Ellery.

"Oh, dozens of indications. That hamper with the bottles of cocktails. Suppose it hadn't been delivered? Suppose, if it were delivered in that crush, it weren't taken along? Or suppose Jack and Blythe were too wrapped up in each other, even if it were taken along, to bother about a drink? Or suppose only one of them drank? So awfully *chancy*,

Ellery; so poorly thought out. Now Jacques Butcher, had he been the criminal, would *never*—"

"All right, all right," said Ellery. "I'm convinced—yes, I'm not. You saw a clever idea with fantastic overtones and poor craftsmanship, and because Lew was that way you said it was Lew. I'll have to recommend the method to Glücke; he'll be delighted. Now, Miss Paris, how about paying off that bet of ours?"

"The bet," said Paula damply.

"Yes, the bet! You said I'd never catch the criminal. Well, I have caught him, so I've won, and you've got to take me out tonight to the Horseshoe Club."

"Oh!" And Paula fell silent. He could sense her panic over the wires. "But . . . but that *wasn't* the bet," she said at last in a desperate voice. "The bet was that you'd bring him to justice, into court. You didn't. He committed suicide, he tried to escape and his parachute didn't open—"

"Oh, no, you don't," said Ellery firmly. "You don't welch on me, Miss Paris. You lost that bet, and you're going to pay off."

"But Ellery," she wailed, "I *can't!* I—I haven't set foot outside my house for years and years! You don't know how the very thought of it makes me shrivel up inside—"

"You're taking me to the Club tonight."

"I think . . . I'd faint, or something. I know it sounds silly to a normal person," she cried, "but why can't people understand? They'd understand if I had measles. It's something in me that's *sick*, only it doesn't happen to be organic. This fear of people—"

"Get dressed."

"But I've got nothing to wear," she said triumphantly. "I mean, no evening gowns. I've never had occasion to wear them. Or even—I've no wrap, no—no nothing."

"I'm dressing now. I'll be at your house at eight-thirty."

"Ellery, no!"

"Eight-thirty."

"Please! Oh, please, Ellery—"

"Eight-thirty," repeated Mr. Queen inflexibly, and he hung up.

At eight-thirty precisely Mr. Queen presented himself at the front door
of the charming white house in the Hills, and a pretty young girl
opened the door for him. Mr. Queen saw, with some trepidation, that
the young lady was star-eyed and pink-cheeked with excitement. She
was one of Paula's elfin secretaries, and she regarded his lean, tuxedo-
clad figure with a keenness that made him think of a mother inspecting
her daughter's first swain come a-calling.

It was absurd, too absurd, blustered Mr. Queen inwardly. Out of my
way, wench.

But the wench said: "Oh, Mr. Queen," in an ecstatic whisper, "It's
simply *wonderful!* Do you think she'll *do* it?"

"Why, of course she'll do it," pooh-poohed Mr. Queen. "All this
blather about crowd phobia. Nonsense! Where is she?"

"She's been crying and laughing and—oh, she looks *beautiful!* Wait
till you see her. It's the most marvelous thing that's ever happened to
her. I do hope nothing . . . "

"Now, now," said Mr. Queen brusquely. "Less chatter, my dear.
Let's have a look at this beauty."

Nevertheless, he approached Paula's door with a quaking heart.
What was the matter with him? All this fuss and nervousness over a little thing like going to a night-club!

He knocked and the secretary, looking anxious, faded away; and
Paula's voice came tremulously: "Come . . . come in."

Mr. Queen touched his black tie, coughed, and went in.

Paula was standing, tall and tense, against the closed glass doors of
the farthest wall, staring at him. She was wearing elbow-length red
evening gloves, and her braceleted hands were pressed to her heart.
She was wearing . . . well, it shimmered and crinkled where the light
struck it—cloth of gold? What the devil was it?—and a long white fur
evening cape over her shoulders, caught at the neck with a magnificent
marcasite brooch, and her hair done up in—well, it looked like the hair
of one of those court pages of the time of Elizabeth; simply exquisite.
Simply the last word. Simply—there was no last word.

"Holy smoke," breathed Mr. Queen.

She was white to the lips. "Do I—do I look all right?"

"You look," said Mr. Queen reverently, "like one of the Seraphim. You look," said Mr. Queen, "like the popular conception of Cleopatra, although Cleo had a hooked nose and probably a black skin, and *your* nose and skin . . . You look," said Mr. Queen, "you look like one of those godlike beings from Aldebaran, or some place, that H. G. Wells likes to describe. You look swell."

"Don't be funny," she said with a little angry glance. "I mean the clothes."

"The clothes? Oh, the clothes. Incidentally, I thought you said you didn't have any evening clothes. Liar!"

"I didn't, and don't; that's why I asked," she said helplessly. "I've had to borrow the cape from Bess, and the dress from Lillian, and the shoes from a neighbor down the street whose feet are as big as mine, and I feel like the original Communist. Oh, Ellery, are you *sure* I'll do?"

Ellery advanced across the room with determined strides. She shrank against the glass doors.

"Ellery. What are you . . . "

"May I present the loveliest lady I know," said Mr. Queen with fierce gallantry, "with these?" And he held out a little cellophane box, and in the box there lay an exquisite corsage of camellias.

Paula gasped: "Oh!" and then she said softly, "That was sweet," and suddenly she was no longer tense, but pliant, and a little abstracted, and she pinned the corsage to her bodice with swift, flashing, red-swathed fingers.

And Mr. Queen said, wetting his lips: "Paula."

"Yes?"

Mr. Queen said again: "Paula."

"Yes?" she looked up, frowning.

Mr. Queen said: "Paula, will you . . . May I . . . Oh, hell, there's only one way to do it, and that's to *do* it!"

And he seized her and pulled her as close to his stiff shirt as the shirt would permit and clumsily kissed her on the mouth.

She lay still in his arms, her eyes closed, breathing quickly. Then, without opening her eyes, she said: "Kiss me some more."

And after a while Mr. Queen said thickly: "I think—Let's not go out and say we did. Let's sort of—stay here."

"Yes," she whispered. "Oh, yes."

But there was iron in that man's soul, after all. He sternly put aside temptation. "No, we *are* going out. It's the very soul of the treatment."

"Oh, I can't. I mean . . . I don't think I can."

Mr. Queen took her by the arm and marched her straight across the room to the closed door.

"Open that door," he said.

"But I'm . . . now I'm all messed!"

"You're beautiful. Open that door."

"You mean . . . open it?"

"Open it. Yourself. With your own hands."

The twin imps of fear peered out of her wide, grave eyes. She gulped like a little girl and her red-gloved right hand crept forward to touch the knob. She looked at Ellery in distress.

"Open it, darling," said Mr. Queen in a low voice.

Slowly her hand turned the knob until it would turn no more. Then, quickly, like little Lulu about to swallow her cod-liver oil, Paula closed her eyes and jerked the door open.

And, her eyes still closed, stumbled blindly across the threshold into the world.